The Derbyshire Dance

A REGENCY ROMANCE

ROSANNE E. LORTZ

MADISON STREET PUBLISHING

Part 1

CHAPTER ONE

The Vicar

DERBYSHIRE, ENGLAND, DECEMBER 1810

"DEAR ME," SAID AUNT Lucy, pulling aside the lace curtain to peer through the window. She had hung the frilly curtains despite her niece's express disapproval, but they did get in the way of a close inspection of imminent company. "I believe the new vicar is coming up the path. Good heavens! The wind has caught his hat, and he is chasing it. I thought him very dignified in the pulpit on Sunday, but now I shall never see him without thinking of those long gams galloping about our garden."

"Aunt Lucy," admonished Bel, sitting across the room and sipping her tea. "Come away from the window. The poor man does not need to see you giggling at his misfortune." It was more of a suggestion than a command, for Bel knew how difficult it was to pry her aunt away from her amusements. Their quiet life in the country was *not* how Lucy would have chosen to spend the final decades of her life, and, predictably, she took full advantage of whatever liveliness she could find in the Derbyshire countryside.

"Oh, very well," said Aunt Lucy with a good-natured huff. She removed herself from the window and walked over to the polished silver candle sconces above the fireplace. Using the silver as a mirror, she straightened her lace cap. "Jenny!" she called with a raised voice. Their maid-of-all-work popped her head into the parlour. "We'll need another teacup and plate, for we're about to have company."

Bel continued to sit steadily in her own armchair, refusing to make a fuss about something so un-fuss-worthy. "I wonder why the vicar would be calling in such unfavourable weather?"

"Upon my word!" Aunt Lucy flounced over to a chair to sit down. "What a question! Perhaps he feared that if the weather were fine, he would never find you here in the house."

Bel was not certain that the vicar's visit hinged on her presence, but she could not argue with the truth of her aunt's statement. She had already been bemoaning the fact that the rain blowing sideways would keep her from walking the perimeter of her estate today. Not *all* hope was lost, however. After tea was over, she intended to don a pair of breeches, wrap herself in a greatcoat and muffler, and check on the sheepfold.

Aunt Lucy leaned forward conspiratorially. "I expect the vicar has already visited the Brownlees at Mullhill Manor as they are first in consequence in the neighbourhood."

"Of course, he has," replied Bel. "Mr. Brownlee was the one responsible for his appointment. The vicar must have been known to him long before now."

"Yes, well, I daresay, after the Brownlees, he may have tried to call on the Audeleys. But the Audeleys are away in London.

So, *we* must be his second visit." Lucy's eyes grew bright with anticipation. "Or, considered in another light, his *first* visit with unmarried ladies."

"His first visit with the parish spinsters, don't you mean? I daresay his predecessor warned him that a pair of old tabby cats lived at this farm."

"Tabby cats! Upon my word—"

Bel's eyes sparkled at her aunt's sputtering denials. Aunt Lucy was fifty years old if she were a day. Bel herself was still on the right side of thirty, but it had been years since she considered herself an eligible miss. If it were not so impractical, *she* would be wearing a lace cap too. Between the two of them, there was certainly no one in this parlour to attract the attention of a young bachelor clergyman.

"Mr. Davies would never speak so ill of us to the new vicar," protested Aunt Lucy. "I gave him ever so many remedies for his gout, and he was particularly fond of my strawberry preserves. He could eat half a jar of it in one sitting."

"Which may have been the reason his gout never got better." Bel arched an eyebrow—the left one, the one that always gave her a cynical appearance. "You must admit that his convalescent trips to Bath almost always happened shortly after you dropped off a jar of preserves at the vicarage."

Aunt Lucy made another feeble protest, but she could not deny the truth of the matter. For the last several years, their previous vicar, Mr. Davies, had refused to amend his diet and had instead been making regular visits to Bath to buttress his ailing health. This year, in early autumn, the ponderous cleric had opted to retire to Bath permanently. The Derbyshire living had sat empty for two months while Mr. Brownlee, the largest landowner in the parish, decided where to bestow the living next. The parish folk had begun to wonder why the process was taking so long. Surely, there must be a respectable curate *somewhere* in search of a promotion?

Finally, just in time for Advent, Mr. Brownlee had made his decision, and the new vicar had arrived. Hopefully, Mr. Horace Townsend would be abstemious enough with the strawberry preserves and robust enough in constitution to avoid gallivanting off to a spa town at regular intervals. But as yet, no one knew enough about the new vicar to predict anything.

"Bel," said Aunt Lucy, leaning forward in her armchair. "Before he comes in, I want you to promise me something."

Bel wrinkled her nose. "Not until you've told me what it is."

"Promise that you won't bring up anything peculiar—like crop rotation, or grain prices, or hoof diseases!"

Bel crossed one leg over the other beneath her grey kersey skirt. "What on earth is peculiar about those topics? I heard Mr. Brownlee himself discussing agriculture with the vicar as we walked past after the Sunday service."

"Yes, but you know it is peculiar for *you* to discuss such things. A lady does not show interest in such *earthy* endeavours."

Aunt Lucy was of the mind that true ladies could only dabble in embroidery, painting, pianoforte, and strawberry preserves, but none of those pursuits appealed to Bel. She debated whether to respond to her aunt or to let the matter lie. But before she could say anything, a fast-moving bundle of fur catapulted onto her lap and began to nuzzle into the waist of her woollen day dress. She uncrossed her leg and began to scratch the creature behind the ears.

"There you are, Magpie," Bel said soothingly. "Wishing for the wind and drizzle to stop, no doubt." Her cat was as much a creature of the outdoors as she was, but the finicky puss did draw the line at parading through puddles. On a clear day, there was nothing Magpie liked better than a long ramble through the fields, but on a rainy day, going to sleep on Bel's lap was often a second-best option. Bel balanced her teacup carefully as Magpie's tail swished against her arm.

The two ladies heard a knock on the front door. Aunt Lucy clutched the arms of her chair with visible excitement. "Mr. Horace Townsend," announced Jenny, bobbing a curtsy to the ladies in the parlour.

"Ah, Mr. Townsend," said Aunt Lucy, bounding from her seat to take the vicar's hand. The man was tall and lanky and dressed in a dark coat and dark trousers that hid the raindrops well. It was impossible to tell the colour of his bedraggled hair, but Bel suspected it might be an ashen blond. She wondered if it would be impolite to offer him a towel to dry himself off—she certainly would have wiped down a horse if it had entered the stables in that condition.

Aunt Lucy beamed at the wet visitor. "How kind of you to call on us so soon after your arrival. I am Miss Lucy Morrison, and this is Miss Belinda Morrison."

The vicar took Lucy's hand, and she held his fingers as reverently as if they belonged to the archbishop.

"You'll pardon me for not rising to greet you," said Bel dryly. "My cat Magpie does not like to be disturbed, even for clergymen."

"Ah, yes, quite all right," said Mr. Townsend. His alert blue eyes took in the purring white cat with its patches of black. "I understand that cats are a particular favourite of ladies. I must admit that I prefer dogs."

"How interesting," murmured Bel, predisposed to discount his opinion already. She might have *known* that he would have liked dogs based on his Sunday sermon. It had been overly authoritarian in herding people about, just like a young sheepdog who needed a few years of maturity under its fur.

"What part of the country do you come from?" asked Aunt Lucy, gesturing for him to be seated. "And won't you have some tea?"

"I'm a Shropshire lad. Most recently from London, but born and bred in Shropshire. And yes, tea would be splendid."

A Shropshire lad? Bel managed to keep herself from rolling her eyes. One should stop referring to oneself as a *lad* after leaving the hallowed halls of Eton, and she was quite certain that Mr. Townsend had not darkened the door of Eton for a dozen years or more. He looked almost the same age as she was, the perfect age for a spinster to relegate herself to the shelf...and the perfect age for an established gentleman to marry. Such was the irony of life.

Since Magpie was still purring contentedly on Bel's lap, Aunt Lucy assumed the office of hostess and made up Mr. Townsend's tea. To Bel's surprise, he wanted no milk or sugar in his drink. He did not seem like the sort of fellow who would enjoy a bitter beverage, but perhaps his enthusiasm for religion affected his enthusiasm for tea.

"Are you married, Mr. Townsend?" asked Aunt Lucy, offering him the question along with the teacup. There had been no wife with him on Sunday, but maybe the vicar had come ahead of his family to settle into his new position, and his spouse was still *en route* from London...or Shropshire.

"I do not yet have that privilege." Mr. Townsend displayed no embarrassment about the subject. "The curacy I came from in

London was quite impecunious, without a residence or stipend large enough to support a wife. And the women of London were godless, all vanity and pomp, with more care to be seen than to be sanctified."

"But now you are a vicar," said Aunt Lucy, stemming his more dire reflections, "with a vicarage large enough to house a family." She cast Bel a sly look. "Let us hope that there are more opportunities for matrimony in Derbyshire than there were in London—"

"What do you think of the countryside in our part of Derbyshire?" interrupted Bel. Mr. Townsend's matrimonial prospects were no concern of theirs, and Aunt Lucy could *not* be allowed to continue mining that vein of conversation.

"Very reminiscent of the twenty-third Psalm," said Mr. Townsend approvingly, "especially this valley in which we are situated. Although perhaps the greenness is due to the incessant rainfall of late. I believe it has rained every single day since I arrived last week."

"I believe you are right." Bel kept a close catalogue of the weather since it impacted her own activities so profoundly. "But that is hardly unusual. One expects rain in every county of England at this time of year."

"Indeed," said Mr. Townsend, his head bobbing up and down with affirmation. "You are most perceptive, Miss Belinda." He looked between the two ladies. "Since I am new to this parish, you ladies must enlighten me as to your relationship. Can it be that you are...sisters?"

"Oh, dear me, no," said Aunt Lucy, with a gasp. "Belinda is my niece. Her parents passed away five years ago, and due to her youth, I came up from London to Derbyshire to be her companion. It would not do for such a *young* lady to be alone on this large estate."

Bel's fingers curled into Magpie's fur with more force than was necessary. What game was her aunt playing, trying to pretend that Bel was a spring lamb? It was true enough that she had needed a chaperone—her brother had already departed for India by the time her parents passed away, and she had been obliged to invite her aunt to live with her for propriety's sake. But Bel was handily and happily aware that she could no longer be considered young.

"It does seem like a good deal of property," said Mr. Townsend. He hesitated and then plunged ahead. "Five hundred acres?"

"Six hundred." Bel was surprised that he had estimated it so closely. But then, perhaps Mr. Brownlee had told him how she was situated. The thought that her holdings were being discussed with a stranger was an uncomfortable one. Although, they were not exactly *her* holdings, but land she managed in trust for another....

"And a diversity of sheep and grain, I believe."

Again, he seemed singularly well informed. Either he was as interested in agriculture as she was, or he was interested in the profits that agriculture had the potential to bring. "Yes, wheat and barley and a flock of nearly three hundred."

Mr. Townsend put a hand close to his face and took a deep breath through his nose as if he were about to sneeze, but then, after a moment, the sensation seemed to subside without any explosive effects. "Gritstone sheep?" he asked. "You are so close to the Peak District that hill sheep would be most practical...or, at least, so I've heard."

"Some are Gritstone," said Bel, "but we also have a finer-woolled variety, so we are able to deal in both meat and wool."

Aunt Lucy gave Bel a warning yawn as she adjusted her cap. No doubt she meant to imply that although Mr. Townsend might *ask* about her estate, it would not improve his opinion of Bel were she to continue speaking on the subject.

"What a large holding for a woman to manage on her own." Mr. Townsend's lips pursed as he drank his dark tea. "I daresay you apply to Mr. Brownlee for advice when you find yourself at a loss."

Bel bit her lip. It was true. She had asked her late father's friend, Mr. Brownlee, for advice multiple times, especially when the estate had first fallen to her control. But that was hardly due to her feminine nature. All novices in any endeavour needed advice, whether members of the stronger or the weaker sex. In the past years, those visits to Mullhill Manor had become fewer and farther between. Bel considered herself quite competent at management of the estate, and she disliked the insinuation that management of an agricultural holding was beyond her, simply because she was a woman.

Mr. Townsend was too oblivious to notice the dark cloud on her brow. He accepted a piece of cake from the elder Miss Morrison and took several bites while Aunt Lucy opined on the kindness of the Brownlees to a poor orphan like Belinda. "It is very hard for poor Bel not to have a father or brother to advise her. But Mr. Brownlee has been a guardian angel. Can you believe that he offered his own steward's services to help bring Belinda's flock to market last year?"

"In exchange for a sizable share of the profits," objected Bel. "I refused him. I hope that I am not so poor-spirited that I cannot sell my own livestock."

"I daresay no one could accuse you of being poor-spirited, Miss Morrison," said Mr. Townsend, "but to bear up under such a responsibility for five years is remarkable. I wonder that you have not considered matrimony to relieve yourself of such a burden." Once again, he inhaled convulsively and put a hand up to his nose, but the sneeze never came.

Bel shifted in her seat, waking the gently dozing Magpie. The cat began to stretch and flex her claws. "Matrimony?" Bel echoed.

Aunt Lucy's eyes shone with excitement. For the vicar to introduce the topic on his first visit was a coup beyond anything she had ever dreamed. Aunt Lucy's pink lips parted, doubtless about to make another sly remark.

Bel, however, spoke first, determined to approach the matter directly and put an end to any possible presumption. "Dear me, Mr. Townsend." She set down her teacup and arched her left eyebrow. "Are you proposing to me so soon?"

———ele———

"Well, you mishandled that monstrously," said Aunt Lucy with a longsuffering sigh, peering out from the lace curtain at the retreating form of the vicar. "Why on earth would you think that Mr. Townsend was proposing to you? The poor man was mortified. He almost had an apoplexy from choking on his tea. And he couldn't put his teacup down soon enough to escape from the house. His hat was still dripping wet, and he never even had time to finish his plum cake."

"I simply took my lead from you," said Bel innocently. "You were hinting so openly at my eligibility, and my property was under such close scrutiny that I assumed Mr. Townsend had gathered his courage and made me an offer."

Aunt Lucy squeaked in irritation and went back to her chair. "Hinting is all that should be done on the first encounter! You were not supposed to be forthright enough to force him into a declaration. You were supposed to blush and say something complimentary to the male sex that he could have interpreted as a compliment to him!"

"Is that a rule?" Bel walked over to the window and noted that the rain had finally stopped. "I'm sorry, but I'm not familiar with how this game is played."

"Oh, I think you are more cunning than you let on," said Aunt Lucy, shaking a finger at her niece. "Admit it. You scared Mr. Townsend away on purpose."

"I admit nothing," said Bel with a smirk. She looked around the parlour, searching for something more important than Mr. Townsend's good opinion.

"I don't know why you dislike him. He had an air about him—as if he were an authority in the room. He reminded me of—"

"—of Mr. Brownlee," said Bel. "He has that same dictatorial good nature, a man who commands the conversation so benevolently that he cannot understand why anyone would disagree with him or have their own opinion on a matter."

"Well, I for one saw nothing disagreeable in what he had to say."

Bel frowned, her mind already elsewhere. "Where has Magpie got to? She must have slipped out the door when Jenny released our guest."

"Never mind your confounded cat. This is serious. It's not every day that an unmarried vicar comes to Derbyshire."

"Oh, Aunt Lucy, leave me be! Can you imagine me tethered to an insufferably enthusiastic clergyman who wants to tell me how to run my estate and wants to lift all my burdens by doing it himself?" He had apparently sounded out the extent of her holdings and flocks, but if he thought that marriage to her would bring him six hundred acres, he would be in for a rude awakening when Charlie came home.

"Belinda dear," said Aunt Lucy, with a sigh of sadness. "It's true that Mr. Townsend might not be your ideal, but what other eligible suitor is likely to arrive in this remote part of Derbyshire?"

"No one," said Bel cheerfully. "Which is why I intend to put on some trousers and make sure Jer and Tam have safely put the sheep into the pen for the night." She deposited a kiss on her aunt's cheek. "Don't wait dinner for me. It may be late before I get back."

CHAPTER TWO

The Duke

NIGEL YAWNED. HE WAS tired of not being tired. He had always favoured lazing about till the late hours of the afternoon, but somehow, that luxury could be better savoured when one had enjoyed some sort of gaiety the night before. The problem with rusticating here in Derbyshire was that there was *nothing* to do.

The Audeleys' home contained a medium-sized library, but he was so unused to reading in the past several years that opening a book seemed daunting. The Audeleys' home held a pianoforte with a large chest of sheet music, but he was so out of practice that it was painful to hear his own clumsy efforts. The Audeleys' home boasted the largest rose garden in this part of Derbyshire, but he had no use for walking unless he had a companion with which to converse. And besides the coachman John and the gardener Archie, there was no one at all to talk to. It had been benevolent of Mrs. Audeley to let him stay at her empty house—especially since London was too hot to hold him at present—but he did not know how much more of his own company he could take without going mad.

One part of him was glad there was no one of consequence around, for he was beginning to feel smelly and unkempt. He had only packed a trunk for a week-long journey, and now he was running out of clean shirts, resurrecting rumpled cravats, and wondering why he had thought he could do without a valet on this trip. He briefly contemplated sending a message up to London and requesting that Simpson post to Derbyshire with all haste. But he could not shake the niggling worry that word of his whereabouts might leak out. If Solomon Digby was watching his house in London, his spies might follow his valet Simpson back to Derbyshire. Then Nigel would have more to worry about than unwashed linens.

No, Nigel must send no letters that might be traced back to him—neither to Simpson, nor to Lady Maltrousse, nor to any of his other gaiety-loving friends back in London. And he must keep his identity mum in this dull Derbyshire neighbourhood—which would add even further to the interminable dullness.

Meandering about the house, Nigel poked his head into the kitchen. "What are we having for dinner tonight, John?"

"Eggs, yer grace," grunted the coachman. "And ham."

"Excellent," said Nigel, "my favourite. And no need for 'yer grace,' I must remind you." It was the exact same meal that they had enjoyed for the whole of Nigel's stay. But John could hardly be blamed. He was a coachman, not a cook, and he was doing his best to provide board for the gentleman who had been foisted on the skeleton household. Besides the gardener and the coachman, there was only Mrs. Garrick who stopped by daily to empty the chamber pots, dust the furniture, and scour the dishes.

Nigel looked down at his sad shirtfront, stained from previous wear. Slowly, a brilliant idea crept upon him. "Do you think the lady who comes in to do the washing up could launder my clothes as well?"

"Don't see why not, yer gr—sir," said John. He nodded at the spotty faced young man sitting agape on the wooden bench by the kitchen table. "She be Archie's mother."

"Excellent," said Nigel again, not quite sure that he was using that word to the highest level of its lexical potential. "Normally, my valet handles my laundry, but I am without his expertise at present." In truth, Simpson's expertise was quite extraordinary. Nigel had inherited him from his brother, the previous duke, who had in turn received him from the clever Lady Maltrousse. Simpson seemed to understand the need to uphold the Warrenton standard of modish masculinity.

Archie dropped the spoon that had been travelling toward his open mouth. It fell on the wooden table with a clatter. Nigel averted his eyes. He had already noticed that the youthful gardener looked utterly stupefied whenever he was in the exalted presence of a guest, and he did not want to add to the lad's awkwardness. "Yer grace," the young man managed to gasp, like a fish on land taking his dying breath.

"Er, yes, what is it?"

"Might you be needin' a valet while yer stayin' here?" The boy's fingers began to drum on the table with nervous energy. "I could help wi' that."

Nigel paused. This unprepossessing creature was not exactly the model of a metropolitan gentleman's gentleman. Simpson would be horrified if Nigel let the lad brush his coats or iron his cravats. But Nigel was no longer in London, and when one was in the country, one had to make shift as best one could.

"Very well, you can attempt it." Nigel looked down at the scuffed toes of his once-proud Hessians. "But you must stop calling me 'yer grace,' and your first task will be to put some shine back into my boots."

"Yes, yer g-good sir!" said Archie, his Adam's apple bobbing like a bottle at sea.

John gave a snort. "But don't you be forgettin' the rose garden while you're playin' valet, Archie, or Mr. Audeley'll have somethin' t'say to you when he gets back."

The youth began to assert his ability to do both jobs at once. As Nigel listened, he felt something rub against his leg. Zounds! What was that?

A white cat with black patches on its back and face was acquainting itself, quite affectionately, with his boot. Throughout the past week at Audeley House, Nigel had never caught sight of the creature. "John," he interrupted. "Do the Audeleys keep a cat?"

"A cat? No, sir. The Audeleys don't own any such creatures." John lumbered around the corner of the kitchen table and saw the interloper. "Come here, you scamp. It's back out into the rain for you." The coachman reached down and tried to seize the feline, but it darted behind Nigel's legs. John paused, clearly unsure whether to risk mauling their exalted guest in the attempt to seize the intruder.

Nigel bent down and held out a friendly hand. The cat nuzzled against it. Within seconds, Nigel had picked up the cat and was rubbing its rounded head between the ears. "I think this cat would like to stay for dinner."

John gave him a puzzled look. "An' do ye want it to?"

"Of course. Set an extra plate, if you please."

Ignoring the look of confusion that passed between John and Archie, Nigel exited the kitchen and made his way to the parlour, still holding the trespassing feline. A cat might not be as good as a human companion, but at least it would give him *somebody* to talk to.

———

By the following afternoon, Nigel was beginning to appreciate just why lonely spinsters kept a cat. The creature alternated between resting calmly on his lap and darting wildly about the room amusing him with its antics. It had none of the annoying slobber or loud barking of a dog.

It soothed and settled Nigel to have another presence in the room, so that he could speak aloud without feeling like a candidate for an asylum. He loved a cheerful chat, even though he had to keep up both ends of it. In younger days, he used to drop in at the Society of Eccentrics for some captivating conversation, but he had all but given that up after his rise to the dukedom two years ago. After all, if he was ever to come out of his brother's shadow, he needed to take the ton by storm, not waste time dabbling in science, history, philosophy, and philanthropy. But he missed those days when one could talk deeply about the variety of life instead of desperately stroking the vanity of others.

"How many new stars do you think they've discovered since I've been in Derbyshire?" Nigel asked the cat.

The cat cocked her head and meowed.

"Twenty! That's rather optimistic. Have you been to the Kew Observatory then?"

The cat meowed again.

When he tired of discussing astronomy with the cat, Nigel found a ball of string from a workbag Mrs. Audeley had left in the parlour. He twirled the end about for the cat's enjoyment until John came to the parlour and cleared his throat. "The neighbour Miss Morrison is here, sir. She's askin' about her cat."

Nigel's spirits sunk. He might have known this furry amusement belonged to some local spinster. What a pity that he would have to surrender it and return to his state of listless boredom.

"Show her in," he said in a resigned voice. Head bent, he began to roll up the ball of string.

"I was not aware that the Audeleys had a houseguest," said a low, feminine voice.

Nigel looked up and saw a slender woman in a loose brown walking dress. It was not the sort of gown any of his London acquaintances would ever think of wearing—in public, in private, or in any circumstance outside of indentured servitude. But despite the unfashionableness of her gown, the woman had a lithe build, a firm stride, and sun-browned skin. Her face was not beautiful, but it was striking, and even more so since Nigel had not set eyes on any woman in the last week besides his new laundress, Mrs. Garrick. From beneath an unadorned chip bonnet, her clear grey eyes were assessing him thoughtfully.

This was not the aged spinster he had been expecting.

Nigel rose from his seat, dropping the ball of string to the floor. The cat sprung upon it with virulent vigour. "Nigel Lymington, at your service." He flashed the woman a scintillating smile and held out a hand with practiced grace.

"Pleased to meet you," said the lady, ignoring his outstretched hand. It might have been her matter-of-fact tone, but to Nigel's ear, she sounded anything *but* pleased. "I am Belinda Morrison."

Nigel paused. This was a far different reception than when he usually approached a lady at the theatre, at a ball, or in Hyde Park. Thunder and turf! He was considered a handsome fellow. Still in the prime of life. Possessed of all his hair. Well-muscled in physique. And with a title to boot! His carefully cultivated rakish reputation might be a deterrent to the more prudish members of the ton, but he had never encountered a matchmaking mama who would treat him with a lack of enthusiasm.

And yet, this Derbyshire gentlewoman looked decidedly put out by his presence in her neighbour's house.

"I'm sorry my cat has disturbed your peace," continued Miss Morrison, focusing all her attention on the truant feline. "She tends to wander far afield, but she usually ends up in a neighbour's barn, not their house." She half-knelt, letting the skirt of her drab dress drag on the floor. "Come here, Magpie."

To Nigel's amusement, the white-and-black creature backed away. It took the end of the string in its mouth and darted under the sofa. Apparently, Magpie—like any self-respecting feline—had no intention of coming at its owner's beck and call.

Nigel reached down and seized the ball of string, tugging gently to lure the cat out of its hiding hole. But even though he was able to dislodge the string from the cat's claws and draw it out from under the sofa, Magpie did not follow suit.

"I fear that you must take a seat," said Nigel, "until your cat decides she wants to be caught."

With a shrug, Miss Morrison sat down on the edge of the sofa, perched like a bird who planned to take flight as soon as a prevailing wind could be found. Her grey eyes swept over Nigel like a broom. He was relieved that he had obtained a clean shirt from Mrs. Garrick this morning and that he'd had the wisdom *not* to let the inept Archie tie his cravat—although why he should care about that was beyond him! Miss Morrison was clearly no arbiter of fashion.

"How are you acquainted with the Audeleys, Mr. Lymington?"

The word "Mr." grated on him. He supposed it was providential that this provincial miss was unaware that he was a duke. But still, where was the fluttering of fans, eyelashes, and hearts that he had come to expect? He had spent the last two years seeking to impress the whole world with his ducal position, and now he must hide it under a bushel like a pile of rotten apples.

And yet, even if he did reveal it, he had the distinct suspicion that it would impress this woman no more than his appearance had. She had neither the giddy exuberance of inexperienced debutantes nor the sly innuendo of more experienced ladies of the ton. Her cool indifference annoyed him. And intrigued him.

"I met Mrs. Audeley and her son during their stay in London."

"So, the Audeleys have returned home at last?"

"They have not. Mrs. Audeley was kind enough to offer me a place to stay as I had business in Derbyshire."

Her grey eyes opened wide. "What sort of business?"

The business of avoiding the seamier side of London society—although that was not exactly an answer one could share. Nigel cudgelled his brain for an excuse. What sort of business would take a man to this part of the world? Sheep? Boulders? Umbrellas? "Er...I'm investigating some mining rights."

"Who is your contact? Mr. Brownlee?"

"Among others." He waved a dismissive hand with more confidence than he felt. Who on earth was Mr. Brownlee? Was he a neighbour of the Audeleys? And did he have a mine on his property?

"Are you an investor?"

"I'm considering it." Nigel had no funds at present to do any such thing, but he attempted to imbue his answer with an air of mystery. This Miss Morrison was nothing if not inquisitive. He did not remember any London lady questioning his business in such a determined tone of voice! He wished she would stop asking questions…and take off her bonnet so he could see what colour her hair was.

"Welcome to Derbyshire," said Miss Morrison, giving him a nod as she finished her interrogation. She did not remove her bonnet.

Nigel looked at the low space beneath the sofa. The cat continued its refusal to come out. "Your cat is still delinquent, Miss Morrison, so you must tell me something about yourself while we wait. How do *you* know the Audeleys?"

"Oh, they have been my neighbours ever since I can remember. Mrs. Audeley, as you must already know, is a dear woman and a credit to the county."

"And Mr. Audeley?"

"We do not see eye to eye on agricultural practices, but Mr. Audeley is a sincere young man with romantic sensibilities."

Nigel's dark eyes blinked. Eye to eye on agricultural practices? What kind of antidote was this spinster? And he was fully aware that Mr. Audeley was filled to the brim with romantic sensibilities. It was Gyles Audeley's romantic sensibilities that had led Nigel, Mrs. Audeley, and the infinitely aggravating Lord Kendall on a wild goose chase from London to Grantham to Nottingham to Derbyshire—only to discover that Gyles Audeley had *not* eloped hither with Nigel's niece Louisa and had instead vanished into thin air!

"How good to hear that the Audeleys have your stamp of approval," said Nigel dryly. "My visit will be all the better knowing that my hosts are respected by their neighbours."

The woman's grey eyes narrowed. "Why, Mr. Lymington, I do believe you are having fun at my expense." Before he could reply, she bent down and collared the cat that was nosing its way out from under the sofa. "But now that I have Magpie, I shall intrude no further on your time. I daresay I shall see you at church tomorrow morning." She stood up to leave, holding the unprotesting feline against the brown wool that swathed her breast.

"Unlikely," said Nigel, standing as well. The shapeless dress hardly revealed anything of Miss Morrison's figure, but he was certain that she had one there, somewhere, under all that fabric. He had the sudden urge to unsettle her with his libertine views. "I rarely attend services."

She stared at him with a hint of scorn on her brow. "Are you irreligious, Mr. Lymington?"

"Er, no, I am not an atheist. But I cannot abide how vicars love to make a man feel guilty for everything he does."

"No smoke without fire," said Miss Morrison promptly. "Perhaps you feel guilty because you *ought* to feel guilty."

Nigel nearly took a step backwards. A society woman would have tittered and laughed and agreed with him how dull vicars were. His friend Lady Maltrousse would have batted him with her fan and invited him to play cards with her instead of going to church. But Miss Morrison knew how to turn a witticism into a criticism, and in the process, find a man's weak spot and press in the blade to the very hilt.

"I feel guilty right now," said Nigel, "for taking up so much of your time." He made a dramatic step toward the door to the parlour, indicating his readiness to bid his guest adieu.

"I forgive you," said Miss Morrison cheerfully, making quick work of the distance to the exit. "And thank you for occupying my cat. I hope she will not trouble you again."

"*She* was no trouble," said Nigel, unable to resist sending another barb her way.

Miss Morrison ignored him and stepped out the door.

He watched her plain chip bonnet and unfashionable brown dress disappear down the path and took a deep breath. As troublesome as Miss Morrison had been, he almost wished she would have deigned to stay and vex him longer. At least it would have given him *someone* to talk to.

As matters stood now, the only chance he would have to chat with her again would be hoping her cat returned to visit the scullery or visiting the nearby parish church.

CHAPTER THREE

Church

I T WAS RAINING AGAIN the next day, and despite that, Bel and Aunt Lucy rode to church in the open wagon. Bel held the ribbons, trying to avoid the largest puddles. Aunt Lucy clutched the side of the vehicle, alternately begging her to go slower or faster, depending on whether the rough road or the driving rain was currently providing her greater distress. "I do not know why we could not invest in a carriage, my dear. There is a veritable deluge coming down on my head. We are practically *swimming* our way to church."

Behind them Jenny, Jeremiah, and Tam sat on the bench, wrapped in thick woollen cloaks made from their own flock's shearing. Jeremiah—normally called Jer—was Jenny's brother, a large lad who was handy with a whittling knife and a pitchfork. Tam, a few years older than him, was a quiet fellow who performed his chores with silent precision. Tam had offered to drive that morning, but Bel preferred holding the reins, particularly in a downpour. She supposed she would have let Charlie drive, had he been there, but aside from him, she had a hard time trusting anyone to keep the horses on the road as well as herself.

"I don't want the expense of a carriage," she explained to her aunt. "If Charlie chooses to buy one when he returns, that's his affair. But for now, we'll save our guineas."

"Hmph!" said Aunt Lucy, trying to shield her head in the open conveyance with a cap, a bonnet, a cape, and an umbrella. It was so windy that her words carried only to Bel and not to the servants behind them. "I do hope Mr. Townsend will not mention you in the sermon. It's a dangerous thing to embarrass a vicar, for the whole parish might hear of it. But let us hope that he has forgotten your impertinence."

"I don't know why he would have," said Bel, "as I have not forgotten *his*." She reflected that she had met *two* impertinent gentlemen in the last two days, but somehow Mr. Townsend's inquisitive presumption was less endearing than Mr. Lymington's highhanded teasing. She had recapitulated her annoyance with the vicar more than once to Aunt Lucy, while at the same time, inexplicably, failing to mention Mr. Lymington's existence. After all, it was not likely that she would meet Mr. Lymington again—he had made his views on attending church quite clear.

"Upon my word! It was not presumptuous of the vicar to make conversation. You *like* talking about your estate just as much as I like talking about porcelain shepherdesses and pearl necklaces."

"Yes, but I don't like being told it's too much for me to handle. And I don't like strange gentlemen casting an eye on how much acreage I own. And besides, if Mr. Townsend had asked Mr. Brownlee a few more questions, he would have discovered that the estate does not belong to me but to Charlie."

"I daresay he would have discovered nothing of the kind," said Aunt Lucy, too miffed to remember that she was treading on sacred ground. "Charlie's been gone for nearly seven years now. There's no likelihood of him ever returning, so I think Mr. Brownlee and the rest of the neighbourhood have safely concluded that—"

"No!" Bel pulled on the reins and slowed the horse to a walk as they approached the churchyard. "There is no proof that Charlie is dead. You know what a terrible correspondent he is—it's no surprise that he's never written. India is a long way away, but I'm certain that someday we'll hear news of him. Or maybe he'll turn up on our doorstep without warning, a wealthy nabob who will be surprised to learn how many sheep he now owns in Derbyshire—"

"Oh, my dear girl, no one can fault you for wishing as much, but the reality is—" Aunt Lucy's words broke off, confronted by the bright glitter in Bel's grey eyes and the firm set of her chin. "Never mind. We shall argue no further and simply get through this Sunday as best we can, no matter how much my cape smells like wet sheep. Oh, look! There is Mrs. Brownlee as dry as can be after *her* carriage ride. And she is wearing another new gown."

Bel looked at the stone porch of the church and saw their pretty, plump neighbour dressed in green velvet beneath a holly red cloak. It was the perfect attire for a dreary December. Bel would never think of purchasing such an ostentatious ensemble herself, but she could admit that Mrs. Brownlee looked very fine in it. She suspected Mr. Brownlee must give his wife a great deal of pin money, to distract her from the fact that she had never been able to bear a child—and to distract her from his frequent absences from home.

The church bell was ringing as Bel steered the wagon over to the right side of the building where carriages were parked. Jeremiah jumped down and took the horse's head. Tam handed down Aunt Lucy from the wooden step beside the front wheel and escorted her to the porch of the church. Were the wagon parked at home, Bel would have climbed down without assistance, but here in the churchyard, she had enough presence of mind to remain seated and wait for Tam to help her descend.

"Allow me, Miss Morrison."

Surprised, Bel turned to the right and saw Mr. Lymington dressed in a many-caped greatcoat and crowned with a stylish top hat. There were no waterfalls pouring over the brim of his beaver, so he must have arrived in the Audeleys' closed carriage rather than an open conveyance like their own.

"I thought you did not attend divine services," said Bel without any pleasantries or preamble.

"I had no choice. A certain lady made me feel guilty for avoiding them."

Bel lifted an eyebrow.

His hand stretched out. Waiting.

With unusual self-consciousness, Bel placed her gloved hand in his. He helped her down onto the squelching ground and offered her an arm. It was a different sensation than holding on to the forearm of one of her farm labourers, and Bel supposed it must be because this fellow had taken her by surprise with his presence. On the porch of the church, Bel could see Aunt Lucy ogling them, hands fixed into a primitive telescope, trying to ascertain who Bel's companion might be.

"Ye all right, Miss Bel?" asked Tam, jogging back to retrieve her. He did not recognise the stranger either, and his concern had overcome his taciturn nature enough for him to inquire.

Across the churchyard, the wealthy Mrs. White turned her bonnet in their direction, and half a dozen lowlier members of the parish stood behind her gawping.

Bel disliked being such a spectacle for the neighbourhood simply because she was walking on the arm of a strange gentleman. "Yes, I'm fine, Tam. See to Jenny, if you please." Tam nodded and helped Jenny dismount from the back of the wagon.

Bel quickened her stride so that Mr. Lymington would not have to shorten his own to accommodate her. They reached the porch steps. The organ had already begun to play. Aunt Lucy looked at the gentleman guiding Bel through the church doors, opened her mouth, and shut it again. Bel could sense that her aunt's flood of curiosity was barely dammed, held back only by the organ prelude that precluded all possibility of conversation.

The Morrison ladies and the stranger proceeded through the church toward the box pews by the choir. "I daresay you would like to sit in the Audeleys' pew," said Bel nodding to the high-backed pew directly in front of their own.

"I daresay you would like me to," said Mr. Lymington. He released her arm without further comment and slid into the open bench directly below the Morrison ladies. Bel was relieved that he was not in *her* pew. It was bad enough that she had entered the church on his arm, creating a spectacle for the whole parish of Upper Cross.

"Belinda May Morrison," hissed Aunt Lucy as the organ reached the final cadence. "Who is *that*?"

"Hush, Aunt," said Bel. "He can hear you."

"Yes, I can," he said, turning halfway in his seat and flashing Bel's companion a charming smile. Aunt Lucy's wrinkled face began to glow, and Bel almost shook her head in disgust. Why did her aunt have to be so susceptible to every handsome countenance?

"*That* is Mr. Lymington," said Bel in low tones. "He is staying at Audeley House."

"I didn't realise the Audeleys had returned from London—"

"They haven't," whispered Bel, trying to silence her aunt as the vicar walked in front of the altar to begin the service. "Mr. Lymington is merely utilising their house for free lodging."

"What a delightful construction to put on my presence," whispered Mr. Lymington. "I'm pleased to meet you, Auntie."

Aunt Lucy began to giggle.

"Almighty God," said Mr. Townsend, beginning the prayer with far too exuberant a tone, "give us grace that we may cast away the works of darkness, and put upon us the armour of light, now in the time of this mortal life in which thy Son Jesus Christ came to visit us in great humility...."

Bel straightened her back and looked forward between the narrow confines of her bonnet brim, willing herself to ignore the man in the pew in front of her. But every time she succeeded in freeing her mind from considering Mr. Lymington, it veered off into an inner criticism of the vicar's method of reading the liturgy. Did not this "Shropshire lad" understand that there should be a certain reverent gravity to his cadence? One did not read the litany as if announcing the next act at a circus. The vicar's enthusiasm for the service was excessive—the exact opposite of Mr. Lymington's, as he sat inspecting the fingers of his gloves rather than giving the readings his full attention.

At least Mr. Townsend's hair was not dripping like a sheepdog's coat right now. Bel could see that her earlier supposition was correct and that it was a dark shade of blond, even darker about the sideburns than it was on top. Whereas Mr. Lymington's hair was a uniform shade of deep, dark, rich brown—

Bel forced her attention back to the service and tried to keep her mind from wandering around the corners of her eyes. She could sense that Aunt Lucy, with her customary curiosity, was having the same difficulty. Even Mrs. Brownlee across the building was having a hard time keeping her eyes off Mr. Lymington. The attention which had been reserved for the new vicar last week had been inexorably diverted to the mysterious visitor from London.

Finally, the service was over. Mr. Townsend proceeded to the back of the church where he could take leave of his new parishioners. Bel vacated the wooden pew and sensed Mr. Lymington's shadow over her shoulder. He fell in step behind her and Aunt Lucy, almost as if he needed a guide or protector to see him out of the building. She wondered if the unusual experience of attending a church service had made him uncomfortable. Good. It ought to.

A crowd of others were surging about them, doubtless hoping for an introduction to the newcomer, but Bel had no proprietary claim on his presence and was not about to halt and introduce him to everyone. As Bel and Aunt Lucy approached the back of the church, Mr. Brownlee asked the question that everyone was wondering. "Good morning to you, Miss Morrison. And to you, Belinda. Is this a guest of yours?"

Bel raised one eyebrow, surprised that Mr. Brownlee did not already know the man if he were here to confer with him on mining rights. "It certainly might seem so since he trails on our skirts so closely, but no. He is a houseguest at Audeley House." She closed her lips firmly, forcing the gentlemen to make their own introductions.

Mr. Lymington held out his hand to Mr. Brownlee. "Nigel Lymington."

"Harold Brownlee."

The two men shook hands. They were much of a height, but Mr. Brownlee's shoulders were more stooped, and his blond hair had greyed and begun to thin. Mrs. Brownlee, with her bright red cape waited hopefully at her husband's elbow, desirous of an introduction. But as usual, her husband seemed to have forgotten her existence.

"What brings you to Derbyshire, Mr. Lymington?" Mr. Brownlee's craggy face was full of enthusiasm.

"I came to admire the landscape," said the dark-haired visitor.

Bel looked at him sharply. What about his claim that he was here for investment purposes? Was that a sham? Or was he trying to find the lay of the land before letting the principal parties know of his interest?

"We certainly have landscape aplenty to admire," said Mr. Brownlee. "Although the winter is not as conducive for sightseeing." He stepped out to expand the circle and admit the vicar into the conversation. "I've been showing Mr. Townsend the sights, but it's wet work."

"Yes," said Mr. Townsend, shaking his head energetically. "Rainy but rewarding. I believe I'm acquainted with half the parish now and can find my way from the vicarage to Upper Cross quite credibly. I called on the Miss Morrisons just two days ago and enjoyed their *warm* hospitality."

Aunt Lucy gave a little gasp, no doubt still mulling over Bel's forward questioning of the vicar that had sent him sprinting for the door.

"I'm glad that it was not *too* warm for you," murmured Bel. She saw Mr. Lymington's dark eyes send her a sideways glance. The import of that comment seemed to fly right over the vicar's head, however.

"We are holding a dinner in Mr. Townsend's honour this week on Wednesday," said Mr. Brownlee, also oblivious to any undercurrents. "Perhaps you would care to join us, Mr. Lymington? And Miss Morrison and Miss Belinda too—we would not think of excluding you."

"How thoughtful of you," said Bel. She was not entirely sure that a dinner in the vicar's honour would be a pleasant experience, but if he was to become a fixture in the neighbourhood, then perhaps it was best if she became used to him. She stopped herself from looking at Mr. Lymington as she wondered whether he would accept the dinner invitation.

Before the dark-haired newcomer could answer, the vicar jumped in. "Indeed, you have been nothing but affable since my arrival." Mr. Townsend beamed at Harold Brownlee. "I know you are acquainted with my mother from bygone days, but I had not expected to find such a welcoming or involved patron."

Mr. Brownlee clapped the vicar on the shoulder with good-natured bonhomie. Plump Mrs. Brownlee reached for her husband's arm and nodded her head toward Mr. Lymington, trying to assert her own part in the dinner invitation. But once again, her inattentive husband failed to make the requisite introduction.

"We shall send around invitation cards tomorrow," proclaimed Mr. Brownlee, "and it shall be a magnificently merry party." He cleared his throat. "And now, Mr. Townsend, have you become acquainted with the Ferris brothers?"

A new crowd of parishioners surged forward to shake the vicar's hand. Bel found herself pushed by the tide out onto the porch of the church, with Aunt Lucy snuggled beside her and Mr. Lymington standing far too close for comfort so they could all keep out of the rain.

"Do you think it will let up if we wait here a moment?" said Aunt Lucy.

"Not likely," said Bel briskly. "Those grey clouds go on for miles."

"Miss Morrison and Miss Morrison," said Mr. Lymington, his face bending low between their two bonnets as the front of his greatcoat grazed against Bel's shoulder. "I came in the Audeleys' closed carriage, and it would be no trouble for Coachman John to drop you at your house."

"Oh, I see no reason to impose," countered Bel. She had been wet to the skin before without dying a lingering death. Further association with strange gentlemen seemed a far more dangerous malady.

"I can't imagine that it's an imposition," said Aunt Lucy quickly. She smiled up at Mr. Lymington. "Besides, it will give you the chance to see where we live in case you wish to call on us."

Bel bristled. They had not had callers for weeks on end in their provincial little part of Derbyshire, and were they now to be put to the trouble of *two* gentlemen callers within one sennight?

Mr. Lymington smiled as if aware of her irritation. "It would be my pleasure, Miss Morrison." He gave a half-bow to Aunt Lucy; then he inclined his head toward Bel. "I hear you give a *warm* welcome."

"Oh, Belinda is the best of hostesses," said Aunt Lucy, with more artifice than accuracy.

Bel glared at her aunt. She was glad she had never agreed to Aunt Lucy's proposals that they take a house in London together—not if this was the way her aunt thought a companion ought to behave when gentlemen were in the vicinity.

John exited the church, and Mr. Lymington sent him round for the carriage while Aunt Lucy explained to Tam that the Miss Morrisons had found another way home. Bel, waiting on the porch of the church, set her lips into a firm line, thankful at least that the ride home was short.

Chapter Four

Sheep

THE RAIN INCREASED OVERNIGHT and, by the time morning came, Nigel was expecting to see Gyles Audeley's rose bushes floating away on a liquefied landscape. Surely, it was indoor weather today. There were too many puddles and too much mud to even attempt an outing.

Nigel recalled a house party he had attended last winter where it was too wet to leave the premises. But even though there was rain outside, the lively gathering had been filled with drink, dancing, and mild debauchery—Lady Maltrousse would not have her reputation sullied with accusations of ennui when it could be sullied with accusations of dissipation and depravity.

But the confines of Audeley Manor held no such lively group to while away the weather. After breakfast, Nigel gave a dilatory effort on the pianoforte. He sat in the parlour opening and closing a book for twenty minutes. He paced about the house, mourned the loss of his feline companion, and rewound the ball of string into a tight globe of yarn. And then, after the rain abated at the noon hour, he decided that a walk would be just the thing.

Yesterday's carriage ride had provided him a sketch of the geography of the neighbourhood. The Miss Morrisons lived in a cosy stone house of three storeys with three windows across each floor. Beyond the house was an old barn and several tenant cottages, with drystone walls dividing out different portions of the acreage. Miss Lucy Morrison, as she thanked him for the carriage ride, had been assiduous in inviting him to call. Bel Morrison, on the other hand, had been pointedly silent, refusing to add her voice to her aunt's.

The thought of irritating the younger Miss Morrison with his presence was all the encouragement Nigel needed. He had memorized which turn to take on the road and, puddles or no, he was determined to drink his tea with the Morrison ladies that very afternoon. He stepped out the door and looked down at his boots. Archie had done his best by them, but they would need a thorough cleaning once again after this excursion.

It was not more than ten minutes' walk before the Morrisons' house came into sight on the green horizon. Nigel was still a good distance off when he noticed several labourers in a nearby field working to extricate a sheep from a mud pit. The poor creature had slid into a depression in the ground, and it was too full of mud and water for the beast to climb out again. Nigel paused and peered over the hedgerow to watch the fellows at work.

Two sturdy labourers were down in the mud pit, trying to seize hold of the frightened animal and put a noose around its shoulders. Five yards away, a much slighter fellow—dressed in sturdy boots, an oilskin coat, a large cap, and a pair of buckskin trousers—held the end of the rope.

"Lift her right leg, Jer," said the smaller fellow, seemingly the leader of the bunch even though his young voice had not yet deepened, "and put it through the noose along with the neck so we don't strangle the old girl."

The fellow named Jer complied and, with the harness attached to the sheep, scrambled back out of the mud pit to help the slighter fellow pull on the rope.

Nigel's eyes narrowed. There was something familiar about that lad in the buckskin trousers. He wished that the lad's cap was not covering his hair and shadowing his face so that he could see him clearly. He resolved to tarry a little longer to see if the project of extricating the sheep was successful.

"Give him a shove, Tam," said the lad, and the man still in the mud pit hit the sheep's haunches with an encouraging thwack. The slender fellow and Jer began to haul on the rope, and after a few minutes of straining, the mud released its victim. The ungainly sheep scrambled up the sides of the mud pit, without so much as a thank you to its rescuers, and pulled impatiently while they untied the rope harness that had wrought its salvation.

"Well done," said Nigel, clapping his gloved hands from his side of the hedgerow and alerting the farmhands to his presence. The younger lad seemed startled, almost bashful, at the presence of a gentleman and immediately knelt behind the sheep to work the knot on the harness.

"Thank'ee, sir," said Jer, giving Nigel a nod and pulling his forelock with a dirty hand. The one named Tam grunted in acknowledgement, and Nigel recognised him as one of the Morrisons' manservants from the churchyard. They stood staring at him until the situation became uncomfortable.

Nigel decided to continue his walk to the Morrison house. He turned toward the road and stepped forward without considering his surroundings. His boot splashed into a puddle with such force that the water flew between the sides of his unbuttoned greatcoat and spotted the front of his pantaloons.

"Fiend take it." Nigel frowned and skirted the rest of the puddle. He had wanted to appear his best when calling on his neighbours, and now he looked like he had been dancing in a mud pit just like the rest of these Derbyshire locals.

From the corner of his eye, he saw that the sheep had been freed from the rope, and the muddy mass of wool was trotting happily away from its rescuers. The slender lad stood up again, his large cap still covering his hair, but the grey eyes below the brim of the cap were watching Nigel make his way down the lane, and they were filled with unspoken laughter.

❧

"How kind of you to call," twittered Miss Lucy as soon as the housemaid showed Nigel into her parlour. "And so soon after our invitation! I'm afraid that Bel has gone...out for the afternoon. She will be disappointed to have missed your visit."

"Yes, I'm sure she will," murmured Nigel. He had his suspicions just where Miss Morrison had disappeared to, but he kept those locked tightly beneath the breast of his grey woollen jacket and green paisley waistcoat. At least only one woman would behold him in his bedraggled pantaloons—Lady Maltrousse would have laughed him out of her salon to see him so untidily dressed. He wondered how he would keep the elder Miss Morrison entertained for the time it would take to drink a cup of tea, for he had been hoping to see another lady entirely and quiz her about her comment to the vicar.

"You must tell me all about London," said Lucy, oblivious to his disappointment. "It has been five years since I was there last. Has much changed?"

"Er, no," said Nigel. "The king is still on the brink of madness. Almack's is still as dull as ever. And the Thames still stinks to high heaven."

"But what about the shops and the theatre?"

"The shops still sell ribbons and gloves, and the theatre is still too bawdy for the Methodists, too frivolous for the critics, and too tedious for the ladies who only come to see and be seen."

Lucy sighed in satisfaction. "How I should like to visit once again! You must be quite a favourite in London, Mr. Lymington."

Nigel cleared his throat. "I am occasionally in demand by the less discriminating hostesses." It was a modest way of phrasing his popularity, but then, Lucy Morrison did not need to know that Lady Jersey, Lady Sefton, and Lady Maltrousse all counted on him to make up their numbers for a dinner party.

"But what set do you frequent? You are not a Corinthian?"

"Heavens, no. I despise curricle-racing and boxing and every other sport that induces a man to perspire."

"But you are also not a dandy?"

"No, indeed. I like my collar points to be low enough to see who's sitting beside me."

"Then what are your interests, Mr. Lymington?"

Nigel cocked his head. He did not know how to answer. For the last two years he had never asked himself that question once. He had merely looked for the next luxurious house party, the next risqué ridotto, the next exclusive card game to prove that the Duke of Warrenton could play and partake with the best of them. His interests, of late, had been scrambling for money to maintain his social cachet. But now, here he was, immured in the countryside—and it had taken him less than a week to discover that his own company was as perishingly dull as Parliamentary proceedings.

"I suppose I can only claim a passion for collecting interesting people to talk to."

Aunt Lucy nodded perceptively. "You'll enjoy my niece then, for she's as *interesting* as they come."

Nigel grinned. He was positive Miss Morrison would not be pleased with her aunt's efforts to continually thrust her niece forward as a conversational topic. "Perhaps I shall have the chance to speak with her at dinner on Wednesday," said Nigel lightly. Or perhaps fate might contrive an encounter even sooner.

CHAPTER FIVE

Names

"**M**AGPIE! MAGPIE!" BEL SHOOK her head in disbelief. She'd searched the house and the barn three times over. That troublesome cat had disappeared again. There was always the fear of foxes or other predators taking her, but Bel had a suspicion that Magpie might have gone wandering again to the very place her mistress was most loath to follow. "If you've gone to ground at the Audeleys' again," muttered Bel, "so help me, I'll—"

She did not finish that statement. She had already avoided tea with Nigel Lymington yesterday, tending to the sheep while he was visiting Aunt Lucy. It had disconcerted her when he stopped in the lane to watch Jer and Tam pull the errant lamb out of the mud, and she hoped he had not recognised her. She had started wearing male attire a few years ago when working on her own land. It was easier than fussing with a skirt—although Aunt Lucy had made her promise not to wear it in the house or around any of the gentry. So far, she had managed to avoid encountering the Brownlees, or the Audeleys, or any of the other upper crust of Upper Cross while wearing trousers, but Mr. Lymington's perspicacious gaze had taken her by surprise.

Addressing Magpie's truancy would require a change out of her utilitarian clothing. Bel took off her jacket and shirt, untucked her thin chemise from the trousers, and fastened a pair of stays over her bosom. Then, she pulled a serviceable brown wool gown over her head. She disliked having to call Jenny to help her dress, so she wore her clothing loose. That way, her arms and fingers were nimble enough to reach behind and fasten all the ties that feminine clothing sported.

Finished at last, she wound her full hair into a bun and placed her old chip bonnet over it. She would dress well enough not to embarrass Aunt Lucy, but not well enough to hint that she had any care for her appearance when entering the presence of Nigel Lymington.

Instead of walking on the lane, she cut through the long field that separated the Morrison estate from Audeley House. Archie let her into the house when she told him her errand and showed her to the parlour when she asked after Mr. Lymington. "I was just about t'make tea for his gr—I mean, for Mr. Lymington," he said proudly.

Bel ignored Archie and pushed open the door of the parlour. The sight that greeted her eyes might have awakened tender feelings in a woman yearning for domesticity, but the image of Nigel Lymington—eyes closed, leaning against the wing of an old armchair, cradling a fluffy feline in his lap—filled Bel with more annoyance than sentiment. What was he doing with that cat? The creature clearly belonged to her! She cleared her throat.

Mr. Lymington's dark eyes sprung open. He straightened in the chair. "Ah, Miss Morrison. I'm used to more warning from my butler when I have a caller." He paused. "You'll pardon me if I don't rise to greet you. The cat is napping."

"The cat will have to be wakened," said Bel briskly, ignoring the fact that she had caught Mr. Lymington napping as well, "for she is coming home with me." She looked at the gentle breathing of the furry bundle that sat atop Mr. Lymington's muscular legs. "Magpie," she said in a firm tone. "Magpie!"

The cat continued to sleep.

Mr. Lymington shook his head. "I must say that your naming skills leave something to be desired."

"What on earth do you mean, sir?"

"All I am pointing out," he said, hand raised in a conciliatory fashion, "is that Magpie is not a particularly clever name for a magpie cat. It leaves me wondering if you had a black pony when you were a girl and named it Blackie. Or a pet fish in a bowl that you named Fishy."

Bel froze. How did he know that? The pony had been brown with the name Brownie, but the principle was the same.

"Perhaps it's not the cleverest name," she said her hackles beginning to rise, "but what would you have called a cat?"

He shrugged. "Princess? Guinevere? Melisande?"

She blinked.

"Dido? Coricopat? Scheherazade?"

"Point taken, Mr. Lymington. You are far more clever with names than I am. However, the cat belongs to me, not you, and I shall be taking Magpie home now."

Reluctantly, Mr. Lymington lifted the furry creature off his lap, rose to his feet, and deposited it into her arms. The cat stretched and flexed its claws, dismayed at having its slumber disturbed so abruptly. "*Au revoir*, Magpie," said Mr. Lymington, kissing the air with exaggerated gallantry.

Bel rolled her eyes. How did this fellow manage to be so humorous and so irritating all at the same time?

At that moment, the Audeley's undergardener came into the parlour bearing a little plate of ham, minced finely.

"What is that?" demanded Bel.

"Tea for Miss Magpie," said Archie, attempting to stand to attention like a London footman in livery.

"Tea for a cat?" Bel stared at Mr. Lymington in disbelief. So, this is what Magpie had been eating at Audeley House, an unheard-of indulgence when Bel often expected the cat to catch her own supper in the barn.

"Perhaps you ought to stay to tea and investigate why it seems to be that Magpie prefers my company to yours."

"I can clearly see why Magpie prefers your company. It is because you bribe her with the choicest cuts of meat from your larder. And in the process, you make her wholly dependent on your table and wholly useless as a mouser."

"Nonsense," said Mr. Lymington. "A little ham never hurt a true hunter. You don't see peers of the realm giving up fox hunting simply because they have a French cook in the kitchen."

"I daresay you have *no* cook in the kitchen, Mr. Lymington, so I don't understand how you expect to serve me tea."

"Ah, you are not reckoning with the talents of Mrs. Garrick. She has a plum cake waiting for us. And I happened to walk into Upper Cross earlier this morning and secured some sweetmeats." He looked at her pleadingly, like a boy hoping for a holiday from his books.

She could not understand why he would want her company, but she grudgingly conceded the point. "Very well, I shall stay for tea, but I shall be certain to scold you and put you into a temper." She put the cat down on the floor and let it pick fastidiously at the plate of minced ham.

Mr. Lymington clapped his hands together. "Excellent. And I think you'll find that I keep my temper quite well. It will be a challenge for you to make me lose it."

Within moments, Archie brought in a tray with a teapot, the plum cake, and Mrs. Audeley's gold-rimmed teacups and tea plates. He set it down on the tea table, and Mr. Lymington leaned forward to pour. He seemed quite comfortable playing hostess. In other circumstances, Bel might have found his confidence charming, but somehow, it only made her warier.

"No sugar, I assume?"

"Why would you assume that?"

"Because you are not a sugary person, Miss Morrison."

"Which makes one wonder what lunacy caused you to walk all the way into Upper Cross to obtain sweetmeats."

"Perhaps *I* have a sweet tooth," said the dark-haired man. He gave her a lopsided grin. "Or perhaps I suspected that you would call on me for tea, and I am trying to make you sweeter than you are by nature."

"Upon my word, Mr. Lymington, did you invite me to tea to insult me?" Bel was beginning to wonder if he would make *her* lose her temper before she had landed any hits of her own.

"Not at all." He handed her the dark beverage with no sugar and no cream. She looked down at it and was reminded, uncomfortably, that she took her tea the same way as the vicar. Perhaps it would not hurt to try a little sugar next time.

"I am still puzzled as to why Mrs. Audeley, after such a short acquaintance, would allow you to stay in her house while she is not here."

"It is really quite simple," he said with a drawl. "I attempted to seduce Mrs. Audeley while she was in London, and in the process, we became friends."

Bel had been about to take a drink, but she paused in stunned silence. "I believe I misheard you. You were attempting to...?"

"Seduce Mrs. Audeley." He flashed her an apologetic look. "It seemed the thing to do—to put Lord Kendall's nose out of joint."

Bel had no idea who Lord Kendall was, but at all this talk of seduction, her ears began to turn red. Fortunately, they were well hidden by her narrow-brimmed chip bonnet. She knew Mrs. Audeley as well as one could know a neighbour. She was a modest and unassuming Derbyshire widow, and Bel was certain that Mr. Lymington's attentions would *not* have been welcome.

She changed the subject. "How did you enjoy the vicar's sermon?" Apparently, Mr. Lymington was in more dire need of divine services than she had initially realised.

"I found it very edifying," murmured Mr. Lymington, so meekly that Bel could easily see the deviltry lurking behind his eyes. "The wolf shall lie down with the lamb, and all that."

There was something very wolf-like about Mr. Lymington's face as he considered her countenance. Were all London gentlemen like this, or just this one?

She put down her teacup and bent down to gather up Magpie. "Thank you for the tea, Mr. Lymington. I will bore you no longer with my presence and will take my cat home where she belongs."

"Bore me? Certainly not. Your aunt assures me that you are a very *interesting* person to talk to. And I am still waiting for you to put me in a temper."

It seemed, almost, like a plea for her to stay. Bel had no intention of yielding. Mr. Lymington, despite his charm, was a highly inappropriate person to take tea with. And now that she had retrieved Magpie, she had other chores to complete.

Bel rose to her feet. "I daresay you can amuse yourself, Mr. Lymington, since you are on holiday here in Derbyshire. But for those of us who live here, there are many duties to attend to."

Mr. Lymington looked crestfallen at that although Bel could not understand why. He abandoned his comfortable armchair to stand as well. "Your servant, Miss Morrison." Before she knew what he was doing, he took her hand—the one not holding Magpie to her chest—and pressed it.

Bel started. She had touched hands with dozens of men in greetings at church, in business at market day, and on the dance floor for assemblies, but she had never felt such a frisson of excitement. Why should contact with the impertinent Mr. Lymington affect her so?

At least she was wearing gloves. And at least her bonnet was covering her ears like a shield. "Good-bye, Mr. Lymington," she said crisply without a hint of sympathy in her voice.

Then she fled the room, determined to lock Magpie away until the Audeleys' guest should have left the county.

CHAPTER SIX

Compliments

N IGEL HAD NOTHING TO do the following day other than dress for dinner at the Brownlees'. He had
allowed Archie to attempt a waterfall cravat, but the daft
lad had ruined so many squares of pressed cloth that Nigel
finally had to wave him away and tie it himself. He had not
brought evening wear for this trip of the sort that he would
wear for the ballrooms and dining rooms of London, but
he suspected that a dark morning suit would be more than
adequate to dine with the local squire in honour of the new
vicar.

His truncated tea with Miss Morrison yesterday continued to amuse him and parade through his thoughts more
frequently than it should. Clearly, the woman disapproved
of him. He guessed that she was ten years his junior but still
old enough to be set in her character. And that character, he
suspected, was almost impervious to charm.

Almost.

He had seen her blush when he took her hand in farewell. Apparently, the touch of his hand had done something to her. Blast! It had done something to him too.

Nigel snorted. He had been away from London far too long if the unwilling handclasp of a village spinster could set his pulse racing. Still—it was not the worst thing to have an average-looking female to while away the time with.

He had challenged Miss Morrison to make him lose his temper—a feat that only his niece Louisa had ever been able to achieve. He would challenge himself to bring down her defences. Could he make her smile? Could he make her laugh? Could he finally discover what colour her hair was without a bonnet covering it up?

It was true what he had told her, that he had attempted to seduce Mrs. Audeley merely to put the Earl of Kendall's nose out of joint. But somehow, Rose Audeley had seen through his philandering façade to the person he'd been before his brother had died. Before he'd tried to impress the ton by frittering away a fortune. Before he'd become the wastrel Duke of Warrenton. She had seen him and taken pity on him. And that was how he had found a place outside of London to go to ground like a fox, hoping that Mr. Digby's hounds would not sniff him out anytime soon.

But if he had to maintain his anonymity in the countryside indefinitely, he might as well make his own amusement while he was there. Mrs. Audeley might have been a more tempting armful, but getting up a flirtation with the no-nonsense Miss Morrison sounded amusing indeed.

"Archie! Where's my beaver?"

The aspiring valet rushed into the room, his spotty face lit up with pride and his hands reverently holding the one hat Nigel had brought with him. "Right here, yer grace."

Nigel took it in hand, looked it over, and frowned. "Did you brush it?"

"The best I could," said Archie.

"I'm afraid you've *over*-brushed it," said Nigel. "The gloss is gone, and you've almost worn a hole here in the side. Egad! It's not like scraping moss off a garden wall."

Archie gaped and tried to take the beaver back, but Nigel waved him away. "Never mind, never mind. It can't be helped now." He would have given the lad the sack had they been back in London, but somehow, the botched brushing of a beaver was all part of this rusticating adventure. He was "Mr. Lymington" here in Derbyshire, not the immaculate Duke of Warrenton. And that meant making allowances for Archie Garrick, spots and all.

When Nigel came downstairs, he saw that John had readied the horses to deliver him to the Brownlees'. The coachman had a pleasant smile on his face. Perhaps he was happy not to have to prepare another meal for an inconvenient houseguest. Or perhaps he simply enjoyed the opportunity to harness up the horses after a few days of indolence.

The Brownlees kept country hours for dinner, but it was already dark outside when it was time to depart—dark and dank with the fog that had come down from the hills into the valley. Nigel squinted out the carriage window and discovered that the Brownlees were on the *other* side of the triangle that formed the Morrison property. Apparently, Miss Morrison's holdings were pincered between her neighbours like Switzerland between France and Italy.

The windows of Mullhill Manor gleamed brightly. It was twice the size of the Morrison home and larger too than the Audeley residence. Clearly, Harold Brownlee was the premier landowner in this part of Derbyshire, which is why Miss Morrison had assumed that Nigel's "business" must be with him. John coaxed the horses round the circular drive and dropped Nigel off at the entrance to the house.

A footman—one of a matching pair—opened the door, and Nigel began to feel that he had entered civilisation once again. The plump lady who had been hanging on Harold Brownlee's arm at the church smiled and approached. She was much of an age with Miss Lucy Morrison, but her soft blond hair had not yet begun to grey and the skin about her eyes was still luminescent.

"A very charming home, Mrs. Brownlee," complimented Nigel, handing his beaver, greatcoat, and gloves to one of the footmen.

The lady of the house glowed at this praise. "We are honoured to host you tonight, Mr. Lymington. You must let me know if there's anything I can provide to see to your comfort."

"Good company is all that I require," said Nigel, "and I seem to have found it already."

Mrs. Brownlee put a hand to her heart, showing that Nigel's dart of flattery had struck just the place intended. "I've seated you next to Miss Morrison," she said with a quiet voice. "She cannot fail to keep you entertained during dinner."

Nigel decided to be purposefully obtuse. "Ah yes, I had tea with Miss Lucy this week, and she regaled me with her memories of London."

"Dear me, did I say Miss Lucy? I meant Miss Belinda, for I supposed that the young people ought to sit together. Miss

Belinda, the vicar, and you—and if the vicar starts to prose on, why, Bel will keep him in check."

Nigel gave her an encouraging smile. At the advanced age of eight-and-thirty, he did not consider himself young anymore, but the prospect of teasing Belinda Morrison was a delight that he had been looking forward to all day, even if he did have to endure a prosy vicar.

"My ears are tingling," said the woman of whom they spoke. Miss Morrison approached with fearless step. "What are you telling him about me, Mrs. Brownlee?"

"Nothing, my dear, merely that he is to take you in to dinner."

"Is that so?" said Miss Morrison, without the hint of a simper or the bat of an eyelash.

Nigel stared at her. Her hair, no longer covered by a prim bonnet or a farmhand's cap, was finally revealed to him as a rippling shade of loamy brown, containing as many colours as a patch of freshly turned earth in the summer sun. And her dress, for once, was the expected attire of a gentlewoman—a high-waisted silken confection in navy blue that confirmed she had a lovely collarbone, lovely shoulders, and other lovely parts as well. It was the first time Nigel had seen Miss Morrison in any colour other than a drab brown or grey. It was also the first time that her dress had any shape to it—hinting that her body might be less angular than he had heretofore observed.

Nigel began to consider Mrs. Brownlee a very commendable hostess to arrange matters as she had. He would take Miss Morrison in to dinner, even if it meant enduring the proximity of the clerical guest of honour, and he would tease her mercilessly. After all, one needed *something* to do when one was rusticating.

—ℓℓ—

Bel sensed Mr. Lymington looking her over with an appraising eye. She had allowed Aunt Lucy to select her a gown for the dinner, and predictably, Aunt Lucy had chosen the most expensive gown in Bel's wardrobe with the most beadwork, the most embroidery, and the least coverage. It was not immodest by any means, but it showed far more skin than her usual wool gowns that buttoned up to the neck. More than once, Bel wished she had longer sleeves or a sensible fichu to tuck into her neckline. Mr. Lymington's flippant mention of seducing Mrs. Audeley had put her on her guard—although, she had her doubts whether a real rake would mention a *failed* attempt at seduction so blithely.

As Mrs. Brownlee moved away to greet the elderly Ferris brothers, Mr. Lymington took a step nearer. From the glitter in his eye, she thought he might be about to give her a compliment, but instead, he leaned closer and whispered in her ear. "Miss Morrison, upon my word, I scarcely recognised you without your governess' dress...or without your trousers."

Bel's ears flamed red, with no bonnet this time to shield them from sight. So, she had *not* escaped notice in the muddy sheep field two days ago. Mr. Lymington had taken note of her in trousers and was apparently scandalised—or intrigued—by the picture. "How curious," she shot back, "for I scarcely recognised *you* without a stolen cat on your lap."

"Stolen? Tsk, tsk. Your cat simply knows how to follow her heart."

"Say, rather, her *stomach*."

"A less noble organ, but not to be despised. I must confess that my own stomach is a-quiver with excitement to enjoy something besides Coachman John's cooking tonight."

"What a sore trial it must be to you to stay at an establishment with limited staff. I take it you have a full complement of servants at your usual London estate?" It was not exactly polite to demand if a gentleman was well-heeled and well-housed, but Bel had no qualms about plain speaking with Mr. Lymington.

"Er, yes," said the dark-haired man, but tentatively, as if he did not wish to brag about his status. It was the first mark of humility that Bel had witnessed in him.

"You must be eager to finish your business so you can return to them. What *was* your business in Derbyshire, Mr. Lymington? Mining rights? Or was it landscape appreciation?" Bel cast him an innocent look.

"Something of the sort."

She lifted one eyebrow. She would wager that it was *nothing* of the sort. Why *was* Mr. Lymington here in Derbyshire? And how long did he mean to stay? If he meant to needle her about wearing trousers, she would needle him back about his unjustified presence in these parts. One did not simply come to Upper Cross in rural Derbyshire for relaxation. One went to Brighton. Or Bognor.

"Miss Morrison," said a cheerful voice in tones loud enough to fill a pulpit rather than a mere drawing room. It was the vicar, beaming brightly, nodding at his surroundings, and looking for all the world as if *he* were the host here at Mullhill Manor. "How delightful to see you again. Mrs. Brownlee tells me that I shall enjoy your company at dinner."

Bel would not have thought that her company would provoke such delight, but she gave a warm smile that was more for Mr. Lymington's benefit than the vicar's. "I hope that Mrs. Brownlee proves correct, Mr. Townsend. I shall endeavour to mind my manners so that I do not send you into distress once again."

"Distress?" echoed the vicar. "I can see that I have given you a false impression of me. I must have appeared very pigeon hearted when I left tea early the other day."

"Left tea early?" echoed Mr. Lymington, still at Bel's elbow. "Good heavens! What could have frightened you away? Surely it was not our dear Miss Morrison?"

Bel's lips set into a firm line, and she refused to let them smile. Would the insufferable Mr. Lymington ever stop tormenting her? The worst part of it was that she could not help but find him amusing, wretch that he was.

"Certainly not," replied the vicar. "The fact of the matter is, no sooner had I arrived than I felt a sneeze coming on. And when I tried to stifle it, it came on in greater force. Since I had been soaked to the skin on the walk over, I decided I should curtail my visit and seek dry clothes lest my sneezing fit develop into a wheeze or a croup. A clergyman cannot be too careful with his voice. It is the clarion call to faith, the trumpet from which the Gospel soundeth forth. 'How shall they hear without a preacher?' if you take my meaning?"

"How indeed?" murmured Mr. Lymington, his own urbane voice a pointed contrast with the stentorian tones of the vicar.

"I am relieved to hear that you did not take ill from your outing," said Bel, "and that you did not take offence from my conversation." Aunt Lucy had certainly attributed the vicar's sudden defection to Bel's frank manner, but perhaps his sneezing was really to blame and his breast harboured no such sensitivity.

"Harold explained to me," said the vicar confidently, nodding in the direction of Mr. Brownlee who was about to throw open the doors to the dining room, "that you have a penchant for levity."

"A penchant for levity?" said Mr. Lymington in low tones, his lips quite close to the edge of her ear. "My dear Miss Morrison, have you been making a cake of the new vicar?"

"Certainly not," said Bel. She would have ended the conversation there, but somehow, under the odious influence of the witty Mr. Lymington, she had the wish to be a wit too. She turned and spoke to him in a half-whisper. "I was under the mistaken impression that Mr. Townsend was proposing marriage to me, and I merely asked him to clarify his intentions."

Mr. Lymington gave a wicked laugh. "Why, Miss Morrison, I never would have suspected that you had it in you."

Mr. Townsend, observing the intimacy of their muted conversation, looked ready to administer a reprimand, but the gong sounded before anything further could be said. Mr. Lymington offered Bel his arm, while Mr. Townsend was obliged to take in their hostess, Mrs. Brownlee. Aunt Lucy entered on the arm of wizened old Jack Ferris while his even older brother James Ferris shuffled in behind them without a partner. And then Mr. Brownlee, beaming and benevolent, led in Mrs. White, a wealthy widow who kept a house in the village.

Chapter Seven

Dinner

T HE BROWNLEES KEPT A good table, and Bel, as loath as she was to admit it, was forced to compliment the hostess on the superior quality of Brownlee mutton. "Thank you, my dear," said Mrs. Brownlee, "but that is all due to Harold. He keeps the sheep quite plump and happy, and Cook has little work on his own to make them tender for the table."

Bel nodded. No wonder Mr. Brownlee's steward could command a premium for his flock at the market. Brownlee sheep were famous at auction. She had spent five years increasing the size of her flock and had only begun to sell them at market in the last two years. Ignoring Mr. Lymington's quizzical look, she began to calculate how much lower she would have to price her flock to convince more buyers to take a risk on an untried sheep owner.

The hostess turned to the vicar, eager to draw out the guest of honour. "You must tell us about your home country, Mr. Townsend."

"Indeed," said the vicar, setting down his water goblet with a smack of the lips. "My mother resides in Shropshire, which is where I was raised. My father, regrettably, died before I was born." The vicar's voice held little evidence of sorrow over that fact, but Bel supposed that it was difficult for him to diminish the enthusiasm of his tone, no matter the subject matter on which he spoke.

"Goodness, me!" said Mrs. Brownlee. "So, you never knew him?"

"No, he was an officer in the navy and perished in battle shortly before my birth. My mother received a regular pension, and we lived comfortably in Shropshire with enough for my school fees to be paid when I came of age to go to Eton and Oxford."

Mr. Brownlee, at the other end of the table, began to speak loudly to Mrs. White and the elder Mr. Ferris about the up-coming Christmas season. Apparently, he was already familiar with the vicar's family history and had no need to hear it again. Caught in the middle of the table, Bel found it difficult to follow either conversation, but her neighbour at her elbow leaned in with remarks of his own.

"Who would have thought our British naval administration would be so generous?" Mr. Lymington's dark eyebrows lifted, and his mouth took on a faintly sardonic twist that seemed to be there more often than not.

"Generous?"

"To the good vicar and his mother. I have never heard of naval pensions taking care of women and children so admirably."

"Such a matter is outside my knowledge," said Bel, "but my experience is no doubt narrower than your own. Have you lived in London your whole life, Mr. Lymington?"

"London, primarily, but also here and there."

"Where is here? And where is there?"

"In Lincolnshire, if you must know. My family seat—er, my family *seems* to have put down roots there shortly after the Conquest."

"I've heard Lincolnshire has prime land for farming."

"Does it?" Mr. Lymington swirled the wine around in his glass. "I wouldn't know. And for the past few years I've resided almost exclusively in London."

"What is it you *do* while you are in London?"

"My dear Miss Morrison, must I *do* anything?"

"You are far less forthcoming than Mr. Townsend. At least we now know who his parents were and how his school fees were paid. For I assume you *did* go to school. However annoying you are, you at least go about it in an educated fashion."

Mr. Lymington smirked and Bel could see that she had amused him rather than provoked his temper. "My father paid my school fees."

"And how did your father get the money for that?"

"From his father before him."

"So, you come from a moneyed family?" Although Aunt Lucy might deplore it, Bel had no reticence in talking about finances.

"Er, yes. Although I find myself rather short of the stuff right now." Mr. Lymington gave a longsuffering sigh. "In truth, I have to tell all the ladies that—to stop them from throwing themselves at me."

"How difficult that must be for you. I hope you did not mistake my questions as a declaration of interest."

"I believe I am sufficiently acquainted with you to avoid making that fatal presumption."

Bel could see the vicar eyeing them suspiciously, no doubt trying to make out what their conversation was about. Her acquaintance was of no longer date with Mr. Townsend than it was with Mr. Lymington, but somehow the former seemed quite put out that the latter had her attention. Perhaps it had something to do with his role as shepherd of the flock to which Bel belonged. Or perhaps he knew something untoward about Mr. Lymington. After all, they both had arrived recently from the same metropolis.

Mr. Lymington addressed himself to his food, took a bite of the pheasant, and let out a moan of satisfaction. "Seasoned to perfection, wouldn't you agree, Miss Morrison?" Without waiting for an answer, he plunged ahead. "Magpie would enjoy this pheasant. Perhaps I ought to bring some home for her—"

"Magpie will not be visiting you again," said Bel curtly, "so you can leave your pheasant on your plate."

"I wouldn't be so sure of that. She seems to know where she is valued."

"Upon my word, Mr. Lymington, just because I do not take tea with my cat does not mean I do not value her. It's just like a Londoner to pamper a cat instead of putting her to use. Magpie is a valuable mouser—"

"Not everything's value is predicated on its use."

"Where else is value derived?" demanded Bel.

Mr. Lymington's eyes narrowed thoughtfully. "In the joy that it gives to us. Or in the beauty that it gives to the world."

Bel stared back at him. If he had been more flippant, she would have suspected that he was still flirting with her. But he seemed to be in earnest about the subject—and looking *through* her rather than at her.

His philosophising was faintly demoralising. She knew she was no beauty, but she also knew that her diligent industry and her care for the people beneath her were enough to render her valuable to the community. And as for joy, she knew that to be the least essential of all her emotions. Duty was what sent a person out to the sheepfold on a stormy night. Duty was what kept the barley and rye planted on time each season. Duty was what kept a woman summing the ledgers for a brother who had been gone for nearly seven years.

For Mr. Lymington to predicate value on beauty and joy was the outside of enough! But it was typical of a Londoner who cared about little more than the surface of things. Bel's lips parted to say something cutting, but plump Mrs. Brownlee interjected before the words came out.

"You must tell us, Mr. Lymington, how long you mean to stay in Derbyshire? Will you be here for Christmas?"

"Why, that's yet to be determined, ma'am." Mr. Lymington gave Mrs. Brownlee a warm smile.

"Will the Audeleys be back for Christmas?" asked Bel. She could not imagine that it would be appropriate for Mr. Lymington to stay under the same roof as Mrs. Audeley, not after his startling confession about how their acquaintance came to be.

"I think...not," said Mr. Lymington. "In fact," he said, his tone turning conspiratorial, "it is highly likely that you will soon hear some *news* about Mrs. Audeley."

"Oh?" said Mrs. Brownlee, her cheeks pinking with interest.

"What news would that be?" asked Aunt Lucy, catching wind of an interesting subject from her seat farther down the table.

Mr. Lymington held up a hand in protest. "I am sorry, dear ladies, but it is not my news to tell. Although, the one hint that I can share is that Mr. Townsend will likely be the first to know of it." He cast a sly look at the vicar.

Bel's forehead furrowed. Why would the vicar be the first to know? He had not even met Mrs. Audeley—unless he too had become acquainted with her in London. But she had no intention of teasing Mr. Lymington further about the subject. For some inexplicable reason, she disliked hearing Mr. Lymington talk about their attractive widowed neighbour.

Bel cleared her throat and looked away from her dinner partner to Mr. Townsend across the table. "Have you found the church in satisfactory repair?" she asked the vicar, ignoring the smirk of humour on Mr. Lymington's face at hearing her voice such a dull question.

"In the main," said the vicar. He began to elaborate on the repairs that his predecessor had made recently and the repairs that would need to be done in the next twelvemonth. "The ledgers at the vicarage have made most informative reading. At least the roof is now in good repair, for the rainstorms that we've had this past week would have wreaked havoc on the chancel had Mr. Davies not possessed the foresight to have the steeple repaired two seasons ago."

"Indeed," said Bel. "I have some tenants whose roofs need attention before long."

"My dear Miss Morrison, what a burden for you to carry. Surely, Mr. Brownlee's steward could assist you with finding labourers for the work?"

"I have men of my own who can do the work," said Bel brightly, trying not to grit her teeth at the vicar's officious sympathy.

"Townsend," interrupted Mr. Lymington, "you must have found current information about the parish tithes in those ledgers. How does it look, eh? Are you glad you took the position?"

The vicar cleared his throat in dismay at the Londoner's forthright question. "Mr. Lymington, I don't believe that is quite a topic for dinner conversation—"

"Ah, but you only get the lesser tithes, I suppose?" said Mr. Lymington, ignoring the vicar's discomfort. "And the greater tithes go to whom? Brownlee, I would wager?"

"It's no wagering matter," said the vicar, now visibly put out. "Of course, he receives the greater tithes as he had the right of advowson."

"But he does give you a stipend as well," ventured Mrs. Brownlee.

"Indeed," said the vicar, his bright blue eyes sparkling with annoyance, "but that, again, is nothing that need be discussed." His frown put a full stop to that topic of conversation. "Mrs. Brownlee, perhaps you might tell us what charity cases there are within the parish and how well they are being tended to?"

The plump hostess changed the subject as the vicar desired. Bel addressed herself once more to her mutton, and Mr. Lymington, after those teasing comments toward the vicar, behaved himself for the rest of the dinner. But every so often Bel caught him staring at her with a cheeky smile on his face as if all the world was a joke that the two of them could share.

Chapter Eight

Regrets

W HEN DINNER CONCLUDED, NIGEL felt a modicum of disappointment as Mrs. Brownlee led the ladies to the withdrawing room and left the gentlemen to their port. Mrs. White cast him a speculative glance as she left the room. Her hips swayed provocatively as she looked at him over her left shoulder. He knew that type—restless, rapacious, and eager for male company.

Strangely, however, he felt no urge to investigate Mrs. White's obvious interest and instead continued to mourn Miss Morrison's departure. The only clever conversationalist in the county had left the dining room, and he was to be immured with a half dozen provincial gentlemen to talk about the weather, the countryside, and the roads.

Once alone with the male members of the party, however, Nigel found the Ferris brothers more congenial than expected. They were dressed in the styles of yesteryear, with silver buckles, stockings, breeches, and even brocade frock coats rather than the more modish dark evening wear. As the port flowed freely, the two old men were soon regaling him with local stories about the mythical Derby Ram and the headless horseman of Bolsover Castle.

"I saw the horseman once when I was a boy," said James Ferris, his back curved forward with age, "but Jack never did. Not a once."

Nigel clucked sympathetically. "I daresay a headless horseman is selective about whom he haunts."

Jack Ferris slapped his knee with a hoot of laughter. "Hardly, Mr. Lymington. He has no head, you know, to see who's about when he goes riding."

"I'll wager even *I* can see better than the headless horseman," said James, his grin missing a half dozen teeth. The old fellow was no longer as sharp as his brother, but he still had his old-fashioned charm.

"But he must have some sort of directional sense," speculated Nigel, "even without eyes, ears, or nose. Or else how would the fellow racket about through the forest or make it into the castle courtyard without hitting the walls?"

"A sixth sense," cackled Jack Ferris. "One that points him in the direction of the pretty ladies." He gave Nigel a gleeful grin. "I've been observing you at dinner, Lymington, and it seems that *you* have that sixth sense. What do you think of our beautiful Belinda?"

As the younger Mr. Ferris asked the question, Nigel discovered that Belinda Morrison had been lurking in the back of his mind ever since she had left the room with Mrs. Brownlee, Mrs. White, and her aunt. But it was not until Jack mentioned it that he had even considered her appearance.

Beautiful Belinda?

She was not what society would deem beautiful with her loamy brown hair and less than classical features, but there was something about her forthright spirit that lit up her face like a sky in the middle of a lightning storm.

"Very charming," Nigel drawled, keeping an air of affectation in his voice. It would not do to seem too eager. That was not how the game was played—or, at least, not how it was played in London. "But egad! She has a way of letting a fellow know when he doesn't measure up. I daresay a headless horseman would find himself far too short in her estimation."

Jack Ferris gave a hearty laugh at that witticism and repeated it to make sure his brother had heard it. Nigel, meanwhile, cast an eye over to the corner where Mr. Brownlee was deep in conversation with the vicar. There seemed to be something more serious to their conversation than galloping ghosts, and more than once he caught the name *Morrison* floating across the dining table.

"Are there any other sights that I should look for hereabouts?" asked Nigel, keeping one ear attuned to the left as he tried not to ignore the garrulous old gentlemen on his right.

"There's the Jester's Arms right here in Upper Cross," said James Ferris. "You'll run into Jack there more often than not on cold afternoons."

"And if you can find your hat again once you've sat down," said Jack, "then you're more clever than you look." His old eyes sparkled. "Hats, canes, coats—they've a tendency to go wandering off. The jester takes them, you see. Likes to play pranks on folks hereabouts."

"Another phantom from days of yore?"

"Aye." Jack leaned in conspiratorially and tapped his drooping nose. "But best to keep quiet about it. The old vicar liked a pint of ale and a pie at the Jester's Arms often, and he even left a penny for the jester like we all do. But I don't think the new vicar holds truck with ghostly doings."

Jack rose to pour his feebler brother another glass of spirits.

Nigel, his attention his own once more, looked back across the room at the vicar. His profile bore a strange resemblance to their host's. They leaned towards each other at the end of the table, clearly engaged in private conversation, but neither man able to modulate the sound of his voice enough to keep it from carrying.

"...but he could always return," said Mr. Townsend, combing a hand through his dark-blond hair.

"Pfft!" said Harold Brownlee, snapping his fingers in disdain. "He's been gone seven years come January. No fear of him coming back now, except as a ghost. I'm one of the executors of her parents' will, and as soon as the New Year comes, I can apply to have the boy declared deceased. It's just like I told you last week—the house and land's all hers. And she's respectable. Well-spoken. A little older than a man might like, but she'd be a credit to a man of the cloth, and your income would treble or quadruple."

"You've been more than generous with the stipend," said the vicar. "I'm not in *desperate* need of additional income."

"Nonsense. Every gentleman, even a vicar, looks to increase his fortune. Think of your mother. If your income increased, you could house her here in Upper Cross."

The vicar pursed his lips. "Indeed."

Nigel wondered whether any grown man, including a moralistic vicar, would want his mother in such proximity.

"I have noticed Miss Morrison's way of speaking is a little unsettling," observed the vicar. "I've never heard a Shropshire woman talk so boldly."

"You could mend it in no time," said Harold Brownlee dismissively. "There's nothing about a woman that can't be changed if a man has a mind to do it."

Nigel squirmed. He had had those same thoughts before—and tried and failed to bend his niece Louisa to do his bidding. But to hear the sentiment on someone else's tongue was a revelation of how repulsive it truly was. Miss Belinda Morrison was unique. He could not imagine trying to mould her into something other than what she was.

Nigel's dark eyes flashed with disgust, but instead of making a scene, he rose from his chair and approached his host with a friendly smile. "The port is good, Brownlee. I'm warm to the gills. And I'm learning my way about as well. I hear the Jester's Arms is the place to go for a proper pint."

"I'm fond of it myself," said Mr. Brownlee, rising from his chair and allowing Nigel to split up his *tête-à-tête* with the vicar. Whatever they had been discussing must wait till they were private once again. "We dined there last week, Mr. Townsend, you must recall?"

The vicar frowned. "It seemed a superstitious place. I had not thought Derbyshire so benighted—"

"Superstitious it might be," said Mr. Brownlee blithely, "but the ale is strong, and the food is hot. And besides, it's the only inn in Upper Cross." He nodded to Mr. Lymington. "If you have no cook at Audeley House, I wager you'll be dining there more nights than not. Their public room is large—I hire it once a year to give Mrs. Brownlee a dance on Boxing Day."

"What's that, Harold?" said James Ferris, shuffling over with a glass of port and spilling a few drops in the process. "Is there to be a dance again this year?"

"Of course there is," said their host. "I must keep Madge happy and give her something to do with herself. You should see how many hours it takes her to plan out punch and cakes and garlands and music—and how many hours I get to myself because of it."

The other gentlemen laughed, all save the vicar. "The heavy weight of the cares of this world," uttered Mr. Townsend.

"Well, Jack and I shall be there," said James Ferris, gleefully ignoring the vicar's censorious comment. "And if I fortify myself with enough punch, then perhaps I shall tread a step or two with Miss Lucy."

"Ha, you sly dog!" said Harold Brownlee, clapping the old fellow on the back in uproarious mirth. Nigel, anticipating the blow, seized the glass of port from James' hands and placed it on the table before it spilled further.

"Not if I beat you to it, brother," said Jack Ferris. "And I warrant my legs will last longer than yours."

Mr. Brownlee began to rally the two brothers on their likelihood of making it through a whole reel. Meanwhile, the vicar regathered his composure and turned to Nigel. "Do you dance, Mr. Lymington?"

"What gentleman does not?" In truth, Nigel particularly loved to dance. The sound of violin bows on strings always set his boots tapping; he had looked forward to balls ever since he was a stripling boy. He cast the vicar a teasing look. "But if I were Miss Morrison, I should think you were asking *me* to dance with a question like that."

The vicar took a deep breath, shocked that Nigel was aware of his teatime conversation with Miss Morrison. "That woman can be purposefully obtuse."

"A rare compliment. Or perhaps she simply enjoys catching you out."

"Not a very feminine quality," said the vicar. "But perhaps Harold is right, and she can be trained."

"Trained?" echoed Nigel. "Like a sheepdog?" His voice had a silky purr to it that would have hinted danger to anyone who knew him better.

The vicar was not one of those people.

"Why not?" said Mr. Townsend. "I had a dog once, when I was a young man. He had high spirits as a puppy, but it was not long before I trained him to obey my every command. He used to wait for me outside the church in Shropshire until I'd finished my duties as curate and then walk home beside me, no matter the weather. He was a friend that sticketh closer than a brother, Mr. Lymington. Unfortunately, he...did not survive in London."

"How sad," said Nigel dryly. "Did the town air not agree with him?"

"It was a phaeton, Mr. Lymington." The vicar's blue eyes glinted like glass without a curtain of humour to soften them. "One of those godless society women was driving it around the corner, making a spectacle of herself. She did not see my dog, or if she did, she did not stop. He was crushed by the wheels."

Nigel blinked. "My condolences." Apparently, Mr. Townsend had reason to be sententious. Somebody had run over his dog.

"Shall we rejoin the ladies?" asked Mr. Brownlee. He gave a great guffaw. "I think the Mr. Ferrises would like to press their suit with Miss Lucy and secure some dances at the Boxing Day Ball."

Nigel smiled politely. As long as the vicar refrained from pressing his opinions on Miss Belinda Morrison, Nigel would be content. For, as he had seen at dinner, she clearly did not enjoy a man who questioned her competence or belittled her abilities.

Again, Nigel squirmed inwardly. How often had he discounted his niece Louisa's opinion or belittled her choices? He had inherited both his position as duke and his role as guardian at the death of her father, and in his mad scramble to take the ton by storm, he had never stopped to consider Louisa's feelings, Louisa's hopes, Louisa's dreams.

When he had run through the money—little of it as there was—Lady Maltrousse had suggested that he find Louisa a husband willing to split her inheritance with him. And so he had. He'd found Solomon Digby, a man more at home in a mill or on the docks than he was in a London ballroom. A man with a prodigiously large belly and a prodigiously bad taste in waistcoats. No wonder Louisa had taken exception to the plan and run away with Gyles Audeley!

"Are you coming, Lymington?" asked Jack Ferris, poking his head back into the dining room after the rest of the gentlemen had departed.

Nigel took a deep breath. "I think I'm for home. Could you make my farewells to our host and hostess?"

"But the night is young," urged the old fellow.

"Aye," said Nigel, "but the port has made me melancholy." The port and his own poor decisions for the last two years. Had he really been as insufferably selfish as Horace Townsend? The vicar was in a position of guardianship as well, spiritual guardianship of his parishioners. And the way he was regarding Miss Morrison as a potential boost to his income rather than a person to be respected was, quite frankly, disgusting. But had Nigel's approach to Louisa been any different?

"Shall I tell Miss Belinda she's put you into a brown study?"

"No need for that," said Nigel. He was already rebuking himself for trying to get up a flirtation with her. "I've a bit of a headache, and I'd rather not draw attention away from the good vicar. After all, this dinner is in his honour. Just a quiet word to our hostess, if you please. I'll find the front door and let myself out."

CHAPTER NINE

Cap

A s Mr. Lymington had suggested, the vicar was indeed the first to hear news of Mrs. Audeley. At the end of the service on Sunday, Mr. Townsend trumpeted out an announcement: "I publish the banns of marriage between Rose Audeley of Upper Cross, Derbyshire and Bertram Gale, Earl of Kendall, of St. George's of Hanover Square. This is the first time of asking. If any of you know cause or just impediment why these two persons should not be joined together in Holy Matrimony, ye are to declare it."

"Upon my word, Mr. Lymington!" said Aunt Lucy, leaning over the edge of the Morrison box and barely able to contain her excitement until the announcement had finished. "Rose Audeley and an earl? Did you know this betrothal was forthcoming?"

"I had my suspicions," said Mr. Lymington. Bel noticed that although he had hinted about the announcement at the dinner earlier in the week, he seemed quite sombre hearing the words from the pulpit. She wondered if he had developed a *tendre* for

Mrs. Audeley. Their neighbour, though a few years older than him, was still a beautiful woman with a sweet spirit, a sensible nature, and manners that set everyone at ease. Mr. Lymington, if he had been in the market for a wife rather than a romantic conquest, would have done well to secure a woman like that.

"But an *earl!* I would not have thought Mrs. Audeley would enter such prestigious circles. How did they meet?"

"I am not privy to that information," said Mr. Lymington, refusing to assuage Aunt Lucy's curiosity. He offered Bel his arm as they both exited their boxes at the same time. Bel accepted his arm stiffly. She did not know why he should be so attentive unless he was simply used to having a woman—any woman—hanging on him.

He had left early from the dinner at the Brownlees, and today he seemed less cheeky. Less self-assured. Had something mellowed him in the intervening days? Or had the vicar's sermon finally convinced him that he ought to amend his way of life? Bel turned her chip bonnet so she could study his face and discovered that he was already looking down at her.

"It is not raining," he observed.

"No, indeed, so we shall have no need to share your carriage. We walked here and shall walk home again."

"You have a robust constitution."

"I am not sure if that is a compliment or an accusation."

"Take it as you will." He smiled and pulled her closer, allowing Mr. and Mrs. Brownless to pass them in the aisle. The capes of his greatcoat crushed against her shoulder, and he tucked her forearm neatly against his side.

His proximity and his scrutiny caused Bel to consider her own appearance. She had dressed in a brown wool pelisse over a grey wool dress to combat the cold and pulled on a pair of serviceable half-boots to guard against puddles. It was practical, but was it...pleasing? That was not a question she often asked herself. But why should she care if Nigel Lymington was pleased with her attire? Why should she care if she evoked "beauty" and "joy" for him?

"May I walk you home?"

"And muddy your boots?" She raised an eyebrow.

"Come now, you must think all Londoners lily-hearted poltroons. I am not afraid of a little mud."

"Perhaps *I* am afraid we shall be obliged to invite you to dinner if you walk home with us."

A little of his teasing smile surfaced. "No doubt that was my object in asking."

"And there's no reason why we shouldn't invite you!" interrupted Aunt Lucy. "I declare, having a handsome gentleman at the table and some cosmopolitan conversation would not go amiss."

"You are too kind," said Mr. Lymington. He cast a triumphant look at Bel who had been outmanoeuvred by her aunt. "I would be happy to accept the invitation."

Bel tried to put a frown on her face, but somehow her mouth would not cooperate. Her own countenance was conspiring against her to give Mr. Lymington the false hope that she wanted him to dine with them today!

She chastised her face severely, and as they walked home through the chilly Derbyshire air, she considered how best to make Mr. Lymington aware that she had no interest in his highly superfluous attentions.

"A vast improvement over ham and eggs," said Nigel appreciatively as the Morrisons' maid served the roast beef, vegetables, cheese, bread, and strawberry preserves. "And over the fare at the Jester's Arms too."

"Have you been dining there often?" asked Aunt Lucy.

"On occasion this week, to give John a rest from his culinary labours."

"I would have thought Archie Garrick would cook for you," said Bel.

Nigel saw the plain-faced maid's ears perk up; she paused as she was about to fill his water glass. Apparently, his spotty valet was of interest to this country domestic.

"No, no," said Nigel. "Archie's talents lie in...other directions." Nigel was not sure what directions those were, but he maintained impressive control of his face while uttering the sentiment.

It was more control than he'd been able to maintain when Miss Morrison had first come downstairs after refreshing her wardrobe in the upper storey of the house. She had removed her half boots and her bonnet, but on her head was a prominent and particularly dowdy cap. Her burnished brown hair that he had been hoping to examine more closely was covered as thoroughly as if she had worn a nun's wimple. All through dinner she had kept the beastly thing on—as if she were some sort of aged spinster who had crept down from the attic to eat soft-boiled potatoes and cabbage soup.

"It's quite warm in here," said Nigel when they adjourned to the parlour, "with not a draught to be found." He stood before the fireplace, hands behind his back. "I'm surprised you find the need for a cap to keep away the cold, Miss Morrison."

"Oh, I care nothing about the cold. I merely wear one out of deference to my advanced years."

"Your advanced years," repeated Nigel.

"Indeed." She looked at him defiantly.

"And does your rheumatism also keep you up at night when it rains?" He looked at her dryly. "Old age does bring so many aches and pains."

"Pish-posh!" said Aunt Lucy, bustling over to an armchair and taking her seat with a cup of tea in her hands. "You're both of you far too young to be complaining of anything of the sort. Sit down, Mr. Lymington. There—on the sofa by my niece. You cannot possibly mean to leave so soon after dinner, so you might as well make yourself comfortable."

Nigel obliged one of his hostesses and ignored the narrowed eyes of the other. He had no sooner sat down than his lap was invaded. "Ah, Magpie," said Nigel, delighted to see Miss Morrison's cat curl up on his legs. He enjoyed the creature's soft fur—and the triumph of having the cat like him better than it did its mistress.

"How do you keep Christmas, Mr. Lymington?" asked Aunt Lucy.

"How do I keep it?" Nigel began to cudgel his brain. "Poorly, I suppose. My parents did not enjoy the Yuletide festivities. My brother and his wife enjoyed them too much." Nigel remembered the frivolous house parties that the last Duke of Warrenton would hold. He remembered buying his niece some sugar plums and a little doll and taking them up to the nursery while her parents were revelling with their riotous guests. By last year, of course, he had been duke himself, and he had not even remembered to mark the day with any baubles for Louisa.

"Enjoyed?" asked Bel Morrison, the edges of that odious cap bobbing about her face. "You speak as if—"

"Yes, they are deceased," said Nigel with a self-deprecating shrug. "I have little family left."

"Oh, you poor dear," said Aunt Lucy. "All the more reason for you to keep Christmas with us. That is, if you are still in Derbyshire?"

Nigel scratched Magpie behind the ears. "My plans remain...uncertain." The cat began to purr.

"It seems as if you and Belinda have much in common—"

"Aunt Lucy," said the younger Miss Morrison, an edge of warning in her voice.

"I mean your affection for that cat, of course," said Aunt Lucy. "And she clearly adores you both." The old lady shifted in her armchair and gave a little squeak. "Good heavens! I've gone and spilt my tea." She rose to her feet and placed the cup and saucer on the table nearby. "No, no, do not stand on my account, Mr. Lymington. I would not have you disturb Magpie for all the world. I must go find a handkerchief, but never fear. I shall return momentarily." And with that, Aunt Lucy vacated the room.

Miss Morrison's lips set into a firm line, and she turned her head to meet Nigel's eyes as the door to the drawing room swung closed. "I must apologise for my aunt, Mr. Lymington. She is incorrigible where matchmaking is concerned."

"Certainly, there can be no harm in leaving two such *elderly* folk as you and me alone in a room."

"One would like to think so—but then, there are your unsavoury claims about trying to seduce Mrs. Audeley."

"Er, yes," said Nigel. "I am afraid that I must admit to being the villain in that piece." Indeed, he *was* the villain, but it would never have occurred to him to pursue the Derbyshire widow had not Lady Maltrousse suggested a way to put the Earl of Kendall's nose out of joint.

Miss Morrison stared at him. "You don't seem very accomplished at your role."

"Accomplished? What on earth can you mean, Miss Morrison?"

"You admit to having been foiled in your object, and now Mrs. Audeley is betrothed to an earl and completely out of your reach. And what is more, if you truly were proficient in your rakishness, one suspects you would have capitalised on Aunt Lucy's absence already to—"

"It's the cap," interrupted Nigel, shaking his head with a sigh. "A cap on a lady's head deters rakes just as effectively as a scarecrow in the wheatfield deters birds. But you must have realised as much when you put it on." With enough goading, Nigel hoped that his hostess would remove the displeasing head covering, but Miss Morrison was not such a slave to vanity.

"You surprise me," she replied. "I did not expect you to know anything at all about wheatfields."

"I know very little. You have ascended to the summit of my knowledge."

"Ah well, if you have no land and live only in London, why bother expanding your knowledge on the matter?" She spoke sarcastically as if a lack of land and a predilection for the metropolis were posting inns on the road to moral failure.

Nigel continued to rub his thumb behind Magpie's ears. He did have land. A great many acres of it in Lincolnshire. But it was all in the hands of the steward his late brother had inherited from his late father, and he had little conception of whether it grew wheat, or barley, or bramble bushes. He remembered the steward sending him a letter when he had received the title, and he remembered skimming the letter briefly and then tossing it into the fire.

"If you were to remove your cap," he said cheerfully, "I suspect you would still be in little danger. For Magpie would have something to say if I attempted to move any closer to you on the sofa." The cat was stretched out on him like a princess in her four-poster bed and luxuriating in its place of rest.

"How fortunate then that you have captured my cat's affections, but I warn you that you'll not be taking her home with you."

"Yes, ma'am," said Nigel with a false show of meekness.

The conversation lapsed into silence, but still Aunt Lucy did not return.

"Might I ask you a question?" asked Nigel.

Miss Morrison raised one eyebrow, her left one. "Ask it."

"You already know that my brother and his wife are dead. Do you have any brothers or sisters of your own?"

Her face froze as if she had caught sight of something unpleasant in the mirror and was too disturbed to look again to see if it were real or a phantom. "Yes, an older brother. Charles Morrison. He is in India."

"India?" repeated Nigel. "That is a long way away. Did he join a regiment?"

"No, he embarked on his own. He had a longing for adventure, and India is everything that Derbyshire is not."

"Indeed." Nigel kept his voice soothing, both out of deference for Magpie's catnap and to keep Miss Morrison from bristling and becoming silent. "How long ago was that?"

"Six years," she said. "Almost seven, really."

"Did he marry there? Start a family?"

She hesitated. "I don't know exactly. Correspondence is so difficult from such a distance. But if he did, it would explain why he hasn't returned yet. A wife and children make the journey more difficult."

Nigel nodded. It was a far different story than the one he had overheard Harold Brownlee telling the vicar. Was it possible that Mr. Brownlee did not know the truth of the matter? Or was Bel Morrison simply trying to put the best construction on a miserable situation? She said that correspondence was difficult—had she ever heard from Charles Morrison since his departure almost seven years ago?

The parlour door opened slowly, first a crack with an eye behind it and then wide enough to admit a person. Aunt Lucy re-entered the room, still wearing the same dress sans any imaginary tea stains. "Dear me, have you run out of things to talk about? I have just the thing. A game of piquet."

"With you, Miss Morrison?" said Nigel gallantly. "I would be delighted."

"No, no, with Belinda!" said Aunt Lucy, her wrinkled cheeks pinking at the compliment. "She is far more clever than I." She advanced to a cupboard and found a deck of cards. "To the table," she said, urging them both to rise from the sofa.

Magpie stretched reluctantly as Nigel shifted her off his lap. Bel Morrison rose with almost the same reluctance. "Surely not on Sunday," she said, forestalling her aunt's eagerness.

"As long as there are no wagers, Mr. Davies never did complain about a hand of cards on the Lord's Day."

"Yes, but we're under a new regime now," said Miss Morrison, alluding to the new vicar.

"I'm certain that Mr. Lymington will say nothing to Mr. Townsend about it," protested Aunt Lucy. She placed the deck of cards on the table.

"I would as lief say nothing to Mr. Townsend about anything," murmured Nigel.

The younger Miss Morrison, who had caught the full import of his words, gave him a sharp look. "I daresay you play cards a good deal in town, Mr. Lymington."

"It does pass the time for us indolent metropolitan folk," said Nigel mischievously, "since we have no other occupation besides going to the theatre or making sport of our neighbours."

Bel looked at him as if she was not sure whether he was making sport of her now. Satisfied that her work was done, Aunt Lucy seated herself in a chair by the window with the best light for her embroidery, as far as possible from the card players. Miss Morrison and Nigel walked over to the little table at the back of the parlour, and Nigel noticed that Miss Morrison seated herself hurriedly so she would not have to wait for him to pull out her chair. She began to separate out the deck of cards into the requisite thirty-two. "Will you be the younger or the elder hand?"

"Surely, I must be the elder," said Nigel, robbed by her quick action of the chivalrous gesture of a gentleman. He seated himself in the chair across from her. Despite Belinda Morrison's claim to spinsterhood, she could not be more than thirty years old while he could claim the advanced age of thirty-eight. As the elder hand, he would exchange his cards and make his declarations first.

He leaned in conspiratorially. "Shall we keep your Mr. Davies' prohibition against wagers, or—since we are already transgressing the Lord's Day—wager as we like and ask repentance for another transgression as well?"

Bel's clear grey eyes, incongruously youthful beneath that wretched cap, met his own gaze with a spark of deviltry in them. "If I win," she said, "you must promise never to feed my cat again."

"And if I win," said Nigel, making sure he could not be overheard by Aunt Lucy, "you must promise to burn that cap."

CHAPTER TEN

Charlie

BEL WOKE THE NEXT morning with a smile on her face. Despite her annoyance at Aunt Lucy's match-making ways, she had to admit that she'd enjoyed herself yesterday. Mr. Lymington had been a gentleman—amusing, quick-witted, and generous in everything except his claim to her cat. Despite her competitive play at cards, he had won the game of piquet and taken her dowdy cap away with him. If his boasting words were to be believed, he intended to stuff it in the kitchen grate at Audeley House that very night.

It had been the perfect Sunday afternoon. Often, when the weather was fine and there was work outdoors Bel wanted to be *doing* things—making Sunday feel like a day of drudgery. But Mr. Lymington's companionship had filled the time pleasantly. She could not see spending time with him on a regular basis when there was real life to be lived and real work to be done, but perhaps he would not be so bad as a holiday friend.

She decided that his claims of rakishness had been vastly overrated, for he had said nothing untoward to her during their play at piquet. And other than a penchant for flirtation, he seemed to have no more bad qualities than most men.

Still smiling, Bel slipped out from the bedclothes and weighed her options for how to spend her day. She could dress in trousers and inspect tenant roofs with Jer and Tam. Or she could dress in a gown and sit in the parlour and see if Mr. Lymington would appear. There had been no promises made, but she suspected that if the weather remained fine, Mr. Lymington might call again. He certainly had nothing else to do with his time in Derbyshire.

Feeling a little foolish, Bel dressed in a navy-blue dress that fit her more closely than her usual brown and grey gowns. She could see Aunt Lucy grinning at her, every time she thought her niece's back was turned. At least she could redeem the time by doing some bookkeeping. Eschewing the parlour, she went into the little room—barely larger than a closet—that served as her office. Taking a newly sharpened quill, she updated the household expenses and the costs associated with the livestock.

Around mid-morning, Bel's anticipation was rewarded by a knock on the door. Apparently, Mr. Lymington had been too eager to wait for normal calling hours. Leaving her office, Bel smirked as she waited for Jenny to usher in their temporary neighbour. But instead of Nigel Lymington, the parlour was invaded by the stoop-shouldered Harold Brownlee.

"Mr. Brownlee," said Bel, standing to greet him. "To what do I owe the pleasure?" It was not the same pleasure as she had been expecting from a witty stranger, but she did not *dis*like Harold Brownlee.

"Sit down, Bel, my girl. Sit down."

Bel complied, wondering if Mr. Brownlee had come to offer his steward's services yet again to help bring her sheep to market. Mentally, she began to compose a second refusal.

"I know you'd rather avoid the topic," said Mr. Brownlee, leaning forward in his own seat, "but I've come to talk about Charlie."

"What is there to talk about? We still have no news from him, but everything is in order here. When he returns home, he'll find a tidy sum in the bank and a healthy flock in the field."

Mr. Brownlee looked nonplussed. "Yes, well, you'll recall that I'm one of the executors for your parents' estate." He cleared his throat. "Come New Year's Day, it will be a full seven years since Charlie's been gone."

A rising sense of dismay began to fill Bel's breast, but she tried to quash it with an overabundance of optimism in her tone. "He always did let his adventures keep him out too long to come back home in time for dinner."

"Bel," said Mr. Brownlee gravely, "I don't think he's coming back this time. Seven years is a long time. And by law, seven years is long enough that he can legally be declared deceased."

"What poppycock!" said Bel. "I suppose he *could* be declared that, but there's no reason to do so—"

"But there is. If Charlie is dead, as seems most likely, then this land and this house should be inherited by you." Mr. Brownlee paused. "You can stop worrying so much about maximising profits for Charlie and worry about living your own life."

"My life suits me quite well."

"Come now, my girl. You should be going to parties. Visiting London. Finding a husband." Mr. Brownlee shook a crooked finger at her. "Leave the sheep and the muddy fields to old men like me." He breathed in loudly, as if preparing for an announcement of great significance. "I've instructed my man of business to appeal to the courts for a declaration of presumed death."

"Mr. Brownlee!" Bel rose to her feet. "I give you no permission to do any such thing."

"I don't need your permission, my gel. By making me executor of their will, your parents gave me that power." Mr. Brownlee rose to his feet as well. "The newspapers were not sanguine about the possibility of survivors, and your father was doubtful himself that Charlie would ever come back. The appeal will go through in the New Year."

Bel's fingers, calloused from outdoor work, clenched themselves involuntarily. "No. Please. No."

Mr. Brownlee's stooped shoulders moved towards the door. "I am sorry to see you so upset, but it's best for everyone. Your tenants deserve a living landlord, and you deserve a chance at life."

Stunned into silence, Bel allowed Harold Brownlee to say his farewells and exit the parlour. The door shut with the thud of finality.

Charlie *was* still coming back, wasn't he?

Not even Aunt Lucy's doubts had been able to shake her confidence in her brother's return, but Harold Brownlee had used all his weight to stamp out the embers of hope she had carefully kept burning over the last seven years. His threatened "declaration of presumed death" hung over her head like a sword on a string. She didn't know anything for certain anymore.

Bel looked down at her navy-blue morning gown, a shockingly frivolous choice given how today had turned out. She hurried upstairs to her bedroom and, straining her arms to reach the fastenings, stripped off the dress and tossed it onto the bed. Then, pulling on a pair of worn trousers, a cambric shirt, a woollen vest, and the shapeless brown coat of a farm labourer, she hurried downstairs and out into the grey December. Jer and Tam were already thatching a roof, but she would go to the barn. The barn would be quiet. The barn would help her think.

CHAPTER ELEVEN

The Barn

N IGEL PICKED HIS WAY through the muddy yard to the barn a furlong away. He had ordered Archie to press his coat and had taken time with his cravat, but now fate had conspired to send him somewhere wholly unsafe for a gentleman in buff pantaloons and a coat of pale blue superfine.

When he had called on the Morrisons this afternoon, Aunt Lucy had informed him that Miss Bel was out in the barn. "I could invite you inside to have tea with me," she said knowingly, "or you could bring her some biscuits out there in case she's hungry." Nigel had opted for the latter, despite the prescient notion that there would be no chairs and tea table inside the stone building where the hay and other provender were stored.

The door to the stone barn was open and Nigel went inside without announcing his presence. It took a moment for his eyes to adjust from the grey sunlight outside to the musty darkness inside.

The barn was empty of animals. Whatever horses and cows took shelter there at night must all be out to pasture right now. The open space smelled of leather, straw, hay, and manure, and the rivulets of water coming out of some of the stalls indicated that they had been freshly cleaned. Nigel wrinkled his nose. Where was Miss Morrison?

"What are you doing in my barn?"

As he heard the voice from above, Nigel looked up. A second storey had been constructed beneath the thatched roof, creating storage for additional bales of hay above the stalls. In the darkness, he saw a pair of work boots dangling from the hayloft, attached to a pair of buckskin trousers.

"I brought you some biscuits."

"A barn's hardly the place for those."

"Oh, I don't know. I expect mucking out these stalls would give one quite the appetite." Nigel eyed the ladder on the left side of the barn that reached up to the loft above. "May I come up?"

Hearing no answer, he took the silence as an invitation. He cradled the jar of biscuits against his chest and used his other arm to pull himself up the ladder. When was the last time he had climbed into a hayloft? Back in his Oxford days? Certainly not anytime in the last two years after succeeding to his brother's title.

There was a round window at the far end of the loft that let in some light. Through the dusty rays, Nigel could see the traces of tears on Miss Morrison's face. Something had driven her out to the barn besides a desire to do menial chores. Something had upset her usual equanimity. He must tread carefully.

"I'm afraid that I could not carry tea without sloshing it all over me. But if they're not too dry to swallow down on their own, we have biscuits aplenty to share."

He stooped low as he came closer to her in the narrow loft, handing her the jar of biscuits so that he could carefully lower himself down to a sitting position on the edge of the overhang. His Hessians dangled beside her work boots. He felt a few pieces of straw poke through his pantaloons into his thighs. Ah, well. What was a pair of ruined pantaloons when there was a lady to console?

Reaching into his coat, he removed a handkerchief and handed it to Miss Morrison.

"Am I to scrub my dirty hands with this?"

Nigel shrugged nonchalantly. "Or your face. Don't worry. The handkerchief's clean."

Miss Morrison rolled her eyes and returned the jar of biscuits in exchange for the handkerchief. "I was very worried."

Nigel looked away, allowing her the privacy to pretend she was not wiping her tear-stained cheeks. When he looked back, the traces of her afternoon despondency had disappeared.

He wished the handkerchief could wipe away some other things. Her wonderfully variegated brown hair was covered, as usual, this time by a labourer's hat and her figure was shrouded in a shapeless coat, ideal for keeping out the winter chill.

"Do you want it back?" she asked, holding the begrimed handkerchief between thumb and forefinger.

"Normally, I would say no, but I'm running short on all sorts of wardrobe items since I've been gone from London so long. I daresay Mrs. Garrick can scrub it clean." Nigel reached for the waistcoat and stuck it inside his coat of pale blue superfine.

"Surely, you could send up to London for some more clothes?" said Miss Morrison, distracted from her own distress by his clothing conundrum.

"I can't, actually," said Nigel. "It would give away my location."

"Give away your location?"

Nigel gave a deep sigh. If he wanted her to tell him why she was crying in the hayloft, he ought to share something about himself as well. And somehow, he found himself *wanting* to tell her. *Needing* her to know.

"I've made London too warm to hold me at present. It will be very unpleasant for me if I return before certain things have...blown over."

"Hmm. A jealous husband?"

Nigel winced at the judgement in her tone. Why did he care so much if a country spinster with a dirty face wearing trousers and a farmer's cap looked down on him from her heights of moral virtue?

"No, but you can think that if you like."

They sat there in silence for a moment, legs dangling from their lofty perch. Nigel felt younger than he had in years.

"Mr. Brownlee came by the house this morning," said Miss Morrison abruptly.

"Oh, did he?" said Nigel lightly.

"He's the executor of my parents' will."

"Mmm." Nigel wondered if this conversation was related to the one he'd overheard between Harold Brownlee and the vicar.

"The will leaves everything to my brother Charlie, unless he should predecease my parents. In which case, everything was supposed to go to me." She took a deep breath. "Charlie left home two years before my parents died."

"A goodly amount of time."

"Indeed. It will be seven years in January since our last news of him, and Mr. Brownlee is determined to appeal to the courts to have Charlie declared...dead."

Nigel had no platitudes to offer. He paused, hoping that period of silence would indicate his compassion. "When was your last news of him?"

"The ship he took for India—the *Belladore*—it disappeared on the western side of Africa. Or at least, that's what the newspapers said. It never made it to India at all."

"Were there any survivors?"

"Father went down to London to find out. The ship's owner had claimed it as a total loss—no cargo recovered. But the wreck was not far off the coast. Survivors *could* have made it ashore. Charlie was strong and fit. And from what I've read, not all the tribes in that part of Africa are hostile to Europeans. He would have found a way to survive until another ship came into the area. He could have made his way to India on a different merchantman."

Nigel's tone was gentle. "And yet, there has been no word from him in the past seven years?"

"No."

He opened the jar and handed her a biscuit. Then, he took one for himself.

They nibbled the gingery treats in silence. Nigel decided that the biscuit was much too dry to enjoy without tea.

"I suppose I'm being ridiculous to be angry with Mr. Brownlee," said Miss Morrison with a sudden rush of emotion, "but it feels like he's ringing the knell of finality on the matter. To have the courts come out and make a pronouncement—that finishes everything. Without that, there's still hope. There's still the comfort that Charlie was always a terrible correspondent. He could have made it to India and simply forgotten to write." Her grey eyes were bright as stars beneath the oversized cap that hid her hair.

Nigel's dark eyes met hers sympathetically as he turned the matter over in his mind. "What motive could Brownlee possibly have in wanting to send it to the courts? Does he gain anything if your brother is declared dead and the property devolves on you?"

"No, I don't think so," said Miss Morrison slowly. "I think he's merely trying to keep me from being trapped in the past and bound to the estate." She took a deep breath. "I may not always like his interference with my farm management, but he *has* been a kind neighbour."

"Still," said Nigel, tossing his dry ginger biscuit onto the straw far below, "it's just another kind of unwanted interference. I can see why you are upset."

"Thank you," said Miss Morrison firmly. She put the rest of her biscuit in her mouth and rubbed the crumbs off her fingers by wiping them on her trousers. "Of course, I don't know why I'm telling all of this to a London rake."

"Clearly, I've reformed," said Nigel sanguinely. "For here we are alone in a hayloft for half an hour, and I haven't even tried to kiss you."

It was a gibe meant to be humorous, but as soon as it left his mouth, Nigel realised that abstention from such an activity was a true sacrifice on his part. Miss Morrison's mouth was not the plump rosebud of a London flirt, but those wide, supple lips still seemed eminently kissable. He'd been a saint not to attempt it.

"I'm not in the habit of kissing strangers who steal my cat," retorted Miss Morrison with more force than was necessary.

"Come now, Miss Morrison, we're hardly strangers anymore."

"Aren't we?" She raised her eyebrow. The left one. The slightly crooked one that gave her a perpetual look of cynical amusement. The one that Nigel desperately wanted to rub a thumb over if he ever was allowed to put his hand near her face.

Nigel perked up his ears. "Hush! Is that a mouse skittering behind us?"

"If it is, it's because Magpie's been delinquent. And I think we both know why."

"Too much ham at Audeley House?"

"Indeed," she said, assuming a tone of high dudgeon while trying to contain her own smile.

"Well, since I enjoy feeding the animals," he said, reaching into the jar that sat beside him, "I shall leave our mouse friend a cookie." He removed a ginger cookie from the jar, crumbled it into pieces, and tossed the pieces into the hay behind them.

Miss Morrison groaned. "You are incorrigible." She swung her feet up to the ledge on which they sat and pulled herself up into a crouching position. "Come now, Mr. Lymington. Up you get. You cannot stay here all day and encourage the vermin to congregate."

Nigel picked himself up without hitting his head on the low roof, aware that the legs of his buff pantaloons were somewhat worse for wear. Crouching, he shuffled his way over to the ladder and climbed down.

"Shall I plan on the barn or the parlour tomorrow?" he asked as he reached the bottom of the ladder.

Miss Morrison, at the top of the ladder, was clearly waiting for him to vacate the barn before she made her own descent. A pity. Even without skirts, a lady on a ladder was a tempting view from below.

"What do you mean?" she demanded.

"Where shall I call on you for tea?" Nigel gestured at his fine garb, much too fine for the barnyard setting. "I'd like to wear the right clothes next time."

She shook her head at his persistence. "Neither the barn, nor the parlour, but the cottages by the road, Mr. Lymington. I'll be examining tenant roofs tomorrow to see if Jer and Tam have made sufficient repairs."

"Ah," said Nigel. He supposed his own tenants in Lincolnshire had roofs as well, but it had never occurred to him that he ought to make sure they were well-thatched. "Rain or shine?"

"Rain or shine," repeated Miss Morrison.

Nigel tipped his hat to her and went out the open barn door still carrying Aunt Lucy's jar of dry ginger cookies. Perhaps nothing dire would happen if he sent a discreet missive to town asking Simpson to forward more of his wardrobe. He could already tell that if he spent more time with Miss Morrison, he would destroy the rest of the clothing that had come with him to Derbyshire.

CHAPTER TWELVE

Cottages

"I WONDER IF MISS Belinda Morrison might accompany me on this errand of mercy?"

Bel, clad in her trousers and cap, listened from the top of the stairs as the vicar consulted with Aunt Lucy below. She had been about to strike out for the tenant cottages to help Jer and Tam with the thatching, but Mr. Townsend's knock had sent her in retreat up the stairs.

"Oh, how kind of you to ask," replied Aunt Lucy, fully aware that Bel was nowhere near presentable—indeed, the vicar would have been appalled to see her in trousers. "I believe she may not be...at home. But I can check. If you would just sit here, Mr. Townsend." She gestured to the bench in the narrow hallway.

Aunt Lucy climbed the stairs, silently motioning Bel back into her bedroom so they could talk freely. She closed the door. "You must change your clothes, my dear, so you can go walking with the vicar."

"But I intend to examine the cottages today. The roof repairs are finished. And Mr. Ly—" Bel bit her tongue. She did not want her aunt to think she had an assignation with Mr. Lymington. She had simply mentioned to him where she might happen to be tomorrow. She did not know for certain that he would appear.

"You can examine them just as well in a walking dress. Good heavens, it's not as if you'll be jumping up and down on the thatch! Mr. Townsend would like your introduction to the tenants on Morrison land. He's received word that Mrs. Hogg is taken poorly and would like to offer her some spiritual reassurance."

Bel shook her head in disbelief. Mrs. Hogg was always "taken poorly" whenever she ran out of food at her cottage. What she would want from the vicar was a basket of provisions, not a parcel of spiritual platitudes.

"I can pack a basket for you to take," said Aunt Lucy quickly. "And I can send Jenny upstairs to help you change. Wouldn't you like to wear your navy-blue walking dress with the matching pelisse?"

Bel frowned. This was *not* how she had imagined the day proceeding. But Aunt Lucy could not be deterred, and a quarter of an hour later, Bel found herself holding onto the vicar's arm and walking through the faint mist to the tenant cottages.

"Your aunt was unsure whether you would be at home," observed Mr. Townsend brightly. "But I had just come from the Brownlees, and I knew you could not be there. And where else would you possibly go on a day like this?"

"Where indeed?" murmured Bel. She could think of a dozen places on her land and in the village that could have occupied her time this morning, but apparently, the vicar had no such imagination. As she held onto his arm, she could not help comparing the brisk energy that emanated from him to the more leisurely pace that Mr. Lymington preferred. Normally, she preferred efficiency and enthusiasm, and yet there was something about Mr. Lymington's lazy amble....

"Have you met Mrs. Hogg?" Bel asked, ceasing her woolgathering to hold up her end of the conversation.

"Not yet," replied Mr. Townsend. "I understand that her health does not permit her to attend services." His opposite hand was holding the basket that Aunt Lucy had packed, and he began to swing it so vigorously that Bel was afraid the jar of strawberry preserves would have some mishap.

"Her health along with her inclinations," said Bel.

Mr. Townsend shook his head in disbelief, almost sending his vicar's hat flying. "What do you mean, Miss Morrison? Is she irreligious?"

"She is quite religious when a basket is forthcoming, but at other times—no."

Mr. Townsend tutted in annoyance. "The impiety of the metropolis continues to spread, even to a rural hamlet such as this. I am sorry to hear this. Have you worked to remedy this, Miss Morrison?"

"By bringing her baskets to encourage her piety?" Bel lifted an eyebrow.

"Indeed, but also in exhorting her to a truer form of godliness. *Ye seek me, not because ye saw the miracles, but because ye did eat of the loaves, and were filled.*"

"I am afraid I have not been so bold," said Bel meekly. "I shall observe your exhortation today, so that I may know how to go on in the future."

As they neared the row of tenant cottages, Bel's sharp eyes took in the new thatch. Jer and Tam had finished Mrs. Hogg's cottage—not because it had been in most dire need but because its occupant had made the most dire complaints—and were now hard at work repairing the ridge across the peak of her neighbour's roof. Both Jer and Tam were busy passing bundles of straw up a ladder, so Bel elected not to distract them. She would see their work from inside in a moment's time.

Mr. Townsend let go of Bel's arm and knocked loudly on the door of Mrs. Hogg's cottage. "It's the wrong time of year for woodpeckers!" replied a shrill voice, followed by a string of mild oaths. The vicar stepped back in shock, and held out a hand in front of Bel, possibly to shield her from the old woman's depravity.

"She thinks we're the workmen," explained Bel. She pushed past the vicar and used her voice rather than her knuckles. "Oh, Mrs. Hogg, it's Bel Morrison. I've come to bring you a basket."

There was no reply to that, only a scraping sound, and after a few seconds, a hunched woman came to the door and threw it open. "It's about time you came to see me, Bel Morrison." The old crone sniffed. "Well? Who's this young man you have with you?"

Before Bel could reply, Mr. Townsend swept into the cottage, carrying her along in his wake. "I am Horace Townsend, the new vicar of Upper Cross and the surrounding areas. I believe you are Mrs. Hogg?"

"What if I am?" said the old woman. "What's it to you?" Now that she knew the vicar's identity, her defences were up. "An' who invited you inside my house, you young upst—"

"Careful," warned Bel. "You shan't get your basket if you insult the vicar."

Mrs. Hogg's wrinkled lips pursed in suspicion as she considered Bel's threat. "What's *in* the basket?"

"Whatever it is," said the vicar censoriously, "it is worth far less than the treasure that wisdom brings."

Mrs. Hogg began to mutter, but she managed to keep a civil tongue in her head and keep her complaints of a general nature. Shuffling forward, she took the basket from Bel, laid it on the table and began to sort through its contents. "Ham. Scones and biscuits. And strawberry preserves, hmm? The jar's smaller than last time, I see. What's this bundle?" She put it to her nose and sniffed loudly. "Camomile? I ought t'use it for my headache. Those great oafs have been up on my house all day, shaking the roof to pieces."

"But at least you'll no longer need this," said Bel, collecting a bucket in the corner of the room that had been used to catch the drips from the roof above.

"Hmph," replied Mrs. Hogg. "Seems like a better time for such repairs would have been in the summer before the rains ever started."

"*Today* is always the second-best option to *yesterday*," said Bel cheerfully. She looked at the vicar and signalled him with a nod. "I believe Mr. Townsend has some words of exhortation for you."

The vicar cleared his throat. "Mrs. Hogg, I have not seen you at church since I've come to Upper Cross."

"Not surprising," said the old woman with a grunt, "for I haven't been there."

"*Labor for the food that does not perish and the water of everlasting life.*"

"A fine sentiment," said Mrs. Hogg, "for folks who sit comfortably by with a clean account at the grocer's and a full larder at home. But this basket's what keeps me from perishin' when Miss Bel here can find the time to come by my cottage." She looked at Bel, not exactly in charity with her, but also less in charity with the vicar.

"Miss Morrison's generosity is commendable," said the vicar. "I hope you are duly grateful."

"Hmph," snorted Mrs. Hogg. "I'd be even more grateful if you went away again. Now that I have my basket, I want to put the things away in peace."

Mr. Townsend looked ready to deliver a stern lecture, but Bel knew from of old that it was no use arguing with Mrs. Hogg. She made her farewells, and the vicar was obliged to follow her out of the cottage into the lane. Jer and Tam were still aloft on the roof of the cottage next door, but Bel was intrigued to see another figure coming up the lane, a figure with dark hair, dark eyes, and a faded, ill-fitting jacket over a pair of buckskins.

"I wonder, Miss Morrison," said the vicar, offering her his arm, "if you ought to focus more of your efforts on the *deserving* poor."

"Oh, is that what you did in London?" asked Bel, taking his arm perfunctorily. "Refuse charity to all but the deserving?" She was far more interested in the dark-haired man's long stride than Mr. Townsend's long-faced strictures. Really, Mr. Lymington seemed to be in quite a hurry this morning....

"Indeed. The poor that refuse to amend their way of life should be left to their own devices. It is quite clear that a widow like Mrs. Hogg has *not* washed the feet of the saints in her younger days—"

"Good day, Miss Morrison. Mr. Townsend." Mr. Lymington lifted his hat reverently to the vicar. But just before that, Bel could almost have sworn that he had given her a wink.

"Mr. Lymington," said the vicar, in loud tones, taking in the other man's faded clothing. "You look quite different in your working day clothes than your evening dress."

"Indeed," said the Audeleys' houseguest. "I was afraid I might be required to ascend a roof today, so I borrowed my coachman's clothes for the occasion."

"Ascend a roof?" repeated Mr. Townsend incredulously. His eyes followed Mr. Lymington's gaze until he caught sight of Jer on a ladder tossing a bundle of thatch up to Tam above him. "I'm certain the local men have things well in hand."

"You seem to have things well in hand too," said Mr. Lymington. He eyed Bel's fingers resting lightly on the vicar's arm. Bel sensed the sardonic edge to his voice. She discovered that she was pleased that he was *not* pleased to see her arm in arm with the vicar.

"Miss Morrison was kind enough to accompany me on an errand of mercy," said Mr. Townsend, "however misguided it might have been."

"Good heavens," said Mr. Lymington dryly. "Misguided mercy is to be avoided at all costs."

The vicar's frank face stared at him as if to make sure he was not in jest. "One has limited resources, so it is well to conserve them for the more deserving poor rather than the undeserving denizens of poverty."

"Of course," said Mr. Lymington soothingly. "May I walk with you?" Without waiting for a response, he took Bel's other arm.

She lifted an eyebrow. "I'm certain Jer and Tam would be happy to let you help with the thatching."

"I suspected I might see you on the ladder yourself," said Mr. Lymington, paying her back in her own coin.

"Miss Morrison?" said the vicar. "How preposterous! I'm certain that you would never see a gentlewoman on a roof in Derbyshire or—where did you say you were from?—in Lincolnshire."

"Oh, you would be surprised how enterprising some females can be—the Lincolnshire ones, that is." Mr. Lymington kept his voice deadly serious.

"Once again," said Mr. Townsend, talking over Bel's head as they picked their way down the lane, "we see the contagion of the metropolis spreading to the more rural counties of our country. Whereabouts in Lincolnshire were you born, Mr. Lymington?"

"Quite a way from Lincoln," said Mr. Lymington vaguely.

"What is the closest town?"

"Difficult to say."

Bel tilted her head to look up at Mr. Lymington's firm jaw. Why was he so reticent to reveal anything about his home country? His dark eyes adopted a look of innocent curiosity, and he took his own turn delivering inquiries over the top of Bel's bonnet. "Perhaps you could settle a question that's been on my mind since the Brownlees' delightful dinner party. Your poor departed father—what did you say the name of his ship was?"

"I didn't," replied Mr. Townsend. "I don't believe I've ever known it. My mother does not like to talk about the sad event."

"Ah, of course not," said Mr. Lymington sympathetically. "I simply thought I might look it up in the newspapers when I return to town."

"Whatever for?" The vicar's sonorous voice was filled with confusion.

"To satisfy my general curiosity."

"Hmm. It was quite long ago. I don't think it would be easy to find any mention of it."

Mr. Lymington, who seemed to consider that turnabout was fair play, would not be so easily deterred. "Yes, well, what are you—thirty years old? I suppose one might find an archive of newspapers from the time in London—"

"Gentlemen," said Bel, setting down the soles of her half boots and refusing to move any further. "Where are you taking me?" Their conversation over the brim of her bonnet and pulled them past all the Morrison tenant cottages and back toward the main road that led into Upper Cross.

"I thought perhaps we could get a nuncheon at the Jester's Arms," said Mr. Lymington, looking down at her apologetically. Bel looked back at him in surprise. She would not have expected Mr. Lymington to enjoy visiting an inn in his ill-fitting coachman's clothes, but it seemed that he had fully embraced the part.

"I'm certain Miss Morrison would not want to be seen in a public inn with a strange gentleman," interjected Mr. Townsend.

"Yes, but with me there as chaperone," replied Mr. Lymington, "I'm hopeful that no one will look askance at you."

Mr. Townsend stiffened and sent a glare at the cheeky Londoner, but Mr. Lymington had already detached Bel from the vicar's arm and was leading her in the direction of Upper Cross. The vicar followed with a harrumph, but Bel disregarded his veiled criticism. She was having more fun than she had had in ages. It was easy to forget the farm chores that needed doing, the ledgers that needed balancing, and all her worries about Charlie with Mr. Lymington there to amuse her out of the doldrums.

ele

"Lymington!" said Jack Ferris, clapping Nigel on the back.

Nigel grinned. He had encountered the younger Ferris brother several times in the last week at the Jesters' Arms, and his continued acquaintance had been a delight. He reminded him of several of the older gentlemen at the Society for Eccentrics in London, a society that thrived on conversation about science, exploration, history, philosophy, and anything else that bubbled to the surface. It had been *too* long since he had visited that establishment—another of the simple pleasures in life that he had given up while trying to make his name in the ton.

"And where might be your aunt today, Miss Morrison?" asked Mr. Ferris, with a hopeful glitter in his eye.

"She is keeping to the house today," said Miss Morrison, casting Nigel a grateful look as he manoeuvred her towards a bench against the wall in the public house. She let go of his arm as he seated her, and he immediately missed the warmth of her fingertips pressing against his arm. "Although had she known we might fall afoul of your company, she might have chosen to join us."

"'Fallen afoul,' is it?" said Mr. Ferris with a hoot. "I daresay no gentleman would be sad to have his anchor line entangled with one of the Morrison ladies, eh?" He nudged Nigel appreciatively while the vicar, misliking the drift of the conversation, cleared his throat censoriously.

"No indeed," said Nigel, eyeing his female companion with enthusiasm. He found it faintly ironic that the one day he had decided to dress in tatters, Miss Morrison was wearing the most fetching gown he had yet to glimpse her in. The bonnet was still unmodish, plain, and entirely *de trop*, but the rest of her costume was just as it should be. His dark eyes glinted mischievously. "I found Mr. Townsend thoroughly entangled with Miss Morrison not a quarter of an hour ago."

"I believe you should clarify that you are speaking *metaphorically*," said Mr. Townsend in crisp tones. Nigel wondered if the man was more concerned for Miss Morrison's reputation or his own.

The lady in question lifted her left eyebrow and gave Nigel a slight shake of the head. He was used to ladies tittering at his semi-salacious remarks, but he could sense the disappointment wafting from this Derbyshire lady in his direction.

"Miss Morrison was good enough to accompany me on an errand of mercy to Mrs. Hogg," continued the vicar, determined there should be no doubt about the matter.

"Ah, the *good* Mrs. Hogg," said Jack Ferris slyly, hinting at his opinion of that indigent widow. "You're a braver soul than I, Townsend. But stay," he said, laying a hand on Nigel's arm. "Here comes the even better Mrs. Coleman. We must ask her for a table and a nuncheon."

The party secured a spot in the inn's private parlour. Nigel again offered Miss Morrison his hand and seated her in a chair in the parlour. "Shall I find a place for your bonnet?" he asked, wanting nothing more than to loosen the ribbon ties on the close-fitting chip bonnet that covered Miss Morrison's wild brown hair. That bonnet was a tragedy, and it needed to meet its fatal end.

"No, I always dine with my bonnet on at this inn," said Miss Morrison. She leaned toward him confidentially. "One wouldn't want the jester to take it."

"I've never had the jester take my beaver," commented Nigel, "and I've dined here three or four times already."

"Ah, he might be waiting for you to feel secure in your surroundings," said Jack Ferris, his eyes sparkling, "so that he can manufacture his mischief when you least suspect it."

"What utter poppycock!" boomed the vicar and began to expatiate at length on the folly of idle superstition, ceasing only when Mrs. Coleman brought out the fidget pie and calf's tail soup.

"Mr. Brownlee must be pleased that you are earning your living so well," said Nigel sardonically as he filled Miss Morrison's cup with ale from the pitcher.

"How do you mean?" replied the vicar, pausing before he could taste the repast. His spoonful of soup hovered betwixt bowl and lip.

"Why, here we are receiving a second sermon, and it is not even Sunday," said Nigel. "Is Mr. Brownlee aware that he's bought two sermons a week for the price of one?"

The wizened Mr. Ferris laughed heartily at this gibe, but the vicar stood up indignantly and excused himself from the table. Miss Morrison sent a reproachful look in Nigel's direction, and once again he felt more rebuked than if a dozen dowagers had rapped his knuckles with their fans. He had claimed yesterday in the hayloft that he was a reformed man. Apparently, he must see about amending his speech as well as his conduct if that were to be true.

Chapter Thirteen

Letter

FOR THE NEXT SEVERAL days, Nigel had ample opportunity to amend his flippant speech. Belinda Morrison let him trail behind her as she inspected roof repairs, discussed the spring planting, and examined pregnant sheep. Sometimes she wore trousers, sometimes a serviceable brown gown. Nigel could not decide which he preferred as both were too loose-fitting for her slender figure. What he *would* like to see her in was a gauzy muslin morning dress, with a low neckline and a set of stays to lift—he stopped himself. Apparently, it was not only his deeds and speech that needed amending, but also his thoughts.

"Does your family raise sheep in Lincolnshire?" she asked, catching him in the middle of his improper musings.

"Er, yes, I believe so," said Nigel. He remembered seeing woolly bundles dotting the fields outside his brother's manor house when he had visited. But he had spent no time in Lincolnshire since receiving his inheritance. No doubt those woolly bundles belonged to him now.

"What month do you breed them?"

"Breed them?" echoed Nigel, appalled to discover that Miss Morrison had just put *him* to the blush. Apparently, his thoughts about lady's undergarments had been entirely innocuous compared to Miss Morrison's earthy conversation.

She placed her arms akimbo and stared over the drystone wall at her flock in the wet meadow. "Mr. Brownlee is determined that October is the right month for the rams, but I think November is better for our Derbyshire climate—it lets the weather get warmer for the lambs when they come. We lose less of them."

Nigel could see the corner of her lip twitching as she talked. She was enjoying discomfiting him with her straightforward speech. "I'm afraid I'm more acquainted with the rhythms of the London season than the agricultural season. I know the exact time to order new waistcoats and the best place to find a beaver or Hessians."

"Ah, but the London season does nothing but waste money. A season of successful farming gains it."

"And have all your seasons been successful?"

"Not at first," she admitted, "but I have put by a tidy sum each of the last few years." Her lips no longer seemed ready to slip into a smile, and her chin set itself into a firm angle. "For Charlie, when he comes back."

"Of course," said Nigel smoothly. Their time in the hayloft had been very informative concerning the lady's regard for her long-lost brother. Nigel had a niggling sense that Harold Brownlee was probably right and that "full fathom five her brother lay," but he had no intention of voicing his doubts.

The continued visits to the muddy Morrison farm took their toll on Nigel's wardrobe, but before the end of the week he was delighted to see a large trunk containing additional clothing delivered from the posting inn. His valet Simpson had followed his instructions.

The communication that followed the day afterwards, however, was less of a delight. John came into the parlour while Nigel was playing the pianoforte and cleared his throat, in deference to the music. "A letter for you, yer grace."

Nigel's fingers froze on the keys. He would have reminded John that it was plain Mr. Lymington, but he soon saw that the direction on the letter had no qualms about announcing his title. It was made out, quite ostentatiously, to the Duke of Warrenton.

Thunder and turf! No doubt Mr. Coleman who received the post bag at the Jester's Arms was already gossiping to his wife about Upper Cross' prestigious visitor. Nigel wondered if he would ever be able to take his dinner at the "haunted" inn again.

He gave John a nod of thanks, moved from the pianoforte toward the window for better light, and then broke the seal on the letter. Inside, the tone was less formal, the flirtatious scribbles of a lady that Nigel knew far better than he ought.

Nigel,

Where have you been, your gorgeous grace? There's been no word from you for weeks, and I've been forced to exercise my wiles on your valet to find your location. I learn from Simpson that you've been rusticating in rural Derbyshire, cast out from Paradise like Our First Parents. Can it be? Why, in heaven's name, would you exile yourself from Mayfair so rashly, you sly creature?

I know you are punting up the River Tick, but things are bound to look up. You are a duke, my dearest, and dukes can always stave off disaster by virtue of their title. If your odious niece continues to prove recalcitrant in sharing her inheritance, I will find you a pigeon of your own to pluck. There will be heiresses aplenty in town after the New Year.

Come home again as soon as you can. I daresay you may indulge your desire to rusticate with a countrified Christmas—I intend to watch the roaring Yule log at a country house party as well. But if you are not back by the end of December, I shall come to fetch you myself. I have so many delicious *on-dits* to tell you, and I won't have my most amusing pet missing the season.

With Love,

Callista

Nigel swallowed. He had forgotten how forceful Lady Maltrousse could be. She had been a friend of his late brother's...a very *close* friend. When Nigel had become duke two years ago, she had taken him on as her protege, introducing him to the wonders of wine, women, song, and speculation. It was she who had encouraged him to seduce "that countrified little widow

Mrs. Audeley," and it was she who had helped him run up all sorts of debt until he was ready to buckle under the weight of it.

There was a strange sort of magnetism about Lady Maltrousse. To be singled out by her was an infamous and intoxicating honour. Nigel was both dismayed to learn that she knew of his whereabouts and relieved to discover that she had not forgotten his existence.

That thrill was soon tempered by the wish that she *had*. As enticing as his life in London had been, he was not sure that he wanted to return to it. And while Lady Maltrousse might know that he was punting up the River Tick, she did not know about the greatest of his problems on that sordid stream—a problem named Solomon Digby.

Simpson knew, however. And Simpson, to mince no words, was a *traitor*. Nigel's note had specifically told his valet to send his trunk to Upper Cross under the name "Mr. Lymington" and to tell his location to no one. If Lady Maltrousse could track his whereabouts through his valet, then Solomon Digby could too. All it would take was a handful of shillings, and Nigel would be trussed up like a pigeon by Digby's minions.

His venal valet needed to be sacked. For all of Archie Garrick's bumbling, Nigel much preferred a spotty-faced fellow that he could trust to a sophisticated valet with an itching palm. And thank God for Rose Audeley, soon to be Lady Kendall—a far better woman than Callista Fernley would ever be. Thank God that Mrs. Audeley had lent him refuge in Derbyshire from the worst of his mistakes. He wished he had never succumbed to Callista's flattery in the first place and the lure of belonging to her wild and witty set of lords and ladies.

He certainly did not want Callista coming to Derbyshire to fetch him. Later, he must dash off a quick letter to her, something bland enough not to waken her suspicions that he was defecting from her coterie, but also something strong enough to keep her from flitting to his side. But, in the meantime, he had no desire to have her poisonous letter peeking at him, tempting him to return to his old life. Taking the letter to the fireplace, Nigel tossed it in with a quick flick of the wrist. If only he could incinerate the rest of the incriminating ties that bound him to London.

At least he had a fresh suit of clothing to wear to the Morrisons' when he visited later this afternoon. Aunt Lucy had made sure to let him know that her niece would be "at home" today, in the parlour rather than in the fields. Apparently, it was an arrangement they had—that Bel must keep her company indoors at least twice a week.

Nigel resumed his piano playing, his pace more frenetic and less forgiving than before. Then, when the sun reached its zenith, he retired to his room, wrote a quick note to Lady Maltrousse, and allowed Archie to attire him in a coat of mulberry superfine and a black waistcoat clocked with gold. Callista had told him that waistcoat brought out the sparkle in his dark eyes—confound it! He almost bade Archie change his clothes for something else but then turned about face one more time and resumed his original plan. There was no point in letting Lady Maltrousse have such power over his choices.

"Are ye goin' to the Morrison house again, yer g-guh-mister Lymington?" asked Archie. His Adam's apple bobbed up and down at the heady pleasure of dressing a duke in his finest town togs.

"Just so," said Nigel, wondering if his valet had an ulterior motive in asking.

"Might'nt I come along?" Archie looked at him hopefully. "I could sit in the kitchen while y'take yer tea. All quiet-like with...whoever else is there."

"Dear me," said Nigel, inspecting his valet's face for signs of subtlety. "I can only suppose some nubile female with whom you wish to fraternise tends the fireside kettle in the kitchen there."

Archie blushed, his face a uniform colour for once. "Very well," said Nigel, taking pity on him. "You may accompany me. We'll take the carriage today instead of walking. No use ruining a fresh pair of pantaloons if we run across a wagon driver who likes to souse pedestrians with mud puddles."

Chapter Fourteen

Your Grace

B EL WONDERED WHY MRS. Brownlee had come to call this afternoon. It was not that their plump neighbour was *unfriendly* to Bel and Lucy, but she tended to keep to her own home, busying herself with the upkeep of Mullhill Manor and her own appearance. Today, she clearly had some news of import to convey. Bel could sense that the woman had spent the last quarter hour dancing around whatever it was. But it was not until the appearance of a second carriage outside the window that she came to her point.

"My dear," she said, looking furtively at Bel, "I see Mr. Lymington is coming to call as well. I trust you have heard the news about him?"

"I don't believe so." Bel kept her tone impassive, determined not to show curiosity, especially not in front of her aunt. Aunt Lucy had dropped far too many hints to Mr. Lymington about how well her niece would suit him and how well he would suit her niece. There was no point in giving her further fodder to concoct a romance out of a stranger's overtures of friendship.

Mrs. Brownlee leaned in closer to Bel on the sofa. From the other side of the room, Aunt Lucy lifted the edge of her cap to enable her weak ear to hear better.

"I had it from Mr. Brownlee who had it from Mrs. White who had it from Mr. Coleman at the Jester's Arms that Mr. Lymington is no mister at all. He's a titled peer. A duke!"

"Good heavens!" squealed Aunt Lucy, almost leaping out of her chair. "One of the royal dukes?"

"No, not quite as exciting as that," said Mrs. Brownlee. "The Duke of Wanlington, I heard."

"That's certainly not a duke I've ever heard of," said Bel, her eyes sliding towards the window where she could see Mr. Lymington disembarking from his carriage. He was followed by his spindly valet, Archie Garrick, and his clothing was finer than anything he had worn in the last three weeks.

"You've barely been outside of Derbyshire," said Aunt Lucy with a scoff. "I daresay there are two dozen dukes you've never heard of."

"Have *you*, with your vast knowledge of London, heard of Wanlington?" asked Bel pointedly.

"Well, no," admitted Aunt Lucy.

"But still," said Mrs. Brownlee. "A duke! Even if it is a duke that no one has ever heard of." Her eyes flitted back to Bel. "How many times has he called on you?"

"Nearly every day," said Aunt Lucy proudly, answering for her tight-lipped niece.

"Oh my," said Mrs. Brownlee faintly, agog at the distinction that had been paid to her neighbour. "And to think he dined with us at Mullhill Manor—and it was *I* who bade him take you in for dinner."

Bel heard the front door of the house open as Jenny admitted their next guest. Mr. Lymington—or, should she say, his grace the Duke of Wanlington—would be entering the parlour any moment.

Aunt Lucy must have recognised the same. She began to twitter about the weather to Mrs. Brownlee, trying to manufacture the illusion that they were *not* talking about the new arrival. That illusion was doomed to failure, however, for Mrs. Brownlee's shining eyes were fixated on the door as she gripped the armrest of the sofa.

The door opened. "Good afternoon," said the duke breezily, still unaware what had just been divulged.

Mrs. Brownlee rose to her feet and dropped a curtsy. "Good afternoon, your grace."

The dark-haired man fell silent, and his face fell into a grimace while Mrs. Brownlee held her curtsy far longer than was necessary. "Oh, dash it all, please don't do that." Bel saw his lips set in a disappointed line. He looked from Mrs. Brownlee to Aunt Lucy to Bel, crossed his arms, and leaned against the wall by the doorframe.

"Won't you sit down, your grace?" simpered Aunt Lucy, jumping to her feet as well. She gestured to the place on the sofa that Mrs. Brownlee had vacated and pulled their plump neighbour over to the window. "Mrs. Brownlee and I were just admiring the...landscape."

"Yes, it is so picturesque this time of year," remarked Bel dryly. Anyone with eyes could see that the December garden was particularly barren and colourless except for the boxwood hedge.

Warily, the duke uncrossed his arms and walked over to the sofa, taking a seat next to Bel. She could see that his mulberry coat framed his shoulders impeccably, no doubt the product of one of London's most exclusive tailors. His dark waistcoat was patterned with whorls of gold thread, and his cravat was the kind of snowy white that didn't exist in Derbyshire.

Bel took a deep breath. But he was still the same gentleman who had called on her all this week. The same gentleman who had offered her a carriage to keep out of the rain. The same gentleman who had brought her biscuits when she was crying in the hayloft. She would not do him the discourtesy of either sudden disgust or sycophantic worship.

—ele—

"Mrs. Brownlee tells me that you're a duke, Mr. Lymington." Miss Morrison arched an eyebrow and spoke with the same straightforward confidence that she had always possessed.

"Does she indeed?"

"Mmhmm."

Nigel looked at her sharply. She did not seem the least bit angry or awed. As much as he had worried about the former, he had absolutely dreaded the latter. To see Miss Morrison furious with him for his lie of omission would be a shame, but to see Miss Morrison kowtowing to his title would be the end of his admiration of her.

"Well, are you?" she demanded. Nigel could see the plump neighbour over by the window craning her neck to listen in—while Aunt Lucy kept Mrs. Brownlee from rejoining the couple on the sofa, ostensibly giving them a *tête-à-tête*.

"Yes, I was elevated to the title two years ago, at the demise of my brother."

"My condolences on the death of your brother."

He gave a slight shrug. He had already told Miss Morrison that his brother was dead. They had not been close. Or even fond of each other. Not like a more generous family of siblings. Not like Belinda and Charles Morrison.

The Duke of Wanlington?" she said, continuing her interrogation.

"Warrenton, actually. But I can see how those meddling with my mail could have mistaken the direction on the letter. My correspondent has shockingly poor penmanship."

Indeed, everything about his correspondent was shocking, and he wished fervently that Lady Maltrousse had never written to him.

The elder Miss Morrison could contain herself no longer and flitted back to stand near her niece. "Letters are always of interest in a small village," said Aunt Lucy. "I'm afraid Mr. Coleman—and Mrs. Coleman—have no qualms about sharing word of whatever arrives in the post bag. No, pray, do not get up from your seat, your grace."

"And the rest of us have no qualms about sharing the gossip from the Colemans." Bel pursed her lips at her aunt, and Nigel noticed how the soft winter light caught the sprinkles of red and gold in her brown hair.

"But the Colemans are such dear people," Mrs. Brownlee hastened to add, coming over to have her share in the conversation, "and so accommodating about the preparations for the Boxing Day ball at the inn. I do hope Your Grace will still be able to join us?"

Lady Maltrousse would have encouraged Nigel to squash Mrs. Brownlee like a presumptuous mushroom, but somehow, Nigel could not find it in himself to snub her. He rose to his feet as a gentleman ought. "I am not sure, Mrs. Brownlee. It is possible I may need to leave the neighbourhood sooner than that."

If Mr. Digby sent men looking for him, he would be leaving Upper Cross as fast as a hired horse could take him. Curse Simpson and his itching palm!

"I imagine a duke has many responsibilities at Christmas time," said Miss Morrison, rising from the sofa to make a fourth in the conversation.

"Er...yes, I suppose. To which responsibilities do you refer?"

"Why, it is not only Christmas for you, but also for all your servants, your tenants, and their families. Surely, some gesture of largesse is warranted?"

"Ah. Yes." Nigel had never considered the matter before. "Of course. My steward, naturally, takes care of such things. I leave everything to him, so that I don't have to be bothered."

"How convenient," said Miss Morrison, as if she had seen right through him. "So, your only task is to procure a Boxing Day gift for your steward."

"Just so." Nigel wracked his brain trying to remember the name of the man whose letters he had ignored. He crossed his arms once again and decided to curtail the visit that he had looked forward to all day. "How late it is. I must be on my way now. If you could ring for Archie, Miss Morrison?"

"We have no bells here," she said, "but I can fetch him from the kitchen." Nigel made his adieu to the two older woman and then followed Miss Morrison out the parlour door and down the staircase to the kitchen, seizing his beaver as he went.

There, on a stool by the countertop, Archie was enjoying a biscuit, head bent close to the Morrisons' maid-of-all-work.

"Jenny," said Miss Morrison brightly. "Our guests are leaving."

"Oh," said Jenny, turning red as she saw Nigel following behind her mistress. She slid from the stool and bobbed a curtsy in the messy kitchen, the steam from the kettle causing her dishevelled hair to fall into ringlets. "Your grace."

"I didn't tell 'er," said Archie, red in the face. "She already knew, Mr. Lymington...er...yer grace."

"No," said Nigel smoothly. "I'm certain you didn't. The cat is out of the bag now, is it not, Miss Morrison?"

"Out of the bag entirely," agreed Miss Morrison, "and roaming wherever it wishes." She laid her hands on the flat, wooden surface of the countertop, and Nigel saw that in contrast to the callouses on her hands there were two perfect half-moons on her thumbnails. The desire to trace them with his own fingers was overwhelming, but a new distance had grown between them like an overnight hedge of thorns.

"Good day, Miss Morrison," said Nigel, trying to paper over his frustration.

"Good day, you grace," said Miss Morrison, eyebrow lifted in ironic humour. It was only after he had left the kitchen that Nigel noticed she had not bothered to curtsy to him.

It was something.

Chapter Fifteen

Warning

BEL HAD A SUSPICION that the Duke of Warrenton would no longer call on them so freely now that his identity was being bruited about the neighbourhood. And she was right. He not only missed divine services on the third Sunday in Advent, but he also refrained from stopping by the Morrison manor house the following four days.

When the rain abated mid-afternoon, Jer took Aunt Lucy and Jenny in the cart to the grocer's while Bel lingered at home. For once, she felt her usual indefatigable industry waning. Listless, she leafed through the pages of *Curtis's Botanical Magazine,* wishing that the plants it described were less ornamental and more practical. Gyles Audeley might enjoy a strictly decorative use of his land, but Bel was determined to turn a profit with every acre. It was the least she could do for Charlie.

A knock on the door brought her to her feet. Since Jenny was out, she would answer it herself. Perhaps it was Mr. Lymington—the duke—at last.

"Miss Morrison!" said the vicar in surprise, and Bel felt a pang of disappointment.

"Yes, I live here."

"Of course," said the vicar, a line appearing between his brows, "but I expected your maid to answer the door." He paused. "Might I come in?"

"I am not receiving today."

"It's not in the way of a social call," said the vicar. "It's something more urgent."

Reluctantly, Bel allowed Mr. Townsend inside. She motioned for him to join her in the parlour but kept the parlour door wide open for propriety's sake—a silly precaution since no one else was about in the house. At least Magpie was home. Bel lifted the feline chaperone up into her lap on the sofa and beckoned for the vicar to take the chair opposite.

Once seated, Mr. Townsend cleared his throat. "I imagine you have heard the news about the *stranger* in the neighbourhood."

Bel could not resist pretending ignorance. "Do you mean the Audeleys' houseguest or yourself?"

"I mean the Duke of Warrenton," said Mr. Townsend severely.

"Ah, that."

"Yes, that. How grossly he has deceived us all. And now, I see he has shown his true colours and omitted to attend divine services yesterday."

"Why should he come to church to be stared at?" Without fully understanding the feelings in her own breast, Bel yielded to an undeniable urge to defend the duke.

Mr. Townsend was about to answer, but a violent inhalation indicated that a speck of dust or dander had entered his nasal cavities. He continued to inhale spasmodically until he let out a great sneeze. That sneeze was followed by two more, a short pause, and then another set of three.

Finally, the vicar regained his equanimity and began to resume the conversation. "No doubt he hid his identity so that he could come as a wolf among sheep in this parish. But now that I've heard his name, his London reputation is well-known to me. I regret to tell you this, Miss Morrison, but the Duke of Warrenton is the worst kind of rake."

Bel folded her hands primly on her lap. "He already confessed as much to me."

The vicar's mouth dropped open in surprise. "Confessed as much? So, you already know about his immoral ways? I wonder that you did not send him about his business right away. At the Jester's Arms, you seemed to be *encouraging* his attentions."

"Some might consider that *my* business and not yours." Bel had never spoken thus to a man of the cloth before, but her blood was up, and she could not abide his pomposity.

The vicar put a hand over his mouth as a strangled gasp slipped out. He tried—and failed—to halt another bout of sneezing.

Bel glared at him. If he could not enter her parlour without falling into paroxysms, then it was irresponsible of him to enter the parlour altogether. But the vicar assigned blame in other places.

"If you would simply remove the cat, Miss Morrison," he gasped in between sneezes, "our conversation could continue without interruption."

"I don't believe Magpie is interrupting anything." Bel tried to keep her fingers from tightening into claws as she stroked the cat's soft back. "And perhaps it would be better if this conversation *did* come to an end."

A sound from the window caught the ears of both. It was a carriage pulling into view. Bel almost snorted audibly. How ironic. Their neighbour from Audeley House who had been *in absentia* for the last several days had chosen *this* moment to arrive.

Mr. Townsend rose to his feet, his sharp blue eyes recognising the passenger now disembarking from the carriage. "No wonder you are eager for this conversation to be over. I warn you, Miss Morrison, you are treading a dangerous path. If you continue to consort with this man, it will be your reputation that suffers. As your spiritual advi—"

"Yes, so you've said," said Bel, inconveniencing Magpie by rising from her chair as well. She had no patience for Mr. Townsend attempting to use spiritual authority to circumscribe her actions. If it had been Mr. Davies, installed as vicar in Upper Cross since before her own birth, she might have listened. But for a stranger who had no claim to either years or experience to lecture her was unpardonable. "I will thank you for your advice and bid you good day, Mr. Townsend."

Mr. Townsend's nostrils flared, and his shoulders pulled back stiffly. "I hope that Mr. Brownlee is right about you and that your lack of prudence is not an incurable defect. No doubt the lack of male leadership in this house is largely to account for it." He bowed himself out of the room before Bel could respond to that astonishing statement. "Good day, Miss Morrison."

ele

Nigel had kept to himself for nearly a week, incensed at Simpson for revealing his whereabouts, miffed with Lady Maltrousse for refusing to leave him in peace, and mildly irritated with the curiosity his title had awakened in Upper Cross. As he wallowed in frustration on the Audeley House pianoforte, the sounds of arpeggios and chords had filled the air with his restive spirit.

A few times, he had seen Magpie roaming the rose gardens outside the windows. He had considered setting out a dish of meat to entice the friendly feline inside, but he recalled how vexed Miss Morrison would be if he subverted her cat's affections any further.

His own affections were subverted beyond remedy. After spending so much time in the company of Bel Morrison, he now felt the lack of her keenly. The sensation was different from anything he had ever encountered. Even when he had been on the hunt for his latest conquest, he had not felt this continual dull ache. He had become a master at distraction over the last two years, but there was no distraction that could stop him from meditating on Miss Morrison's low voice, muddy trousers, and bright eyes.

Finally, after no further communication had been received from London and after no minions of Solomon Digby had wandered down the lane bearing cudgels, Nigel decided that enough was enough. He would call on Miss Morrison once again. Unwilling to encounter more curiosity from the village folk, he ordered John to bring round the carriage and set him down at the Morrison house during calling hours.

As Nigel approached on the path, he saw Mr. Townsend exiting the house. But before he could get out a word of greeting, he felt the vicar push past him. Clearly, the fellow was not himself. Perhaps some contretemps had occurred?

There was no servant at the open door, so Nigel let himself in and, removing his own greatcoat and beaver, set them on the table in the entrance hall. Then, knocking on the door of the parlour, he heard a low voice saying, "Come in."

Magpie, seeing him enter, lifted a curious head. Within seconds, the cat had vacated Miss Morrison's lap and was nuzzling against his leg.

"To what do I owe the honour, your grace?" Miss Morrison made no move to rise from her chair. Her eyes were flashing like the sparks in a forge, and Nigel could sense that she was filled with some strong emotion.

"I believe the honour is all mine," said Nigel gently. He looked around the room, hoping to find Aunt Lucy ensconced in the window seat, but the parlour was empty except for the woman in front of him. He swallowed. A lady alone. It was exactly the situation he would have most hoped for in London. But not here. Not with Miss Morrison. It was not prudent to call on her today—both for her sake and his own. "I see Miss Lucy is out...perhaps I should come by another day."

"Oh, the damage is done already," said Miss Morrison, rising from her seat. "Now that you've arrived in plain daylight, everyone will know about it. Mr. Townsend will proclaim to the world that I have disregarded his advice and continue to receive calls from a London rake."

Nigel froze. "I told you my reputation was...questionable."

"According to the vicar, not only questionable but notorious. According to him, you are quite the 'duke about town.'"

"Er...yes, I'm afraid I was." The key word there being *was*. He had been a self-absorbed Lothario with Lady Maltrousse and her set and the worst of all blackguards to his niece Louisa. But no longer. That way of life was in the past. Or at least, he *hoped* it was in the past. He still needed to put his new resolve to the test, and that test could not be performed until he encountered temptation once again.

Miss Morrison breathed in deeply through her nose, and Nigel could not tell whether she was more irritated with Mr. Townsend or with him. "Why don't you go back to London where you belong?"

"Because I can't," replied Nigel evenly. "If I do, I'm likely to have my legs broken and my ears cut off." Once again, the black-and-white cat began to nuzzle the legs in question and audibly purr its regard for them.

She stared. "What on earth does that mean?"

Nigel reached down a hand to scratch Magpie between the ears. "I know it sounds like a Drury Lane theatrical, but it's all too true. I took some money from a fellow named Solomon Digby, in exchange for a promise I could not perform. The money is spent. Digby is angry. And of necessity, I must remain incognito until I scrape together some funds to repay him with interest."

"Surely a duke has plenty of funds to pay his obligations?"

"*This* duke does not." Nigel held out his hands as he shrugged. Should he explain it all to her? Should he put himself into an even worse light?

He sighed. There was something about Miss Morrison that required nothing less than the truth.

"My brother ran the estate into the ground through poor management. And foolishly, I put in no effort to revitalise it when it came into my hands. As matters stand, the income from the Lincolnshire estate is barely enough to support the expenses incurred by my London residence and staff."

He paused, watching with bated breath as the light from the window caught the dozen different shades of brown in Miss Morrison's hair.

She stomped her foot. "Then leave London and turn your attention to rescuing your estate. Or are you unwilling to put your responsibilities ahead of your selfish pleasures?"

Nigel gave her a self-deprecating half-smile. "As usual, the sensible Miss Morrison hits upon the crux of the matter. I don't *want* to go to Lincolnshire. And what's more, I don't know the first thing about running an estate."

"I daresay your steward could inform you."

Nigel took a deep breath. He did not want his steward to inform him. If he had to take lessons on estate management from anyone, he would far prefer that they came from a straightforward Derbyshire lass near Upper Cross.

"In any case," continued Miss Morrison, "it seems more prudent to spend your time in honest toil in Lincolnshire than in dishonourable hiding in Derbyshire. You'll never be able to repay this Mr. Digby if you remain here."

"I'm sure you're right, but I've discovered Derbyshire has attractions that Lincolnshire does not." His dark gaze gave a gleam of appreciation. Despite her plain, practical dress. Despite her refusal to make any concession to fashion. Despite her straightforward way of raking him over the coals.

She arched an eyebrow, that delightfully cynical left eyebrow which Nigel had come to anticipate and enjoy. "Your grace, pray don't insult my intelligence by giving me a compliment. I daresay you've enjoyed the company of dozens of ladies far more sophisticated and beautiful than me."

"As you wish," said Nigel. "I will refrain." He reached out a hand, and surprisingly, she let him take her fingers and bow over them. "But since I *have* enjoyed the company of dozens of ladies, when I do give you a compliment, you must admit that I know what I'm talking about."

She let him hold her fingers for half a moment before she pulled away her hand.

"I intend to stay for the Boxing Day ball," said Nigel.

"How kind of you to condescend to our small gathering."

"I suspect the condescension will be more yours than mine if you agree to sully your reputation even further...and stand up with me in the ballroom.

Miss Morrison's grey eyes flashed. "Trying to fill your dance card already, your grace?"

"Yes," said Nigel promptly. Hopefully. Desperately.

"I'll think on it," she said quietly.

Nigel forced a smile and made his farewells. At least, she had not said no.

Chapter Sixteen

Sweetmeats

"What's this, Bel?" demanded Aunt Lucy, the next day. "I saw Mrs. White at the butcher's, and she let it drop quite slyly, that it was clever of a spinster to bag our friend the duke, when usually widows were preferred by *that type.*"

"How odious," said Bel calmly, but inside her heart was beating a ragged march. "I haven't 'bagged' anyone."

It was true. The Duke of Warrenton wanted nothing more from her than a dance at the Boxing Day ball and a diversion from the dullness of his enforced exile from London. She had replayed their conversation in her head a hundred times over the past three days, and she had no illusions on that score.

"Well, I didn't think you *had,*" said Aunt Lucy, "or I would be the first to know of it. But the way she was insinuating things—it was almost as if she thought there was some sort of havey-cavey business going on between the two of you."

"No doubt that's to be expected," said Bel sharply, "given the duke's reputation." She wondered if Mr. Townsend was to be blamed for the gossip circulating in Upper Cross. Had the offended vicar offered Mrs. White that rumour on a platter?

"What do you mean by his 'reputation'? I must say, he seemed like a very nice man when he was plain 'Mr. Lymington.' Can he really have changed so much now that we know he's a duke?"

"Mr. Townsend seems to think that the Duke of Warrenton is a wastrel and a womaniser."

Rather than showing any shock, Aunt Lucy's wrinkled cheeks rounded in a smile. "Or perhaps Mr. Townsend is simply jealous. Perhaps he seeks to blacken the name of his rival—"

"His rival?" Bel gave a forced laugh. "On the contrary, Mr. Townsend finds my lack of prudence to be highly disturbing—particularly, my lack of prudence in conversing with the Duke of Warrenton."

"Good heavens!" said Aunt Lucy. "The words of a jealous man if I've ever heard them! Why didn't you tell me this sooner?"

Bel shrugged. "I didn't think it important enough to mention. I daresay we have enough on our minds with Christmas, and the Boxing Day ball, and Charlie...." Her voice grew sombre. How easy it was—and how disloyal! —to forget about Charlie in all this hubbub over a rusticating aristocrat.

"I suppose so," said Aunt Lucy doubtfully, the edges of her cap fluttering. Nothing could take precedence in her own mind over the joys of matchmaking. The fact that Mr. Lymington was now "his grace" was a matter as monumental as the Battle of Nile. "We shall see who dances with you more than once at Mrs. Brownlee's ball, and then all will be made clear."

"I am not sure that I will attend."

Aunt Lucy's eyes grew large. "But, my dear, if you do not attend, then there is no reason for me to go. I am your chaperone! And consider—I have already promised a dance to Mr. Ferris—"

Bel could not resist teasing her aunt. "I did not think Mr. Ferris was spry enough to dance a reel."

"No, you goose, the younger Mr. Ferris. He is not so old, I think, as to be incapacitated by a set of dances."

Bel saw two spots of colour form on her aunt's cheeks and finally relented. "Very well, I shall attend. But I suspect it is you, my dear aunt, who will be fending off the bachelors, while I sit in the corner and lament the lack of male leadership in our home."

It was an ironic allusion to the vicar's diatribe from a few days ago, but as she spoke the words, Bel could not help but feel a pang. Oh, Charlie! The sorrow of seven years' absence would rise like the tide at the New Year. She could already feel the saltwater surf of her grief gathering at the pronouncement the courts would indubitably make. Was it right to set aside that heaviness of sorrow for the distraction that a brief dalliance with a duke would bring?

"And what about Christmas dinner?" asked Aunt Lucy.

Bel raised an eyebrow. "What about it?"

"I imagine that poor Mr. Lymington—er, his grace—will be eating it all alone in the Audeley House dining room."

Bel's voice took on a tone of admonishment. "Aunt Lucy—"

"I know, I know, my dear," said Aunt Lucy, holding up her hands in a conciliatory fashion. Then she fled the room before Bel could forbid anything that she was already minded to do.

—ele—

The day before Christmas Eve a box arrived addressed to "the Gentleman at Audeley House." Nigel would have been grateful for the discretion of the direction if his ducal identity had not already been exposed. Inside the box was a selection of wine, sweetmeats, and marzipan from none other than the owner of the house—the former Mrs. Audeley and the new Lady Kendall.

Along with the sweets came a letter, a far more welcome missive than the note from Lady Maltrousse which had arrived the week prior. But still, a letter from the lady of the house might be a kindly reminder that he had overstayed his welcome....

Your Grace,

My coachman John has informed me that you continue to reside at Audeley House. You are welcome to do so for as long as is needful. Lord Kendall and I have no intention of traveling to Derbyshire during the winter months, and I am happy that you can make use of an otherwise empty abode.

I hope you have found good company amidst my neighbours in Derbyshire. The Brownlees are always forthcoming with invitations, and the Morrison ladies and Ferris brothers add charm to any gathering. I daresay the neighbourhood will not let you spend Christmas alone, but I enclose some sweets to add to the cheer of the season.

You will be glad to learn that there has finally been word of Gyles and your niece Louisa. A letter was forwarded to us whilst on our wedding trip. They are in France! Whether they are married is unclear, but a mother's heart always hopes for the best. Gyles will do right by Louisa, if she will let him—which may complicate your own prospects, as I know you have your own plans for her marriage.

Lord Kendall and I are currently in Cornwall, but by the time this letter reaches you, we shall have returned from our wedding trip to Kendall House in London. If Gyles and Louisa reappear in England, I think it likely that they will come there first. But there is always a chance that Gyles will head straight for Upper Cross. Do let me know immediately if there is any news of him.

Yours, etc.

Lady Kendall

P.S. Happy Christmas! You may want to open the bottle of '94 burgundy in honour of the occasion.

P.P.S. Please make a gift of some of the sweetmeats to John, Archie, and Mrs. Garrick for their Boxing Day treat.

When he started the letter, Nigel had been expecting to read an eviction notice. Now, as he came to the end of it, he shook his head in grateful disbelief. What had he ever done to deserve such kindness from the widow Audeley? Perhaps in his younger years as an idle but well-meaning second son, such generosity toward him would have been understandable. But now? After he had behaved so boorishly to his niece Louisa and like an utter profligate to Lady Kendall herself?

He certainly did not deserve the '94 burgundy, but he would accept it in the spirit it had been offered. And perhaps he could pass along his hostess' generosity by sharing the sweetmeats with an even wider circle than the household retainers. Surely, there must be some unfortunates in the neighbourhood who had even less reason to welcome Christmas than he did?

The Eve of Christmas fell on a Sunday. Nigel was tempted to avoid the eager eyes of the country folk by lying abed through the morning church services—it was no great sacrifice to forgo Mr. Townsend's preaching—but the possibility of seeing Miss Morrison drew him there like a lodestone.

He bade Archie lay out his coat of brown superfine with his yellow waistcoat. "No, not the dark pantaloons," he admonished the spotty-faced lad. "The tan ones with this coat. And my brown Hessians." He was still out of charity with Simpson, but he managed to keep his humour with Archie despite the lad's bumbling and even instructed him how to tie an Oriental before John brought round the carriage.

At the church door, he saw that the Morrisons had come in their open cart again, a fact of rustic life that Nigel still found appalling. He had no time to speak with Miss Morrison before he was accosted by the tall, stooping form of Harold Brownlee. "Ah, I hear you've been keeping secrets from us, your grace."

The old man's tone held mild recrimination over the secrecy. "We didn't know we had a duke to dine at Mullhill Manor a fortnight since, or we would have counted *you* the guest of honour."

Nigel demurred. "Surely, the new vicar deserved his day in the sun."

"Indeed, indeed," said Mr. Brownlee, dismissing that topic with a wave of the hand. "I daresay you'll be leaving us soon enough, eh?"

Nigel's eyes flicked over to the Morrison pew. The gentle-woman farmer with the unmodish bonnet was not what had *brought* him to Derbyshire, but she was certainly the thing that made him reluctant to leave. "My departure date is yet to be determined."

The service was about to commence, and Nigel accepted Mrs. Brownlee's starry-eyed invitation to share their high-backed pew. He did *not* accept her invitation to join them at Christmas dinner the following day, however, for he wanted to leave himself open to another invitation if it presented itself—as unlikely as that might be.

If the vicar's brow was a little more thunderous than usual and his sermon against worldliness a little more pointed, Nigel did not regard it, for his eyes continued to stray toward the lady in the brown kersey gown. Miss Morrison, however, seemed determined to keep her own eyes on the straight and narrow. Throughout the service, they never met his. Not even once.

Following the dismissal, Nigel bolted from his seat to intercept the Morrison party, but the younger of the ladies had already hurried outside. Aunt Lucy was more accommodating. She saw him coming and fidgeted with her gloves just long enough to let him come level with her elbow. "Tomorrow is

Christmas," she said, her bright eyes dancing with excitement. "Have you anywhere to dine?"

"No, indeed," replied Nigel, thanking fortune that he had not accepted Mrs. Brownlee's offer to eat the Christmas goose at Mullhill Manor.

"Then you must sit down to table with us," said Aunt Lucy brightly. "We cannot let you 'Christmas' alone."

"I would be honoured," said Nigel. It was quite true. He felt more honoured than if the Queen had invited him to tea or the prime minister had asked his opinion on the Regency question.

But whether the younger Miss Morrison would be pleased was not at all certain. To be unsure of a woman's opinion of him sent Nigel back to his younger years, when he was merely a second son and a second-rate student who had gained all his popularity second-hand from his older brother's much showier personality. He had spent the last two years coming out of his brother's shadow, but in the process, he had entered much darker shadows himself. If only there was a way to extricate himself that did not involve exiling himself to Lincolnshire.

CHAPTER SEVENTEEN

Christmas

O N A USUAL YEAR, Bel would have scoured the woods with Jer and Tam for greenery to festoon the house, but this year, she had no heart for it. What was the point of decorating with Charlie gone on his endless voyage and no one in the house but herself and Aunt Lucy? It seemed too cold-hearted to retire listlessly to the study to do some bookkeeping on Christmas morning, so she sat listlessly in a chair in front of the fire instead while Aunt Lucy bustled about the parlour fidgeting with the weights on the longcase clock and adjusting the lace curtains more than once. Finally, she stopped to make an announcement. "Bel, dear, I have invited a guest to join us for dinner."

Bel eyed her stormily. "I have a strange feeling that I know exactly who this guest is."

Aunt Lucy had the grace to squirm beneath her floppy lace cap. "Yes, I think you might. Mr. Townsend's sermon was so fervent about our duty to the poor, and the fatherless, and the stranger that I thought it incumbent on me to—"

"Surely you did not invite the vicar!" said Bel, her mouth falling open in horror.

"No, no," said Aunt Lucy, her tone full of reassurance. "I invited the duke!"

Bel closed her mouth. She did not wish her aunt to encourage the Duke of Warrenton's flirtation, but at least his presence was marginally preferable to Mr. Townsend's. She sighed. "You'll only encourage further gossip with this."

"If a little gossip gets you closer to happiness, then I'm willing to risk it," said Aunt Lucy. "No, no, don't 'tsk, tsk' me. I'm older than you, and I know what I'm about. I won't have you regretting the time you *didn't* make an effort to secure something better for yourself than this meaningless spinsterhood."

"Meaningless?" Her work to keep the fields sowed, the crops harvested, the sheep sheared, and the market stall open was meaningless? Bel's back stiffened and the firelight glinted off the burnished brown of her variegated hair. "How dare you say such a thing! You may only care for fashionable clothing and folderols and all the follies of the metropolis, but Charlie will value my good, honest labour for what it is and the profit that's accrued from it."

"And what if Mr. Brownlee is right? What if Charlie never comes back? I'll pass on before you do, Bel Morrison, and you'll be all alone, working yourself to the bone until you're nothing but bones yourself. And you'll have no one to leave it to. No one."

Bel's tanned face was suffused with red. She wanted to cry. She wanted to scream. She wanted to protest that nothing Aunt Lucy said was true. But deep in her heart, the weeds of despair had been growing over the last two weeks until the flower of hope had almost been choked out. Perhaps Harold Brownlee and Aunt Lucy were right. Perhaps there *was* no return for Charlie. Perhaps everything she did to secure and improve his inheritance was all in vain.

"Er, am I interrupting something?"

Once again, the duke had let himself into the house at the most awkward of moments. Bel could hardly blame him since neither she nor Aunt Lucy had been in any condition to hear the knocker.

"Indeed, you are," said Bel, more sharply than she meant to. "You seem to have a talent for interrupting at inauspicious moments."

"Your grace," said Aunt Lucy with a forced smile, trying to cover over the embarrassment of being overheard arguing, "how kind of you to join us for dinner."

"The kindness is all on your side," said the duke, gallantly ignoring Bel's discourtesy. "I think Archie was quite relieved that I had received an invitation, for his mother Mrs. Garrick had threatened to invite me to their cottage to keep me from being all alone."

Bel exhaled audibly. "Yes, the prospect of one being *all alone* does seem to be distressing to some people." She sent a fierce look in Aunt Lucy's direction.

"Well, regardless," said the duke, "*I'm* pleased to have company at Christmas." His smile was still affable, but his eyes showed a refusal to enter their argument—however much of it he had overheard.

After a few moments of desultory talk, they sat down at the dining room table. Jenny served a roast goose, the smell of which had been permeating the house for the last four hours. There was fish and vegetables and cheese and venison. Bel reflected that the duke could not complain about such a hearty and flavourful repast, even if it was not so finely sauced or garnished as London food might be. At Aunt Lucy's urging, the duke stood to carve the roast goose for the two ladies and even complimented the brown, crackling skin of the large bird.

Bel, on the other hand, felt the crackling of tension in every polite exchange of conversation. What was the duke's motive in coming for dinner? She was not so foolish as to think that he yearned for the company of a countrified spinster, but every time she raised her eyes to his face, she discovered that his eyes were already lingering on her own features. What did this man want with her?

When they had each sated their appetites, Bel stood up and began to clear the dishes from the table onto the sideboard. The duke stared at her, puzzled. "Surely, that is work for the servants?"

"Jenny was good enough to make the Christmas meal and serve it, but then she and Jer departed to visit their own parents. They took Tam with them, for he hasn't a family of his own. Christmas is for everyone, not just the rich. She's helping Mrs. Coleman at the Boxing Day ball tomorrow night, but we won't see her till then."

The duke stood up and began to clear his own plate and used silverware. "Then allow me to assist you." He helped her gather up a tray of dishes while Aunt Lucy looked on with a knowing smile.

"There's a good deal of goose left," said the duke, bearing the platter with the bird to the wood-topped table in the middle of the kitchen.

"Indeed," said Bel. "When I picked out the goose, I knew it was far too much for three. I had intended to bring some to Mrs. Hogg and the other tenants."

"*Had* intended?"

Bel sniffed. "Well, now that our Christmas has turned into a dinner with guests, I daresay, you and Aunt Lucy expect me to play the fine lady and sit in the parlour and pretend that I love to hear the latest *on-dits* and tittle-tattle of the ton." She looked out the window. "It will be dark soon. If I do not go to Mrs. Hogg's house now, she will have to wait till tomorrow for her roast goose."

"Then, by all means, let us go now. I'm sure your aunt will excuse us on an errand of mercy. I have my own present for Mrs. Hogg."

"You do?" Bel was completely mystified what that could be. Had the duke even met Mrs. Hogg? How peculiar that someone so self-absorbed would think of someone other than himself. As they left the kitchen, the duke retrieved his beaver from the entrance hall. Beside it sat a package of sweetmeats.

"So, you brought a gift for Mrs. Hogg," said Bel sardonically, "but none for your hostesses."

"You've made it quite clear," said the duke, adopting a tragic air, "that you'll stomach no sweetness from me." He put on his greatcoat and placed the beaver on his head at a rakish angle. Bel could not dispel a feeling of attraction for this man, attraction that began somewhere near the seat of her heart and curled all the way down to the tips of her toes.

"It's Christmas Day," she observed, abandoning all sense of caution. "Perhaps I could make an exception."

The duke looked at her curiously, his dark eyes passing over her face and figure as she donned her warm pelisse and placed the practical bonnet on her head. "You'd like me to be sweet to you?" He took the strings of her bonnet and tied them into a neat bow, letting the backs of his knuckles brush against her chin. "I can oblige."

Bel felt a tremor of anticipation that had nothing to do with the cold blast of air from the open door. The duke had been the epitome of a gentleman at dinner. Would he continue to be so on their brisk walk to the tenant cottages? Or would he live up to his reputation and to Mr. Townsend's warnings?

One part of her hoped for the latter. The weary listlessness that she had felt this morning had melted away at Nigel Lymington's briefest touch. It was a distraction most welcome—was she courting folly to entertain it? The Duke of Warrenton would be gone soon enough, hiding from his debts and his responsibilities in some other locality. What harm could there be in neglecting caution just this once before he disappeared from Derbyshire forever?

With Aunt Lucy peering at them out the lace curtains, Bel and the duke set off down the lane, bearing the basket of roast goose, the package of sweetmeats, and an unspoken question about what would happen next.

$$\sim$$

"Marzipan!" said Mrs. Hogg. "Let me see it." Her old fingers grabbed for the box of sweetmeats as Nigel handed it to her. She peered inside, took a sweet, and greedily stuffed it into her gummy mouth. She gave a sniff and looked at the basket Bel had placed on the table. "I sh'pose the goose is cold as a jellied eel."

Nigel could barely understand the woman's garbled words as she sucked on the marzipan treat. "We could heat it for you," he offered, looking at the forlorn fireplace in the little cottage. At least there were some embers glowing that he might be able to fan into a fire.

"Never mind that," said Mrs. Hogg. "I'll put it by for tomorrow." She swallowed the first piece of marzipan and immediately popped another one into her mouth to suck. "I sh'pose I ought to thank you, Miss Bel, that you didn't bring the vicar to sh-ermonise over me this time." She gave a fierce cackle. "And this one's handsh-omer by far. Who is he?"

Nigel gave an involuntary smirk. He was pleased that Mrs. Hogg would compare him favourably to the vicar who was ten years his junior.

"He's a visitor to the neighbourhood."

"Oho! The Audeleys' duke, I'll wager. How do you like our little hamlet, your gorgeous grace?"

"Er, very much," said Nigel, taken aback by her words. It was the same nickname that the incorrigible Lady Maltrousse used for him, but on the wrinkled lips of this leering termagant, it took on a far different character. He wondered if this gummy-mouthed creature was a picture of what Callista Fernley would look like in thirty years—or twenty years, if he was being honest, for it was harder and harder for the hardened temptress to keep up a youthful appearance.

"Well, go on then," said Mrs. Hogg, applying herself to the sweets once again. "You've done your errand of mercy, and you can leave me be."

"Happy Christmas, Mrs. Hogg," said Miss Morrison, laying a hand on the old woman's shoulder in farewell.

"Hmph. Sh-tuff and nonsense," replied the woman, but her eyes softened a little as she looked at her landlady.

Nigel opened the door to let Miss Morrison back out into the piercing wind. He felt the capes of his greatcoat swish about his shoulders as they walked back toward the manor house. His companion's skirts fluttered as well, but her sturdy straw bonnet remained safely fastened to her head. A pity he had tied those ribbons so tight, for he would have been happy to see that bonnet blown to the four winds.

"She was not very appreciative of your kindness," remarked Nigel.

"If we only base our actions on appreciation, we should have precious few good deeds to our name," replied his fair partner—for the longer that he spent in her presence, the more convinced he was that she was as fair as the meaning of her name. Somehow—imperceptibly, incrementally, and irrevocably—this drab-gowned, brown-haired, gentlewoman farmer had captured his imagination and captivated his desires.

"I daresay you have far more good deeds to your name than I have to mine."

"A matter you could remedy if you wished."

"Do you realise," said Nigel stopping in the lane, "that you have never once flattered me or pitied me in the whole of our acquaintance."

"I daresay you find me hard-hearted."

"On the contrary, I find you refreshing. You make me wish I were a better man, Miss Morrison."

She raised an eyebrow. "If wishes were horses, then beggars would ride."

"Point taken. I can't make myself a better man by wishing."

"You can't make yourself a better man by staying in Derbyshire."

Nigel sighed. "I know. But I promised myself I'd keep Christmas here at least—and permit myself the Boxing Day ball for my memories."

They began to walk again, this time their pace unaccountably slower as if neither wished for the walk to come to an end. "Ought we to check on the animals in the stable?" asked Nigel. "With the servants all gone, the horses may need—"

"I'm sure the horses have plenty in their feeding trough," replied Miss Morrison, but she allowed him to steer her towards the stone barn. They ducked inside to the lowing of cows and the nickering of horses, with just enough light left in the sky to make out the dark shapes of the creatures through the open door.

"Well?" said Miss Morrison, turning to face him.

"Well?" he repeated.

"Well, I suppose you had better kiss me," said Miss Morrison. "That's why we're loitering in the barn, isn't it?"

"Er, yes," said Nigel, more nervous than he'd ever been in his life. It was like being sent in a post chaise, all alone, to Eton all over again, with his mother refusing to get up early enough to say good-bye and only Mrs. Grenville and Mr. Randall outside to see him off. He had kissed a dozen ladies in the last year alone, but suddenly, he had no inkling of what to expect. He swallowed. "The thing is, I'm not sure you'll like me kissing you...at least, afterwards, when you think back on it."

"What is that supposed to mean? I'm too much of an antidote to experience pleasure?"

"No, not at all. I mean that if you find the kiss pleasurable you will despise me for having had too much previous practice. And if you find the kiss otherwise...well, then you will despise me for being inept at kissing."

"Hmm," said Miss Morrison, "then I suppose we are at an impasse. Who would have known that a rake could be so introspective about his kisses?"

Nigel could not tell if there was disappointment hidden behind her lightly ironic tone.

"I suppose if I'm not to receive a kiss, we had better go back inside the house. It's getting dark, and—"

He put a hand on her arm, staying her presence, delaying her departure. "Promise me you won't hate me afterwards."

"No," she whispered.

He did not know if that was an agreement to his terms or a refusal to make a promise she could not keep. Perhaps she knew she would despise him. Perhaps she hated him already. But Nigel could tell from the way her body slightly inclined toward him, from the way her lips slightly parted, from the way her eyes played over his face that now, in this moment, she wanted his lips on hers.

He obliged. A soft, tender kiss, kept carefully in place by the narrow confines of her bonnet. He felt her lips push back fiercely against his own. As he had expected, Bel Morrison did nothing by halves. A look of intense desire came into her eyes.

Gathering her in his arms, he began to kiss her more fervently until the edges of the narrow straw bonnet began to scratch at his face. Blast that bonnet! He reached for the ribbon beneath her chin, and his fumbling fingers tried to untie it.

"Mmm, I think that's quite enough," said Miss Morrison, pulling away. Her lips were halfway parted, and her breath came more quickly than before, but apparently, the loosening ribbon had rung an alarm in her head. She straightened her shoulders and took a step backwards.

"Is this your only bonnet?" Nigel demanded.

"Why?"

"Because it's dashed ugly, and it covers up far too much of your face. I ought to buy you a new one—"

"With what money, your grace? Or have you forgotten your financial woes?"

Nigel grimaced. "Always practical, Miss Morrison. So kind of you to mention my debts at this juncture."

The cow nearest to them let out a forlorn moo. It was the exact sound that Nigel's heart was making.

"You're welcome," she said pertly, turning to leave the barn. Nigel followed her, his senses still tingling with the nearness of their encounter and his *amour propre* still smarting from what had followed. As he had expected, she already despised him for causing her practical self to succumb to desire—but, oh, what a kiss that had been! If only she would let him put his lips on her again.

He walked beside her to the door of the stone farmhouse, neither of them willing to link arms even though the wind was increasing. When they reached the steps, she turned around, arms folded across the chest of her pelisse.

"I'll make your farewells to Aunt Lucy. I think it would be better if you didn't come inside."

"I think you're right," he said stiffly.

A movement caught his eye, and from the corner of the house Magpie appeared. The cat came closer and began to purr against the side of his boot. Nigel nudged the feline away. He was not in the mood for sympathy from any creature. "Good night, Miss Morrison."

"Good night, your grace." She bent down and clapped her hands and the cat, with tail held high, minced toward her and deigned to have its chin scratched. The creature purred again.

Miss Morrison looked up at him consideringly, her fingers rubbing in circles over the cat's white chest.

"I didn't hate it," she said brusquely.

"You didn't?" Nigel was unable to hide the surprise in his voice.

"No, in fact, I liked it so much that I think it would be better for both of us not to repeat the experience."

He grinned at her, his nervous tension dissolving like a spoonful of sugar in tea. "I can't promise to listen to that advice."

"I thank you for the warning," she said, lifting that tantalizing brown eyebrow, an eyebrow that he would love to kiss if it were not for that blasted bonnet. "Good night again, your grace."

CHAPTER EIGHTEEN

Preparations

THE BOXING DAY BALL was an all-day affair for Bel. After all, someone must help Mrs. Brownlee with the decorations and the table settings, and as the most competent spinster in the village, that role fell to Bel.

The day after Christmas was a holiday for the servants, so Bel lit her own fire, dressed herself in a plain grey gown, and put on a sturdy pinafore. She also laid out her silk gown that she had worn to the dinner party at the Brownlees and a pair of gloves and a set of dancing slippers. If there was no time to go home in between, she would need to change into her ballgown at the inn.

She felt a strange frisson of anticipation as she tied her close-fitting straw bonnet into place, and for a moment, she held her ungloved fingers to her lips, remembering what had transpired the evening before. A kiss on the mouth from the lips of a London libertine. A tender kiss. A warm kiss. An urgent kiss.

The Duke of Warrenton was a shockingly bad bargain. Her head knew it. Her heart knew it. But his cheeky good humour, not to mention his devilish dark eyes, had slipped under her defences somehow. He wanted to while away his self-imposed exile with a flirtation, and—God help her! —she was quite ready to let him. At least he would be leaving soon. That would save her from getting in too deep.

The arrival of Mrs. Brownlee's carriage helped dispel such thoughts from her mind. Bel climbed inside. After a few moments of happy chatter—mostly on the part of Mrs. Brownlee—the two women arrived at the Jester's Arms. The eager Mrs. Brownlee began ordering Mr. Coleman about as he cleared the tables and chairs from the public room to turn it into a makeshift ballroom.

"Oh, Bel, how good of you to come early with me. Mr. Ferris has promised to bring the boughs and holly, and I've convinced Harold to let me use the beeswax candles." She turned her attention back to the inn's proprietor. "No, no, you must not leave those chairs in the corner, for we can barely fit twenty couples even with the room completely empty. If people want to sit down, they must go into the private parlour where we shall have the tables for the food and punch." She took Bel's hand and pressed it. "What news is there? Will the duke attend?"

"Surely you asked him that yourself," said Bel dryly, "since you shared a pew with him on Sunday."

"Yes, but Harold only asked him about dining with us on Christmas. He declined. I fear he might have left the neighbourhood, which, I will admit, would be a blow. To have a duke at one's ball is a cachet I could never have dreamed of. But perhaps his travel plans have taken him else—"

"He is still here," said Bel, sacrificing some of her own pride for the sake of silencing Mrs. Brownlee's nerves.

"And I've brought him with me!" said Jack Ferris, entering the public room bearing a large bundle of evergreen and trailed by the much taller Duke of Warrenton. Mr. Ferris was in his old-fashioned frockcoat, but the duke wore his coachman's worn coat and carried his own bundle of boughs.

Bel's head turned sharply. This was unexpected. The duke had never said anything about *helping* with the ball preparations.

"Oh, how kind of you, your grace," said Mrs. Brownlee. The plump woman's eyes shone like stars as she realised the guest of honour would still be honouring her with his presence on the most important day of her year. She motioned for the men to place the greenery on the floor so that she and Bel could sort through them and choose the best ones to festoon the doorways and fireplace.

Within the next half hour, the public room of the inn had warmed up considerably. By tacit agreement, the decorators separated into two teams. Mrs. Brownlee and Mr. Ferris began hanging small swags of greenery about the fireplace and windows while Bel and the duke were given the task of making longer garlands to hang from the ceiling. Since Mrs. Brownlee had already ordered the chairs and tables removed, they carried their supplies into the private parlour and found a place to sit.

"Are we out of twine?" asked the duke.

"No, here it is." Bel tossed him the ball of sturdy string. She studied his handiwork. "You must wrap it more times than that, or the garland will come apart under its own weight."

"I know what I'm about, Miss Morrison," said the duke with mock hauteur. Apparently, he preferred a method of interweaving the branches rather than securing them with a more visible wrapping of twine.

"Are you such an expert at greenery then?" demanded Bel.

He looked up at her, and for a fleeting second, she caught a glimpse of the boy who had once inhabited those handsome features. "I have some experience. At my parents' house in Lincolnshire, they barely celebrated the season. But once a year, before I went to Eton, my parents and my older brother would take a trip to London and leave me behind for the holiday. You would have thought I would have been sad, but on the contrary, it was delightful. The housekeeper, Mrs. Grenville, let me keep Christmas with the servants belowstairs. The butler, Mr. Randall, read poetry and organised charades. We wove garlands and heated chestnuts and ate pudding and pulled flaming raisins out of the brandy." He gave her a rueful look, as if in apology for his rapid tone of excitement. "Those were quite the happiest Christmases I've ever had. They were quite the happiest *anything*."

"Were you so unhappy then the rest of the time?"

"Not unhappy, exactly. But there was a decided lack of joy in our house. My parents were not affectionate, and they objected strenuously if their own time or business or pleasure was interrupted. My brother was superior to me in every way that mattered—in horseback riding, in fencing, in conversation. He never let me forget that. And, of course, I was of less use to my parents than he was, seeing as how I was not the heir. I never would have inherited the title if he'd had a son as he ought."

Bel felt a twinge of pity. She had always had the madcap company of Charlie growing up, and a pair of parents who loved them both the same.

"Your brother had a daughter?"

"Yes, my niece, Louisa. I think her childhood was much the same as my own. Being forgotten in the country while her fashionable parents gadded about the metropolis. I felt sorry for her when she was a girl. But that did not last. Louisa is a Lymington through and through—in time, she grew up as cold and hard and mercenary as the rest of us." He gave her an apologetic smile and brushed the stray sprigs of greenery off his lap. "Come, let's hang this above the door."

The duke climbed on a step ladder while Bel fed the end of the garland to him. Thankfully, the innkeeper kept hooks installed directly below the moulding, and the duke was able to secure the greenery without difficulty. They disputed good-naturedly about how low it ought to drape, and their mock argument grew so loud that Jack Ferris warned them they were disturbing the jester's midafternoon nap. "He'll be grumpy as Beelzebub, come evening, and then we'll all be in for it during the assembly."

"Oh, what fustian!" said Mrs. Brownlee. "We've never had any trouble from the jester at any of my Boxing Day balls."

It was beginning to get dark when the decorations were finally finished and the food table arrayed with all the nuts, bread, cheese, and meats for the cold supper. Mrs. Brownlee gave a squeak when she saw how late it had become and hurried out the door with scarcely a good-bye to Bel.

"Shall I take you home to change your gown?" asked the gallant Mr. Ferris.

"No, no, Mrs. Coleman will let me use a room to get ready here at the inn," said Bel. She gave him a knowing look. "But I told Aunt Lucy I would send someone for her later since we have no carriage."

"Say no more," said Mr. Ferris, touching his nose with a wink. He nodded to the duke, who was looking deliciously rumpled in his buckskins, worn coat, and tousled hair. "Come on then, your grace, we'd best get home and do our own costuming and primping. I daresay we'll take longer than Miss Morrison."

The duke smirked. "I think you might be right, Ferris. Miss Morrison has an ironclad efficiency about her that is singularly...appealing."

Bel swallowed. Why must he continue complimenting her in such a charming tone? If she was not careful, she would lose her head completely tonight.

"Don't forget to save one for me tonight," said the duke as Mr. Ferris disappeared around the corner door.

"A dance?" asked Bel innocently

"That, among other things," murmured the duke. He gave her a wink. "There are no bonnets at a ball, so I suggest you avoid dark corners if you don't want to be kissed more thoroughly this time."

Bel meant to think of a witty reply, but all she could do was stare at him with her own lips burning. What was wrong with her that she was so overcome with desire? This flirtation with the Duke of Warrenton was destined to lead to something dire if she did not exercise her good sense and end it soon.

—ele—

As Nigel settled back into Jack Ferris' carriage, he reflected that this was the first time in a long while that he had spoken about his early life. Lady Maltrousse had coaxed some of those stories out of him, but never had he told her about Christmas belowstairs. And never had he felt such an urgent need to get the good opinion of a woman. He cared not only how her body responded to him, but also about her mind. Did she like him? He hoped so. Enough to let him continue to court her? He prayed that this were true.

For he had no doubt in his mind now that he was courting Belinda Morrison. He wanted more from her than a holiday dalliance. He wanted her lifted eyebrow, her hair in all its different shades of brown, her clever conversation across the dinner table, her joyful vigour on a country walk, her confidences entrusted to him, her duty pledged to him and his. At the end of a long day, he wanted both her and her magpie cat to sit on his lap.

From the window of the carriage, he saw a larger, more impressive chaise pulling into the innyard. "Who has Mrs. Brownlee invited this time?" said Jack Ferris, squinting out the window with a wrinkled brow, but neither of them could make out the occupants of the chaise before their own carriage had turned the corner.

Within ten minutes, the younger Mr. Ferris had set down Nigel at Audeley House and was waving cheerfully from the window. Nigel went inside, hoping that Archie had ironed his cravats. If he was going to let the lad make the attempt at tying them, he must be ready for a good half-dozen to be wrinkled beyond use and tossed aside. He took the stairs two at a time and hurried into his bedchamber only to see an unexpected set of shoulders standing by his wardrobe.

"Simpson? Hound's teeth! What are you doing here?"

"Merely my duty," he said with a sniff, only adding a perfunctory "your grace" as an afterthought. "I'm looking for some suitable evening wear amongst the lot I sent down for you. The servants here are a surly bunch, but they indicated that your grace will be gracing an assembly tonight."

"Your duty?" Nigel threw his beaver at Simpson as if he were hurling a quoit. "That stinks like a French cheesemaker. Was it your *duty* to inform Lady Maltrousse that I was in Derbyshire?"

Simpson paled. "Your grace, how was I to know you wanted that kept secret from *her?* You've been *at home* often enough to Lady Maltrousse when no one else was allowed entry—" His eye caught on the worn places where Archie had overbrushed the beaver, and he gave a cry of affronted honour. "Fiend take it! This hat is ruined!"

Nigel ignored the outburst. "You should have known that when I said, 'send my togs to this address, and tell *no one* of my whereabouts.' Basic comprehension, you nitwit." He growled. "How did you get here, anyway?"

Simpson put the beaver down and looked even more uncomfortable.

"I'm not in the mood to be trifled with. Answer me, Simpson."

"She said you would need my services as she didn't intend to ride all the way back to London with a shabby-coated sheep farmer. Begging your pardon—her words, not mine."

Nigel held up a hand. "Are you implying what I think you are implying? Do you mean to say that Lady Maltrousse *brought* you to Derbyshire?"

"Yes, your grace."

"And is Lady Maltrousse downstairs?" Perish the thought! Nigel could think of nothing less desirable than having Callista Fernley's ample charms spilling over Lady Kendall's parlour—charms he had always resisted on his own account since his brother had been there before him.

"No, your grace. She said she'd take a room at the inn."

Nigel froze. She was at the Jester's Arms? The inn where the Boxing Day ball would begin in less than an hour? The inn where Bel Morrison was waiting unprepared for such an apparition? This new development was even less desirable than having her downstairs.

A knock sounded on the door.

"Come in."

It was Archie, his mottled face a bright shade of red, and his voice brimming with affront. "Yer grace, this fellow says that *he* is your valet and will attend to you. But I told him as he's mistaken and that you've filled the position with a local man." Archie stuck out his thin chest proudly, hopefully.

Nigel looked between the two valets. Sartorially speaking, Simpson, who had served his brother and who had been recommended to him by none other than Lady Maltrousse, knew what he was about. But the man was a serpent in the wardrobe whereas Archie was true as a Trojan.

Still, if Nigel was to return to the inn as soon as possible—and forestall any unpleasant encounter between Callista Fernley and Bel Morrison—he needed to be turned out in full kit as soon as possible. Archie might have a heart of gold, but on the outside, he was all thumbs. Simpson was the only logical choice.

"I'm sorry, Archie," Nigel said to the lad. "Simpson will do for me tonight. Run along and tell John I'll need the carriage as soon as possible."

Archie's hopeful face crumpled, and Nigel instantly felt like a cad of the worst sort. As the boy left the room, Nigel pulled off his coat and barked instructions at Simpson. "A fresh shirt. And the mulberry waistcoat. Be quick about it."

Simpson, unusually unctuous, worked his hardest to soothe his employer's ruffled feelings. But Nigel was not amused. He would use Simpson's services tonight, but it would be the last time he let that spy dress him. God willing, tonight he would see the last of both the valet and the vicious harpy that had set his steps on the path to vice.

CHAPTER NINETEEN

Lady Maltrousse

A S BEL CAME OUT of the upstairs room, she discovered that guests had already begun to arrive at the inn. Near the door stood a sumptuously gowned lady in red velvet with perfect blond ringlets dangling on either side of her face. Her cloak had already been discarded into Mrs. Coleman's arms, and her maid was standing nearby with a fan, a lorgnette, and a reticule. "Dear me, what have we here?" said the lady, eyeing Bel as she descended the stairs.

"Even your tavern girls in Derbyshire have few enough charms to recommend them." She looked pointedly at Bel's dark navy dress cut modestly above the bosom. The lady's own "charms" were well on their way to spilling over a narrow bodice that was hardly a handsbreadth wide.

"This is Miss Belinda Morrison," said Mrs. Coleman stiffly, taking offense so that Bel did not have to. "She is no tavern girl but one of the gentlewomen of the village."

Lady Maltrousse gave a trilling laugh. "Oh, I beg your pardon, Miss Morrison. *Not* a tavern wench, I see. And that's just as well, for you look more at home in a nunnery than an alehouse. I came to the inn to find a room, but I hear that there is some merriment afoot tonight. The whole public room rented by the local squire's wife for an assembly?"

"Indeed, there is," said Bel, folding her hands in front of her waist. "But I'm afraid that you have the advantage of me, Mrs.—?"

"Oh, la! Not missus. It's *Lady* Maltrousse, although my friends call me Callista." She approached Bel without hesitation and linked arms with her as if they were bosom friends from seminary long ago. "The innkeeper here says I might have a room if I keep inside it tonight, but I have a mind to join in these country festivities. How might I go about procuring an invitation?"

By the light of Mrs. Brownlee's beeswax candles, Bel could make out the coloured paint on Lady Maltrousse's face around her eyebrows and mouth. Up close, the woman looked nearer to Aunt Lucy's age than her own. She wondered if the blond ringlets about her face were real or the result of art and a careful coiffeur. Did a life of vice really age a person more quickly as the parsons and moralists said it did?

"I'm afraid that I have nothing to do with the guest list."

"Oh, but you seem a clever girl. I can see that the goodwife in charge of the inn looks up to your opinion. Surely, you know the local squire and his wife. In a small village like this, one cannot help knowing *everyone*."

"I am acquainted with the Brownlees." Bel was willing to concede no more than that.

The deep-bosomed noblewoman pressed on. "And surely, you must also be acquainted with any strangers in the neighbourhood. A longstanding *friend* of mine has been staying here for the past month. A tall, dark-haired man, just this side of forty. Handsome, with an eye for the fairer sex—"

"I know whom you mean," said Bel sharply.

The lady's blue eyes glinted. "Ah, I believe you do. Tell me, what name is he giving in this neighbourhood?"

"What name should he give but his own?" countered Bel.

"Ah, so then you already know he is a duke. Is he attending the assembly tonight?"

Bel said nothing, unwilling to tell a lie or to reveal more than she ought.

Lady Maltrousse sniffed. "I have been a friend of the Lymingtons for many years. It would be common courtesy for the invitation to be extended to me."

She had no sooner said this than Mr. Brownlee and his wife entered the inn, Mrs. Brownlee clad in her red Christmas cloak over an expensive new gown of spangled white that sorted poorly with her plump figure.

"What is this that Mr. Coleman tells me?" asked Harold Brownlee loudly. "Another guest in Derbyshire?" He stopped in his tracks as he saw Lady Maltrousse conversing with Bel. He looked at Bel expectantly, and she was forced into the unenviable task of making introductions.

"I was at a house party at Chatsworth," said Lady Maltrousse, "but a little bird told me that one of my dear friends was in the neighbourhood, and I simply had to see him."

"What's this? A friend of the Duke of Warrenton?" said Mr. Brownlee. "How remiss of us not to know of your arrival. I beg that you will stay and grace our evening entertainment with your presence." He reached out his hand for hers and patted it proprietarily.

Mrs. Brownlee, at his elbow, added a superfluous agreement to her husband's invitation, but it was clear to Bel that Lady Maltrousse no longer had any interest in the women of the party. She had got her hooks into Harold Brownlee, and she would stay snug against him until choicer quarry presented itself.

Bel led Mrs. Brownlee into the adjoining parlour under pretence of examining the refreshment table. "Surely, we do not need to have *that woman* at your assembly?"

"But, my dear," said Mrs. Brownlee. "She is a lady. And a friend of the duke's. Just think what consequence she will add to our little Boxing Day ball! Do you think any other of his fine London friends are *en route*?"

"If they are, then it is shockingly rude of them—and him—not to tell you ahead of time. And what do you make of a lady traveling alone?"

"She has her maid with her."

"But no husband," said Bel sceptically.

"You've been listening too much to Mr. Townsend. Our old vicar Mr. Davies would have had a more liberal eye to such things. They do things differently in London, or at least, so Harold tells me. I'm certain that there is nothing untoward." Mrs. Brownlee peered around the corner to see her husband leaning in indulgently towards the white-bosomed Lady Maltrousse while the lady in question tittered and hung upon his forearm. "I daresay it's natural to feel some envy towards her—she is very beautiful, isn't she?"

Bel flamed red. No doubt the Duke of Warrenton thought Lady Maltrousse was the epitome of attractiveness. Was this what he'd been comparing Bel to the whole of the time he'd been in Derbyshire? If so, then he was no doubt sorely disappointed in her lack of ringlets, rouge, and rounded bosom.

The door opened and her eyes darted toward it. The Ferris brothers had arrived, with Aunt Lucy in tow, and on their heels the luxurious Mrs. White swept into the room. Usually, the widow was the best-dressed woman of the village—for while Mrs. Brownlee might possess the most money in Upper Cross, Mrs. White possessed impeccable style—but tonight her dress of diaphanous green net paled in comparison to Lady Maltrousse's daring red velvet. Indeed, Mr. Brownlee was so enamoured with the newcomer from London that he barely turned his head when he saw Mrs. White approaching.

Other gentlemen and ladies from houses further out than Upper Cross began to arrive, and even the vicar's tall figure entered the inn. But the one face Bel was waiting for did not appear. Where was Nigel Lymington, the Duke of Warrenton?

—ℓℓ—

Nigel was three-quarters of an hour late by the time he reached the Jester's Arms. The dancing had already begun, and he had to speak loudly for his voice to be heard above the string quartet. "I apologise for my tardiness," he said to Mrs. Brownlee, hoping that Miss Morrison, standing nearby in the corner with her Aunt Lucy, would hear him. "The wheel of the carriage came off and we were forced to wait until John could walk back to the house and find a replacement from the stable. I was so impatient, I nearly set out in my evening dress to walk here before John returned."

"How unfortunate, your grace!" Mrs. Brownlee clucked sympathetically. "I must own that I was afraid that you had decided not to come, but I should have known better. Especially since your friend from town has arrived."

Nigel's eye followed Mrs. Brownlee's, drawn inexorably to the voluptuous blond who stood across from Mr. Brownlee in a small set on the dance floor. Her front ringlets, parted in the middle, framed her face in the latest style while the rest of her hair was pulled back in an artful bun. Her crimson dress with its daring decolletage was more suitable for a London soiree than the crammed public room of a Derbyshire inn, and she wore the most gemstones of any woman in the room.

"This dance is almost over," said Mrs. Brownlee, continuing her duties as a hostess. "I'm sure you must wish to secure the next one with Lady Maltrousse."

"On the contrary, I'm already promised to one of Derbyshire's finest jewels." Nigel turned hopefully to Miss Morrison who was standing not five feet away, hiding behind a frown that signified she had no wish to be approached. "Will you do me the honour, Miss Morrison?"

"Your grace, please do not think that I was looking in your direction in order to beg for a partner."

"Oh? Were you looking in my direction?" said Nigel with a faint smile. "I had not noticed." His tone turned serious. "But indeed, it is I who must beg for a partner. Will you be so kind as to dance with me?"

Miss Morrison looked at him carefully, a wrinkle between her expressive eyebrows. She was far more reticent than she had been earlier in the day when they had hung the greenery together. Nigel feared that the appearance of Lady Maltrousse had a great deal to do with that. She might not have hated him after that kiss, but she was perilously close to hating him now.

From the corner of his eye, he could see an officious black coat approaching.

"My dear Miss Morrison," he murmured, "it looks as if Mr. Townsend is coming to rescue you. From me. You must make up your mind swiftly. Do I flatter myself that you consider me the lesser of two evils?"

She refused to admit as much, but she allowed him to take her gloved hand in his.

"I'm honoured," said Nigel dryly, taking a perverse delight in leading away Miss Morrison just as the vicar appeared at her elbow. Mr. Townsend gave him a righteous glare, but the good man was not left alone long before Mrs. White shimmered closer to console him and listen to his complaints.

As Mrs. Brownlee had predicted, this dance was just about to end. Nigel had only a few minutes' conversation with his partner while the musicians leafed through their music to prepare for the next set.

"The carriage wheel was faulty, your grace?" said Miss Morrison coolly.

"Yes, John said it looked like it had been tampered with."

"So, not an accident? But who would want to keep the infamous Duke of Warrenton from attending our humble ball?"

"Who indeed?" said Nigel, not liking the tone she was taking. The easy familiarity with which they had spent the morning had disappeared completely. "It is a mystery."

"Lud, I am so warm," said Lady Maltrousse loudly as Mr. Brownlee led her off the dance floor. Her mousy maid, who had been standing on the perimeter of the room, rushed forward to hand her a fan. Lady Maltrousse waved it furiously directing the blasts of air towards her insufficient bodice. "How peculiar that there are no chairs to sit on."

"Oh, but there *are* chairs, my lady, and refreshments as well." Mr. Brownlee's long arm gestured to the adjoining parlour as he exerted all his energy in pleasing their uninvited guest. "You were at Chatsworth for Christmas, you say?"

"Indeed! And a dull enough Christmas it was. The Duke of Devonshire is usually so droll,"—her tittering laughter was loud enough to filter into the main room— "but he's sicklier and sicklier of late. And it's not been the same since dear Georgiana died—indeed, the duke is positively respectable now that he's married to Elizabeth!"

The strings struck up again, covering the sounds of conversation. "You have not greeted your friend from London," Miss Morrison observed.

"I have no friends from London," said Nigel. "At least, no true friends."

"Lady Maltrousse claims otherwise. She says she is a long-standing friend of yours. I wonder, are you friends with her husband as well?"

Nigel winced. "Lord Maltrousse does not move in the same circles as his wife." He led his incisive partner onto the dance floor, aware that each of her subsequent queries would cut like a scalpel.

"But you do. Is Lord Maltrousse as liberally minded as the Duke of Devonshire? As all dukes are?"

"Come now, that's hardly fair," said Nigel. "Devonshire is shockingly loose in the haft—always has been, with a wife on one arm and a mistress on the other." Nigel took her hands to promenade through the set of couples and fell silent for a moment so as not to be overheard.

Miss Morrison, however, was hardly ready to let the subject drop. She waited until the dance brought them back to their own sphere of orbit. "Whereas *you* would prefer to keep a wife and mistress completely separate from each other?"

"It's not what you think."

"What do I think?" She cocked her head and looked up at him as he walked around her in a slow turn.

"You think Lady Maltrousse is my mistress. She is not. She was my brother's *inamorata*."

"So, you acquired her as a...friend...when you became a duke?"

"In a manner of speaking. She was giving me lessons."

"Lessons?"

Once again, the figures of the dance forced them to pause the conversation until they came back to a convenient corner of the set.

"Lessons on how to cut a dash in society. How to be a Lymington."

"And what exactly does that entail?"

"Oh, a certain *joie de vivre*, a devil-may-care attitude. Wine, women, and song. And cards, never forget cards."

"You were taking lessons on how to become a rake?" Miss Morrison's voice was incredulous.

"In a manner of speaking," he said, feeling utterly embarrassed but aware that if he wanted her presence, he could not escape her censure. "I had to uphold the family reputation."

"Upon my word, what absolute rot!"

Nigel could see several curious eyes staring in their direction, no doubt wondering the subject of Miss Morrison's outburst. But he had gone too far in his revelations to stop now.

"Yes, it was. I see that now. But at the time I thought it was all part and parcel of being a duke. My brother, my father, my grandfather—all men about the town."

"And all reasons that your finances are at such a low ebb."

"Not exactly something I like to advertise," said Nigel, wryly. There were even more faces looking in their direction now, including Lady Maltrousse who had apparently recovered her breath in the adjoining room enough to return to the outskirts of the dance floor. She had seized her lorgnette from the attentive maid and was looking at them haughtily through the jewelled spectacles.

As the set came to an end, she traded lorgnette for fan and advanced to where they stood in the centre of the room. "My, my, I was afraid you would have forgotten all your town polish, but here you are arriving fashionably late and dancing with the only tolerable unmarried woman in the room. What? Aren't you going to greet me, Nigel darling?"

Chapter Twenty

The Jester

B EL CRINGED INWARDLY AT Lady Maltrousse's familiarity with the duke. There was so much she did not
know about this man with whom she had shared a kiss in
the barn. And yet, when he told her of his past, she felt the
ring of truth in all his revelations—that, and a wave of pity
for the small boy he had once been thrust into a role he was
never meant to fill.

"What are you doing here, Callista?" he demanded.

"Why, what do you mean? I'm here to see you," she said,
coyly tapping him on the arm with her fan. "I knew you'd
want your valet after a month or more in this godforsaken
countryside, so I brought him along with me to Chatsworth
House. And now that Christmas is over, I've left Devonshire
to his own devices and come to find a duke more to my liking.
Have I come too late? Are you rusticated beyond repair?"

"A month in the country can hardly destroy a man's character," he said, his tone affecting a sophisticated drawl that had

been wholly absent in his fervent conversation with Bel. "But a month in London, on the other hand—" He shrugged.

"Aren't you going to ask me to dance?" Her white shoulders dipped as she fluttered her kohl-rimmed eyelashes, exposing even more of her decolletage.

"I'm afraid that I'm promised to the other Miss Morrison," the duke said carelessly. "You'll have to wait your turn." He paused. "Your servant." Lifting a gloved hand to his mouth, he kissed it.

Bel stood in wooden surprise. Those last two words had been directed at her, and the gloved hand that had just touched the duke's lips was her own. He released her fingers, slowly, like a man holding onto the dice as long as he can before making one last desperate cast. She watched him move to the other side of the room where Aunt Lucy was in animated conversation with the Ferris brothers.

"Oh, you poor dear," said Lady Maltrousse, in annoyingly intimate tones. She did not seem at all offended that the duke had declined to partner her immediately. "I see he's caught you—like a bird in the lime. It doesn't take much for his gorgeous grace to lure a new pigeon in for the plucking."

"Your ladyship presumes too much," said Bel, refusing to be bowled over by Lady Maltrousse's manipulation of events. "His grace is nothing more than an acquaintance."

Lady Maltrousse laughed, and all her blond ringlets bounced with gleeful artifice. "'Pon rep, you coy creature. Are you trying to tell me he has not made *overtures* to become more than that?"

Bel's tan face took on a dusky hue. She could not help remembering that kiss from yesterday evening, or his promise to find her in some dark corner tonight and kiss her again.

"I thought so," said Lady Maltrousse, opening her fan ostentatiously to both shield and showcase their private conversation. "I beg your pardon, Miss Morrison, but you seem both old enough to be on the shelf and naive enough to be an innocent schoolgirl. I feel compelled to warn you that with a man like the duke, his favours are only too fleeting. I've come to take him back to London with me before he can break more hearts here in Derbyshire."

"But what if he doesn't wish to leave?"

"Oh, he will soon enough once he hears what sweets I have in store for him." She tsked. "Men are all the same—easily led by their appetites. I've only to rouse his hunger and he'll hurry back to London to be sated."

"I assume you refer to lust." Bel's tone was completely straightforward without any simpering or embarrassment.

"My, my, what a forward little thing you are," said Lady Maltrousse. "Perhaps you're not quite the innocent I thought you were. Does the vicar know what naughty ideas are lurking in the parish spinster's head?" Her fingers began to fiddle with the neckline of her dress. "Indeed, I do refer to that appetite, but also to the appetite for fame, for acceptance. He has it in spades. He wants to *be* somebody." Her blue eyes raked over Bel's unembellished evening gown. "He would never be satisfied indefinitely with"—she waved a dismissive hand at the cramped assembly room whose greenery had looked so cheerful two hours prior— "all this."

The coldness in the lady's tone appalled Bel. It was the same sort of unalloyed meanness that Mrs. Hogg displayed each time Bel brought her an undeserved basket. But for some reason, it was even uglier in a woman of wealth and means.

"How much does he pay you?" asked Bel.

"Why, what do you mean?"

"For his lessons. For his tutelage on 'how to be a dashing duke.' Surely, you must be turning a profit off him, for it's easy to see that you don't do anything out of the goodness of your heart."

Lady Maltrousse laughed. "How clever you are. I must own that he pays me a small percentage of his winnings at the card table."

"But you do nothing to stake his losses?"

"Of course not. A man's losses are his own affair. And once his niece's marriage is settled, he'll owe me the fee for finding the bridegroom. And then, of course, there's the matter of his own marriage. I'm on the lookout for an heiress for him. Someone whose money is not in...sheep." She looked disdainfully at Bel. "He'll pay another fee for that, once the matter is concluded."

Before Bel could reply, the small maid rushed up to her mistress' side. "Begging your pardon, my lady, but your jewelled lorgnette has gone missing."

"Lud, what did you say? Missing?"

Bel could hear fury building behind the London lady's affected voice.

The maid hung her head. "I set it down, for just a moment, to go relieve myself, and when I came back, it was gone."

"How careless of you, Pinn! Utterly careless!" She turned to take Bel into her outburst. "And who would have thought Derbyshire would be full of sneak thieves?"

"Sneak thieves? What's this?" asked a cheery voice. Bel was relieved to have the spry Jack Ferris join the conversation. Apparently, since the duke had secured Aunt Lucy for the dance floor, dear Jack had no one else to talk with.

"My lorgnette has been stolen," said Lady Maltrousse with feeling.

"Ah," said Jack, tapping his nose. "That'll be the jester. He takes things when he's feeling overlooked." He quickly explained the ghostly legend surrounding the inn and gave a catalogue of things that had been taken in the past.

"And does he give them back?" demanded Lady Maltrousse.

"That depends," said Jack, with a cackle, "whether he's feeling mischievous or malicious."

Lady Maltrousse stormed away with her maid to find the Colemans and lodge a complaint. Meanwhile, Mrs. White sidled up to Bel and Mr. Ferris. "Dear me, what a mercurial creature."

"A fine figure of a woman though," said Jack appreciatively. Then, remembering to whom he spoke, he tagged a compliment on to the observation. "Much like present company, if I do say so. What do you think of her?"

"I think," said Mrs. White from between pursed lips, "that she's no better than she ought to be, despite her lofty title. I wonder Mrs. Brownlee allowed her to attend this function."

Bel, who had always wondered about Mrs. White's morals, thought it quite a case of the pot castigating the kettle. If Mrs. White's dress was more demure, it was only because she did not have the figure to pull off the fleshly display that Lady Maltrousse shared so openly.

Discovering that neither of her interlocutors was keen to gossip with her, Mrs. White soon lost interest and passed on to Harold Brownlee. Mr. Ferris kept Bel company until, once again, the music ceased, and the duke returned with a breathless Aunt Lucy on his arm.

"Your grace knows how to tire an old lady out," said Aunt Lucy.

"Old lady? Where?" said the duke, looking around the room. "I don't see anyone matching that description."

"That's the spirit, Warrenton," said Mr. Ferris appreciatively. He gave Aunt Lucy a wink, and Bel watched her aunt's cheeks pink with enthusiasm. There was clearly something more than friendship forming between these two—she wondered if Jack Ferris would ever have the gumption to give up six decades of bachelorhood to keep that pink on Lucy's cheek permanently.

"My fan!" shrieked Lady Maltrousse from the other side of the room. "I had it in my hand just a moment ago. And now it's gone!" Her maid, the one she called Pinn, hurried to her side again, reaching into the reticule to find her lady's vinaigrette. Lady Maltrousse inhaled the mixture of hartshorn and lemon oil with an angry sniff.

"Is she always like this?" Bel asked the duke, a hint of distaste in her tone.

He cleared his throat apologetically. "Yes." He cast Bel a sidelong glance. "It has a different effect on the circles she frequents in London. She receives approbation for 'feeling things' so deeply."

"Ah, we rustics are too phlegmatic to have such sensitivity."

"*You* certainly did not need hartshorn after pulling a sheep out of a mud pit."

"But *you* might have needed your hartshorn after your pantaloons were splashed with mud by a passing carriage."

"*Touché*," murmured the duke ruefully. "You are made of sterner stuff than I."

"Yes, that's the problem, isn't it?" said Bel. Overcome by the truth of her own statement, she turned her back on him and walked quickly into the adjoining parlour. There, she caught sight of Jenny, her maid-of-all-work who had taken an extra job on her day off helping Mrs. Coleman with the refreshments. "Jenny, I commend you. You've kept the punch flowing all night."

"Oh, that's easy as custard, miss. And Mrs. Coleman has all the trays prepared, so all I need to do is bring them in to replenish." Her brow wrinkled. "Archie's here, though, back in the kitchen. And he's squawking like a mean goose about being turned off from his post."

"Turned off from his post?" asked Bel in confusion. "What do you mean?"

Jenny lowered her voice and came nearer. "It's that harpy in the red dress. She brought his grace's London valet to Derbyshire with her, and now Archie's out in the cold with nothin' but an acre of brown rosebushes to tie cravats on. An' he was so proud of the promotion too! He was hopin' it might…lead to somethin'."

Bel patted Jenny's shoulder comfortingly. She was aware that her maid had hopes that Archie would make enough money someday to set up his own house and make her an offer.

"How angry is Archie?"

"I ain't never seen him so put out. Every time I go back into the kitchen, he rants a little more about Londoners and their kind, an' then he storms outside a bit to cool his head before comin' in again to rant some more."

"Pinn, Pinn!" said the shrill voice again, as the lady in red velvet swept past the door of the parlour. "Go back to that horrid, draughty bedroom and pack my trunk. We won't be staying here tonight."

"But my lady—"

"I'll have no argument. My vinaigrette has disappeared now too."

Bel and Jenny cast each other looks of amusement and kept quiet as they eavesdropped on the conversation around the corner in the hallway.

"My dear Lady Maltrousse," said a voice that must have been Harold Brownlee. It was all care and consideration, so clearly Lady Maltrousse's hysterics had worked their charm on at least one member of the phlegmatic countryside. "It is only two hours till midnight. Surely, you cannot make your way back to Chatsworth so late?"

"No," she said with a huff, "but this inn is a cutpurse's paradise. I'll lose my earbobs next or my necklace. See if I don't!"

"If the inn is unsatisfactory, perhaps you might honour our home with your presence tonight. Mullhill Manor, it's called. Just a half mile down the road."

Bel rolled her eyes. Of course, Harold Brownlee would open his home for an attractive female. And plump Mrs. Brownlee would delight in the honour of the imposition. The conversation faded away with what sounded like an acceptance.

Jenny picked up an empty tray and returned to the kitchen while Bel closed her eyes momentarily, trying to shut out the inanity and insanity of it all.

"Miss Morrison, are you all right?"

Bel opened her eyes. The vicar, Mr. Townsend, was a mere three feet away from her, his blue eyes gazing solicitously at her.

"You seem overcome. May I lead you to a chair?"

Bel almost declined, but a slight wobble in her knees made her think better of it. "Yes, thank you. A chair sounds lovely right now."

"I would offer you some hartshorn, but I don't carry such a thing."

Bel put a hand over her mouth as he seated her in the chair against the wall in the parlour. "No, Mr. Townsend, I don't suppose you do." The thought of the stolid vicar mincing about with a bottle of vinaigrette was too much for her. She began to giggle, and once she started, she was wholly unable to stop.

"This levity, Miss Morrison, is not the most praiseworthy aspect of your character, but I confess I cannot find it as unbecoming as I did at first."

Still giggling uncontrollably, with tears in her eyes, Bel gasped out a response. "What on earth is that supposed to mean, Mr. Townsend? That you now *like* it when I laugh?"

He looked at her a little shamefacedly. "Yes, I'm sorry to admit that I do. But, I daresay, it is a facet of your character that will settle with age." He paused, allowing her a moment to regain her composure. "Miss Morrison, might I call on you tomorrow?"

"As my spiritual advisor?" she said warily. "To warn me away from the Duke of Warrenton again?"

"No, no," he said hastily. "I think you have seen enough on that score tonight to want nothing more to do with the duke and his associates. I would like to...get to know you better, if I may."

It was an unexpected request, and one that Bel might have declined if the moment had been different. But as matters stood, she was currently reconsidering everything that she thought she knew. "Very well," said Bel slowly. "I shall endeavour to be home to receive you."

"Thank you," he said, giving her a nod and leaving the parlour.

Nigel breathed a sigh of relief as Mr. Brownlee escorted Lady Maltrousse out the door of the Jester's Arms to take her to Mullhill Manor for the night. The evening had gone from bad to worse as Lady Maltrousse execrated all the assembly-goers as potential thieves, hung upon his sleeve demanding his protection, and finally exacted the dance from him that he had been most unwilling to yield. "What an odd little country waif you've developed an attachment for," she said as they promenaded down the floor, without a care for who nearby might hear her. "Her skin is positively brown as a nut, and she has no manner, no bearing to even mark her out as a gentlewoman. I've spent months teaching you how to be good ton and conduct properly discreet liaisons with properly ranked noblewomen, and you throw it all away to dance attendance on this nobody!"

Although this London lady might dazzle Harold Brownlee, Nigel knew her better. He could not stop imagining Mrs. Hogg's mean face on Lady Maltrousse's white shoulders. "Perhaps I've finally realised that I don't want a liaison. I want something else entirely."

Her rouged lips fell open. "Are you really considering *marriage*? To a countrified little spinster?" She gave a tittering laugh and was so overcome with the hilarity of the situation that Nigel had to escort her from the dance floor where she could regain her composure.

Lady Maltrousse's outburst had been the final nightmare in an evening that ought to have been divine. Miss Morrison took great care to avoid Nigel for the remaining dances, and he had no opportunity to solicit her hand a second time. Their shared connection from last night and their shared camaraderie from this morning had been stolen as surely as Lady Maltrousse's lost things.

As Nigel stood on the porch of the inn watching the Brownlees leave, John the coachman approached. "It's just as you suspected, your grace," he said in low tones. "It were Archie that sabotaged the wheel."

"Hmm. He was upset with me." Nigel knew that it was no excuse, but he still felt guilty about preferring Simpson over Archie for his toilette this evening.

"With you and with everyone else from London." John looked at the duke gravely. "I caught him hiding a bottle of smelling salts under his coat and grabbed him by the scruff of the neck to turn his pockets inside out. He's been playing Jester all night, pinching things from that red-gowned Rahab." He tugged his forelock as he thought better of that descriptor. "Beggin' your pardon, yer grace."

"No pardon needs begging," said Nigel with a wave of the hand.

"'Twere all on impulse, but the lad's in danger of being hauled up in front of the magistrate for it."

Nigel snapped his fingers. "I know what we shall do. We shall give the lost things to Simpson tomorrow and send him over to Mullhill Manor with my compliments. No one will be any the wiser about the matter, and Lady Maltrousse will hardly report *me* to the magistrate for theft."

John gave a whistle at the temerity of that plan and then lapsed into a low chuckle. "Ingenious, yer grace. It'll serve that fellow right to have a peal rung over his head, and it'll put Archie in better spirits." He watched Nigel place his beaver on his head and shrug into his greatcoat. "Are we heading straight for home, or are we giving anyone else a carriage ride tonight?"

"I assume you mean the Morrison ladies?" said Nigel, cognizant that his partiality was apparent to everyone, including the coachman. "No, no. Mr. Ferris has that well in hand."

Nigel combed a hand through his dark hair. A dark carriage ride with Bel Morrison on the bench beside him would have been bliss. But the evening had turned out far differently than he had hoped. He would have to pick up the pieces the following day and hope that the fragile understanding he had built with Miss Morrison was not shattered forever.

Chapter Twenty-One

Offer

B EL BARELY SLEPT THE night following the Boxing Day
ball.

Aunt Lucy had chattered happily all the way home from the
Jester's Arms while Jack Ferris teased them about their dance
partners. "And both of you partnered by a duke, no less!" But
Bel had refused to join in on the banter. Her nerves, as strong
as they were, had been frayed to the quick by Lady Maltrousse's
tittering laugh and poisonous tongue.

How many other women of that ilk figured in Nigel Lymington's past? If he walked into a London ballroom, would there be
a half-dozen, disaffected married women ready to recommence
a dalliance with him? He intimated that he regretted that way
of life, but did he have the wherewithal to give it the cut direct?
Or would he be perpetually finding some new *chère amie* to kiss
in the dark corner of assembly rooms?

The future looked bleaker than ever. She knew with certainty
now that her flirtation with the Duke of Warrenton had been a

mere distraction to keep herself from thinking about the impending verdict on Charlie's existence.

If there was no Charlie to return to Derbyshire, then her tidy ledgers, her profitable market days, her yield per acre were all for naught. And yet, what if Charlie *did* return? She would keep house for him as a spinster sister until he married. And what then? She would be in the same position as Aunt Lucy, an indigent relative looking for a place to live out her declining years.

Aunt Lucy was right—duty was all well and good, but was it possible that her unflinching pursuit of it would leave her loveless and alone?

The best course of action was for her to marry and marry soon. But what options were open to her in Derbyshire? There was the vicar, who intended to call on her tomorrow. She already knew that she had little sympathy of mind with him, but he was a God-fearing man with a respectable reputation. Perhaps she could grow to care for him and not mind letting go of her "levity" to be the wife he wanted.

There was also Nigel Lymington, the Duke of Warrenton. He was a man who made her laugh—but she had a fear that he would make her weep as well. He would make her weep over his debts at the card table, his associations with moneylenders, his overfamiliarity with other women. She knew she could help him untangle his knotty business affairs; she could talk to his steward, analyse his lack of farming income, and straighten out his estate. But she could not fill that need he had to be accepted into the ton, to be the "equal" of his brother and father in the eyes of the world. In a few months—or a few weeks! —he would see her as just another steward to ignore.

No, if she was to ever find happiness with Nigel Lymington, he would have to find happiness first on his own. He would have to patch his leaky ship, and then she could board it. He would have to find the right road, and then she could walk it beside him. He would have to learn the steps of the dance, and then he could lead her onto the dancefloor.

With thoughts like these racing through her mind, it took Bel half the night to fall asleep. And when she woke in the morning, she had made up her mind. Charlie Morrison, Horace Townsend, Nigel Lymington—she knew what she had to do in every single case.

***

The following morning, Nigel packed Simpson off to Mullhill Manor with a notice of dismissal, a parcel containing Callista Fernley's lost things, and a kennel's worth of fleas in his ear. "And don't expect a reference from me," said Nigel with feeling. "You can ask Lady Maltrousse to find you a new place with some other poor simpleton she wishes to spy on."

Archie, as predicted, resumed his position with nervous apologies about the mischief created and stammering gratitude for another chance. "I lost my head, yer grace. It won't happen again."

"See that it doesn't," said Nigel, feeling hypocritical to the hilt. He had made more mistakes than Archie. Mistakes more serious than sabotaging a carriage wheel. Mistakes far graver than stealing the contents of a noblewoman's reticule. Mistakes so damaging that they might destroy any chance he had of gaining the good opinion of a gentlewoman farmer in Derbyshire.

The very things he liked about Bel Morrison were the very things that would keep her from regarding him with any favour—her good judgment, her sense of duty, her straight-forward manner of speaking. He knew she was attracted to him, but he also knew that her good sense would forestall any imprudent folly. In the eyes of society, his status as a duke made him immediately and eminently desirable. In the eyes of Bel Morrison, he had nothing to recommend himself—nothing beyond a failing estate, a threat of danger from his chief creditor, a reputation as a womaniser, and no earthly idea how to get himself out of any of those predicaments

Still...that question Callista had cast in his face still niggled at him. "Are you really considering marriage?" Yes, he was. But would Belinda Morrison consider it? That was the question.

Nigel tried to relax his nerves on the keys of the pianoforte and waited till mid-afternoon to call on the Morrison ladies. He walked there, disregarding the fine mist of rain. Jenny, the maid, gave him a cold glare when he lifted the knocker—no doubt on account of her friendship with Archie—but he paid it no mind. As he waited by the door, he heard Jenny's voice in the hallway announcing him. "Another caller, miss." Apparently, someone else had been there before him.

When he entered the parlour, he saw that, this time, Aunt Lucy was inconveniently present. Blast! Why was it that chaperones were always absent when you needed them and present when you didn't? Placing his beaver under his arm, Nigel pasted a smile over clenched teeth.

He caught Miss Morrison's eye and nodded outside toward the barn. A walk would be just the thing if he were to get her alone and say what he really needed to say.

"Aunt Lucy," said Miss Morrison, understanding him perfectly, "would you mind if I were to have a private audience with our visitor?"

"Another one?" Aunt Lucy's cap flopped wildly. "Good gracious. Whatever you think best."

She vacated the room and left the door open a mere quarter inch behind her. Enough for propriety's sake, but also enough for privacy unless they raised their voices.

"Another one?" said Nigel quizzically. Did Aunt Lucy know of their private audience in the stone barn two days ago? If so, it was strange that she was leaving them alone once again.

"Mr. Townsend asked for a private audience this morning too," said Bel with a shrug.

"Oh?" said Nigel, trying to tamp down the bile rising in his throat. "And what did the good vicar want?"

"He informed me that he means to call on me once a week so that we can become better acquainted, and that if we suit, in three months' time he means to make me an offer."

Nigel's dark eyes flashed. How dare the vicar presume so much. "And what did you tell him?"

"I said I would allow it." Her tone was flat. "And I will. He's a sensible man with a respectable position. I believe my parents would have supported the match if I were agreeable to it."

"He would bore you to tears," growled Nigel.

"But he wouldn't gamble away our money, or seduce the neighbour's wife."

Nigel winced. He deserved that, of course, but it still stung. "Yes, but you might receive a few more sermons than you have patience for. By all appearances, he would treat you honourably, and yet, there's something in his past that smacks of subterfuge. The unknown father, the excessive navy pension—"

"Oh, pooh! You want to make something out of nothing, simply because you don't like the man—or don't like how his sermons cause you to squirm."

Nigel said nothing. Once again, Miss Morrison's perspicacity pointed at a flaw in himself that he could not deny. He had been about to put his own question to Miss Morrison—now it would seem like a childish reaction to Mr. Townsend's request.

"I did not think you wished to marry," he said with bravado.

"Didn't you?" Her face was unusually disquieted. Vulnerable, even. Her grey eyes widened. "Then what was it you wanted to speak to me about?"

Of course, she had to ask him that! With a woman as plain-speaking as Bel Morrison, he could never put his tail between his legs and quietly slink away.

"Er, I wanted to apologise for my behaviour the past couple days. It was ungentlemanly of me to...flirt with you in such a way when I don't intend to—that is, when I cannot—"

She lifted her left eyebrow, that ironic arc of dubious disbelief, and Nigel was completely undone.

"Confound it, Bel! You know what I want to say to you. And you know why I can't do it. I've nothing but my title and a load of debts and that dashed Solomon Digby hanging like a millstone round my neck. My wretched estate's getting more wretched by the day. My niece Louisa—my last relative in all the world—is lost and ruined, and I'm to blame for all of it. And now I've gone and made an enemy of Callista, and she'll rip whatever reputation I have to shreds when she gets back to London." He took a ragged breath. "I wish I'd met you five years ago, when I was only Lord Nigel Lymington and not the devilish Duke of Warrenton. But now it's too late. I've nothing to offer that you would care about, and I've made a mull of everything in my life."

She kept her distance from him across the parlour and looked him full in the face. Her steady eyes shone on his desperate ones like light from a lantern.

"Then fix it, Nigel," she said, slowly and clearly, her voice punctuating each word with the force of her whole person.

"Fix it?" he repeated, bewildered.

"Yes, fix it," she said. "I know you can." Walking to the door of the parlour, she pushed it open and then stood next to it, hands folded.

"Will you wait for me while I do?" he blurted out. What he really wanted to say was, "Promise me you won't marry that self-righteous bounder Horace Townsend!" But a simple promise that she would wait for him would suffice.

She lifted her chin. "That depends."

He swallowed. That would have to be enough. It was unfair of him to ask for more.

"Good day, your grace," she said.

"Good day, Miss Morrison," he said simply. And putting his beaver on his head, he went down the narrow hallway into the grey December air.

Part 2

CHAPTER TWENTY-TWO

Wedding

JANUARY THROUGH MARCH 1811

T RUE TO HIS WORD, as soon as the New Year came, Harold Brownlee took the necessary steps to have Charles Morrison declared dead, and at that official pronouncement, a little piece of Bel's heart died inside of her. For the first three months, she kept to the house, avoiding all social gatherings and talking with no one but Aunt Lucy. She dressed all in black, a long overdue final mourning for the brother who had already been missed for seven years.

Amid her grief, she rescinded her agreement to allow Horace Townsend to call on her. Conversation with Mr. Townsend could be challenging under the best of circumstances, and in her present state, she could not guarantee civility.

Mr. Brownlee stopped by to offer condolences, batting insinuations at her like cricket balls, saying that she would feel better if she just talked to the vicar. But Bel remained firm. Instead of visiting in person, Mr. Townsend sent her a cordial letter informing her that, "*It is better to go to a house of mourning than a house of feasting.*" He encouraged her to remain steadfast in good works and assured her that he would resume calling on her when she was out of mourning. In the meantime, he planned to establish himself more fully in his parish duties.

The Duke of Warrenton sent a note of condolence to the Morrison ladies but made no attempt to call himself. Indeed, some said that he had vacated the neighbourhood entirely, for he was not sighted at the church or the Jester's Arms for weeks on end. Bel, who had Magpie to observe, knew better. Whenever the cat disappeared for a few days and came back looking fat, sleek, and utterly pleased with herself, she knew that she had been trespassing at Audeley House, keeping Nigel Lymington company and eating like a queen.

She never went looking for the cat, however. That was too dangerous. For she had a strong suspicion that if she saw Nigel Lymington, dark hair ruffled, sleeves rolled up, sleeping in an armchair with her cat on his lap, she would be utterly undone. The endearing domesticity of such a picture would awaken desires in her that needed to remain dormant until the duke could reform his way of living and fix what was broken.

In February of the new year, rumour had it that Gyles Audeley had returned to Derbyshire. But like his prestigious houseguest, he must have been keeping close to his house and his garden, for there were no sightings of him in Upper Cross.

Mr. Townsend, once again, had the honour of knowing coveted news first; at the next Sunday service he announced the banns for Gyles Audeley and Louisa Lymington. A gasp went up from Mrs. Brownlee and several other members of the congregation. "Yes, that's why the duke's been visiting Audeley House," said Harold Brownlee authoritatively, as if he had known the news all along. "He's Gyles' future uncle."

"First his mother becomes a countess," said Mrs. White in disbelief, "and next *he* marries the niece of a duke?" She looked to those sitting nearby for confirmation of her envious inclinations. "'Pon rep! It's unbelievable. One would think that the Audeleys lead a charmed life. And wasn't Rose Audeley's father a mere solicitor?"

Before the third reading of those banns, however, another announcement upended the settled social circle of their Derbyshire village even further. Bel had given up mourning dress for one day to put on trousers and fix a broken gate. When she re-entered the house at teatime, she saw that Aunt Lucy was not alone in the parlour. No, indeed. Her dear aunt was sitting on the sofa next to Jack Ferris, much closer than propriety allowed, her cap horrendously askew and her cheeks as pink as sunset.

"What's this?" asked Bel. She took off the wool cap covering her pinned-up hair and slapped it against her leg. "Do I need to demand your intentions toward my aunt, Mr. Ferris?"

Jack's eyes twinkled. "Only if I need to ask your permission to marry your aunt. After all, you appear to wear the trousers in the family."

"Oh, Bel!" wailed Aunt Lucy, finally noticing her niece's unfortunate clothing. "How could you appear like that in the parlour in front of a guest?"

"I'm not a guest anymore," said Jack, holding up a hand that was firmly attached to Lucy's. "That is, if Bel will allow me to be her uncle."

"I'll allow it," said Bel, and her face which had been sombre for the last eight weeks split into a genuine smile.

Jack stood up from the sofa and helped Lucy to her feet. "Well, my darling girls, it's all settled then. You must name the date for our departure for London."

"London!" cried Aunt Lucy and Bel in unison.

"Aye, London," said Jack. "I know how you love the place, Lulu. And you'll be wanting to buy your trousseau."

"M-my trousseau?" echoed Aunt Lucy, her face taking on a look of beatific joy. Bel suspected that after fifty years of spinsterhood, she had imagined the ship of matrimony had sailed and would never come back to port. But Jack was determined that Lucy would miss out on none of the gaieties that betrothed brides enjoyed.

"I'll take a house near Green Park for you ladies to lay down your heads, and I'll find a hotel on Piccadilly for James and myself—very proper, Miss Bel. Nothing for anyone to complain about. And we'll see the sights and do some shopping and come back to Derbyshire in April for the wedding."

"Oh, Mr. Ferris!" said Lucy, her eyes shining. "You make me the happiest person in the world."

"Impossible," said Jack, lifting her wrinkled hand with his gnarled one in a courtly salute, "for my own happiness cannot be surpassed." He began to laugh. "I haven't told James yet—I daresay he'll complain I stole a march on him. But there's always Miss Bel still unmarried, eh? Perhaps there's hope for him yet."

⁓⁓

Nigel spent the first few weeks of the new year in a black sulk of self-recrimination. Fix it? How could he fix it? He couldn't even return to London without skulking in the shadows—and it was in the shadows where Solomon Digby's men were always lurking. Where could he get two thousand pounds, plus interest, to pay the man back?

But as January wore on, he began to cudgel his brain for what gains he could effect while keeping away from London. Availing himself of Lady Kendall's stationery, he wrote a letter to his steward in Lincolnshire, asking for a brief accounting of the estate's holdings. Embarrassingly, he could not remember the man's name, so he was forced to address him merely by his title. Then, encouraged by the completion of the first letter, he wrote a second one to his solicitor Mr. Childers in London, asking the man to sell all the furniture in his town house—from the billiards table where he had once played with Solomon Digby to the black-lacquered chinoiserie that his brother had accumulated. Without furniture or inmates, there was no need for an army of servants to carry on cleaning the house, so Nigel instructed the solicitor to write them letters of recommendation and let them go. Now his townhouse would be as empty as his bank box at Hoare's.

By February, his letters had received replies, one from Mr. Childers confirming the closing of the townhouse and one from a Mr. Jonathan Billings, whom he rightly assumed must be his steward. With furrowed brow he read through a list of crops and yields from the previous year, unsure whether they were profitable or paltry. At some point, however, it occurred to him that Gyles Audeley was a gardener. There ought to be some books about agriculture in the library. But a gardener, it turned out, was not the same as a farmer. The botanical journals that Gyles kept on the library shelves were all ornamental in nature.

Nigel sent a second letter to Mr. Childers, asking him to use some of the money from the furniture to procure for him the most recent encyclopaedia of agricultural practices and to use the rest to remit his debts to any London tradesmen he owed. A week and half later it arrived, twelve heavy volumes in a leather-bound trunk. Staggered by the size of it, Nigel took three days to gather up the courage to open it. But when he did, he discovered that his natural curiosity had only atrophied over the past two years and not died completely. He began to exercise his muscles of mental acuity and was soon discerning the difference between winter and spring barley and the benefits of four-field crop rotation.

It was in this state of affairs that an unexpected carriage arrived at Audeley House. Archie was the first to meet the new arrivals. Nigel could hear his astonished voice in the hallway and the name *Audeley* wafting through the open door of the library. When he came out into the hallway to see who it was, he found not only Gyles Audeley in the entryway but also his golden-haired niece, Louisa.

The fear in her eyes was palpable—after all, the last time she had seen him, he had threatened to keep her under lock and key until she married Solomon Digby. She held tightly to Gyles' arm and remained wary as a songbird with hawks circling its nest. "What are you doing here?" she demanded.

"That," said Nigel, "is a long story. Perhaps we should sit down in the parlour so I can explain?"

And so they did. They sat in the parlour, and Magpie chose this moment to visit, curling up on Nigel's lap while he explained his peculiar journey from London to Derbyshire, in the company of Lord Kendall and Gyles' mother as they followed the coach in which they thought the young couple had eloped. "Imagine your mother's surprise when only her coachman was here with an empty carriage, and the both of you had disappeared without a trace."

Gyles was unapologetic about the deception. "A regrettable but unavoidable result of keeping Lady Louisa safe from *you*."

"I don't deny that I'm to blame in this," said Nigel, slowly. "In fact, if I'd never bargained with Digby, then Louisa would never have run away."

"There would have been no need! But your own greed wouldn't allow me to make a match of my own. It had to be someone of your own choosing who would pay you handsomely for the opportunity."

"And how well I have been served for that selfishness." With a few choice words, he explained to Louisa how he had been forced to run away from London as well. "I took an advance from Digby, and I spent it. And now I can't show my face until I've paid that debt back—or my face will never look the same again." He looked at her apologetically. "I'm sorry, Louisa."

Her frosty demeanour began to melt. "You seem so different! Almost like the Uncle Nigel I used to know when I was a child."

Nigel gave a hoarse laugh. "Do I?" It was being disappointed in love that had done it. It had made him truly see himself and desire to become a better man. But he hardly intended to confess all that to Louisa and Gyles. The wound was still too painful to let others probe it at present.

"Will you give your consent to me marrying your niece?" asked Gyles.

I don't see why I shouldn't." Nigel considered Gyles, so young in years, but already a man proven in his character. "Your mother's become a friend of mine—that's why she let me take refuge here. You have her eyes, and something of her generosity, I expect."

"With your consent, we can marry in just three weeks," said Louisa, her world-weary tone completely gone and replaced with a squeal of excitement.

"If you will serve as our chaperone," said Gyles, "I would be quite happy to let you live here for three more weeks. But then it's back to London for you, for I shall want my house, and my rose garden, and my wife all to myself."

"Of course," said Nigel. He had been considering where he would go next. Lincolnshire, probably. But not London. "I've been considering where I shall go next. I need to make things right. Or at least, as right as I can make them."

Louisa approached him and took his hand in hers. "Thank you," she said. "I don't know how much of a compliment this is, but I think, in time, you'll be a better duke than any of the Lymingtons ever have."

"A low bar indeed," agreed her uncle, "but I shall strive to meet it."

With everything settled with Louisa's guardian, Gyles paid a visit to Horace Townsend. The banns were read in church the following Sunday, or at least, so Nigel heard, for he was continuing to avoid the place.

"Will you invite the whole neighbourhood to the wedding?" he asked Gyles. He had kept to the house for the last eight weeks, but now that he had least put right his relationship with his niece, perhaps he could allow himself at least a glimpse of Belinda Morrison.

"The ones we have always dined with regularly," replied Gyles. "And we must send a card to my esteemed mother and stepfather as well." He gave Nigel a grin. "I must confess, I was far better pleased to have Kendall for a father than you. Now I must get used to having you for an uncle."

"No one outshines the Earl of Kendall," said Nigel with a snort, but there was none of that bitterness he used to hold, back in the days when he considered the Earl of Kendall his rival simply because of the man's irritatingly unassailable position in the ton.

Louisa, capable as always, sent out the cards for the wedding to Gyles' relations in London and to those in the neighbourhood whom Gyles knew well. She spoke with Mrs. Garrick about the wedding breakfast and determined what items Mrs. Garrick could make and what items they must get from the baker and other provisioners.

The letter they received back from Gyles' mother was more surprising than a simple congratulations. Lord and Lady Kendall, regretfully, would not be able to attend the wedding. The physician had ordered Lady Kendall to the sea for the sake of her health, and now that she had arrived in Brighton, it was not safe for her to travel elsewhere until her lying-in was finished. In August, she hoped to be delivered of a healthy child, a half-sibling to Gyles. In the meantime, her heart and prayers were with them in Derbyshire.

Nigel's eyes widened at that news. Not only had Kendall found the perfect woman for himself, but he had already got a child on her. The old familiar serpent of inadequacy began to whisper in his ear, but Gyles' next words silenced it: "We shall miss them, of course, but at least we'll have Uncle Nigel there to give away the bride."

When the day of the wedding arrived, Nigel saw with one sweeping glance of the church that not only were the Kendalls lacking, but also the Miss Morrisons. It was not until the ceremony was over and the wedding breakfast had commenced that he was able to ascertain the reason why.

"Ah, haven't you heard?" said Mrs. Brownlee, having secured a seat next to the duke at the breakfast table. "But, of course, you wouldn't have for you weren't at church last Sunday."

"What should I have heard?" demanded Nigel.

"Why, the banns were called for Miss Morrison."

Nigel's heart leaped into his throat. Had the vicar convinced her to endure his pomposity for life?

"I never would have thought that Miss Morrison would marry," Mrs. Brownlee continued blithely, "but dear Mr. Ferris has charmed her completely."

"Mr. Ferris!" All Nigel could imagine was Jack Ferris tapping his nose and winking at him, and suddenly, he wanted nothing more than to smack that smug smile off the elderly gentleman's face.

Mrs. Brownlee looked at him with such confusion that his good sense finally overcame his jealous instincts. He slowly unclenched his fists. "Would I be right in assuming that it is the older Miss Morrison who is betrothed? Miss *Lucy* Morrison?"

Mrs. Brownlee's soft chin wobbled with gaiety. "But of course!"

"So that explains the banns," said Nigel, "but not the absence of the betrothed couple at this wedding." He fixed an inquiring look on Mrs. Brownlee. "Where might they be?"

At that moment, Harold Brownlee stalked over to his wife's side and took his own seat at the table. "Who are you looking for? Ah, you mean Ferris? He's gone to buy a trousseau for his betrothed—in London."

"London?" Nigel's jaw almost fell open. So that explained why Magpie had not come around the house for the last week.

"Where else would one go shopping?" said Mrs. Brownlee. "I wish Harold would take me there for the season as well."

"And *both* Miss Morrisons have gone to town?" asked Nigel, determined to stay focused on the salient points.

Harold Brownlee nodded. "Indeed, Miss Bel is gone as well. Our poor Mr. Townsend is quite blue-devilled."

Nigel's nostrils flared, but he said nothing to that last remark. Mr. Townsend had no possible way of understanding what the word blue-devilled meant. Unless one had kissed Belinda Morrison once and then had the privilege taken away, it was impossible to comprehend the concept.

"Is he?" said Mrs. Brownlee doubtfully. "I hadn't noticed any change in his demeanour when he came to Sunday dinner—"

"I daresay it will improve her looks and her spirits to come back with a few new gowns," continued Mr. Brownlee, "although she'll never hold a candle to your niece!" He looked with admiration at the newly married couple seated at the head of the table. Louisa's heart-shaped face was serene as she gazed at Gyles.

"Indeed," said Mrs. Brownlee. "I think they are the handsomest couple to ever sign the marriage register in Derbysh—"

"I've done my duty as an executor," said Mr. Brownlee, "and made sure the will is properly carried out. The house and land are all Bel's now, but she's been as miserable about it as a wet hen. One would think it would be a relief to her to have this business with Charlie put to bed." He shook his head. "But there it is. Sometimes there's no understanding women."

"I daresay you might have more success if you tried listening to them," said Mrs. Brownlee quietly.

"Eh? What was that?" said Mr. Brownlee.

"Oh, nothing at all, my dear," she said with a pinched smile.

Nigel gave polite answers to the rest of the conversation, but his mind was a million miles away—or a hundred and thirty miles away, to be precise.

London! He was so used to picturing Bel Morrison in the rolling green fields and hills of Derbyshire, that he could hardly imagine what it would be like to see her on a London street. Would she break with convention and walk in Hyde Park at dawn rather than waiting for the fashionable hour? Would she wander about town without a footman to hold her parcels or a maid to uphold her reputation? He grinned, thinking of Bel in her wretched straw bonnet striding past Hanover Square.

Part of him wanted to forget everything—his debts, his fear of Digby, his doubts about his own worthiness—and depart for London at first light. But another part of him remembered the task she had set for him. "Fix it," she had said.

He swallowed and looked back to the head of the breakfast table where his niece Louisa sat, radiant in her own happiness. She had sent to London for some of the dresses she had left at Nigel's house—fortunately, the man who had sold the furniture had left those—and the soft blue silk she wore was a perfect foil for her golden hair. She looked up at him and smiled and raised her cup to him. He had fixed that part of his life, but there was still much more to be done.

No matter where Bel Morrison's steps took her, London was a city closed to him at present. His own road lay through Lincolnshire, and it was there he must go if he were to restore his livelihood and take responsibility for the title that had been entrusted to him.

CHAPTER TWENTY-THREE

London & Lincolnshire

APRIL 1811

B EL SLIPPED OUT OF the house on Half Moon Street to go
for an early morning walk. The sights of London were all
foreign to her with the narrow stone streets and the tall white
facades, but it was the smells of London that really unsettled
her. After the fresh air of the countryside, it was overpowering
to be hemmed in by the wafting stink of the Thames and the
ever-present stench of refuse on the streets. She was used to the
scent of manure, of course, but the sweet hay given to the horses
of Derbyshire must have made their leavings less loathsome than
the stale feed given to horses in London. And the squalor of so
many inhabitants in so small an area could not be completely
erased by separating the neighbourhoods of the rich from the
alleyways of the poor.

She had left off wearing black in London. It provoked too
many questions among new acquaintances—questions that she
did not want to answer. Aunt Lucy had insisted that her niece

visit the modiste and have some new gowns ordered, and Bel had insisted that she would pay for them out of her own pocket so as not to be a burden on Mr. Ferris. It was the first time she had bought new clothing in years without feeling like she was robbing Charlie's estate of something that was due to him. But now, Charlie was gone forever. The money was hers—every pound that her parents had put away and every shilling that she had scrimped and saved since her parents' death.

Her parents' bank had always been in London. When she stopped at Hoare's to inquire about her account there, she discovered that the interest had compounded even more than she had anticipated. No one would have expected it, no one who saw her walking down the street in her plain muslin gown and unmodish country bonnet, but Miss Belinda Morrison was the proud possessor of over ten thousand pounds.

Bel rounded the corner onto Piccadilly from Half Moon Street, for the house Mr. Ferris had found for them was quite close to that intersection. She soon came upon a pathway leading into Green Park. The name was less than apt. The manicured walks were insipid compared to her wild rambles on the hillsides of Derbyshire, and the "green" of Green Park was a pale imitation of the vibrant emerald of her own countryside. She had tried Hyde Park the day before and found nothing at all interesting on its curated paths beyond the sight of a little pug dog being chased by a footman, a gentleman sitting on a bench sketching, and a young lady sitting on the same bench watching the gentleman.

Her rambles in Derbyshire, besides being beautiful, had always been useful too. She had gone walking for a purpose—to find a lost sheep, to examine a crumbling stile, to deliver a basket to Mrs. Hogg—not simply to relieve the ennui of sitting in a stifling drawing room hour after hour. She supposed that if she were part of the fashionable world, there would be more to do with herself. She would have afternoon calls, and Almack's, and card parties, and balls to enjoy. But she also supposed she would tire of those as well—unless she had someone at her side to keep her laughing at herself and the artificiality of town and the ton.

At least she had Magpie to keep her company in London, although she often doubted the wisdom of bringing the cat with her. She dared not let the creature outside lest she get lost. And Magpie was as restless as she was. No doubt she was wishing she had fields and hedgerows to explore and a plate of ham waiting for her at Audeley House.

Bel sighed as she remembered the times she had searched for Magpie at Audeley House. Was Nigel Lymington still there, continuing to hide from his nefarious creditor in rural Derbyshire? She would hardly suppose that the newlyweds would enjoy having Louisa's uncle intrude on their honeymoon. Perhaps he had finally removed to his failing estate in Lincolnshire, another bout of banishment for him after the lively company of London. Bel sighed. If there was only some way she could help. She knew he had to stand on his own power, or he would never respect himself, but what if there was some little assistance she could give? Some way to ameliorate his exile from London?

Bel walked through Green Park in a fruitless fashion and then changed directions to return to the house. She had satisfied the physical demands of taking exercise, but she was still as restless as when she had gone out. And she was still no closer to satisfying her desire to help Nigel in some way.

As she entered the house, the laughter in the drawing room alerted her that Aunt Lucy was not alone. Jack, James, and a couple unknown to her had come to call.

"Bel, dear," said Aunt Lucy, standing up from the flo-ral-cushioned sofa to usher her into the cozy gathering. "Jack's nephew and his wife have come to see us. This is Ned and Clarissa Haverstall."

Bel made her curtsy.

"Ned is my older sister Nell's son," said Jack proudly. "As solid as they come." That statement seemed to be literal as well as metaphorical, for although the fellow was short, he was as stocky as a prize fighter. He looked a little like Tam, but with a more refined air about him.

Mrs. Haverstall was a kind woman who quickly found common ground with Bel and Aunt Lucy. "Uncle Jack tells me that you are acquainted with the Audeleys. Dear Gyles is my godson. And I understand he is but lately married."

"Yes, we would have attended the wedding," said Aunt Lucy, "but Jack whisked us away to London as soon as the betrothal was settled."

Mrs. Haverstall patted Aunt Lucy's hand and led her and Bel over to the window seat for a comfortable coze. "He told me you were starved of proper society and dying to see the metropolis. And now here you are arriving mid-season. We shall have to contrive some invitations to a dinner or card party so you can be properly entertained."

"You are too kind," said Aunt Lucy. "Do you go to many parties?"

"Sometimes," said Mrs. Haverstall. "And this season, more than ever. Ned and I have no children," she said, leaning in confidentially, "but we have a young lady staying with us at present. My dear friend Lady Kendall—Gyles' mother, you understand—has gone away to Brighton for her health. The timing is unfortunate, for her husband's ward, Penelope Trafford, came out this year and is in the middle of her first season. Ned and I are well-acquainted with many members of the ton, and we have taken on the responsibility of chaperoning her for the season. She would have come with us today, but she is still abed after dancing through her slippers last night."

"Good heavens!" said Aunt Lucy. "I have been Bel's chaperone for over five years, but she is the one who stops *me* from staying out too late."

"Penelope is certainly very...lively," said Mrs. Haverstall with a gleam in her eyes. "But Ned and I have come to love her enthusiasm." She gave her husband a fond look.

Hearing his name, Ned Haverstall looked over from the opposite side of the room where he and his uncles had established themselves. "Are you ladies talking about us?"

"Just like a man to assume that," replied Mrs. Haverstall merrily.

"Hmm," said Ned, glaring ferociously until they both fell to laughing. "My dear," he said, "you must stop monopolising Miss Lucy. I must get to know my new aunt."

Obligingly, Aunt Lucy rose from her seat at the window to join the gentlemen. Seizing her chance, Bel leaned closer to Mrs. Haverstall as they both looked out the bay window onto the street. "Mrs. Haverstall," she said in a low voice, "I wonder if you might help me with some information."

"What sort of information, Miss Morrison?" Mrs. Haverstall also kept her voice low, as if aware that Bel did not want this conversation to go farther than their own four ears.

"A friend of mine has become indebted to a businessman here in London. I have recently come into some money, and I would like to pay my friend's debts."

"How generous of you," said Mrs. Haverstall. "How can I help?"

"The businessman is named Solomon Digby. Would you happen to know where I can find him?"

Mrs. Haverstall started and put out a hand against the window moulding to steady herself. "Miss Morrison," she said with an urgent whisper, "you cannot be aware of this, but Solomon Digby is a most unsavoury individual. It would not be seemly—or safe—for you to conduct business with him."

"Oh, surely a spinster of advanced years such as myself—"

Mrs. Haverstall shook her head vehemently. "Advanced years? Ha! You cannot be more than five and twenty."

"I am nine and twenty."

"And a very lovely nine and twenty too," said Mrs. Haverstall, amending her error. "All the more reason *not* to enter the orbit of Mr. Digby. Our dear Penelope had a most unfortunate encounter with—but perhaps there are some things better left unsaid."

Bel looked at Mrs. Haverstall thoughtfully. "I am quite determined, ma'am."

Mrs. Haverstall wrung her hands. "I can see that you are."

"If you will not give me his address, I'm sure I can learn it elsewhere."

Mrs. Haverstall took a deep breath. "No, no, don't do anything rash. I shall talk it over with Ned and see what he thinks. But mind you, I make no promises. Perhaps Ned can go in your stead. Or perhaps, we can persuade you to forget this whole idea."

—ele—

Nigel looked out the window of the carriage. The dramatic peaks of Derbyshire had given way to the flat fields of Lincolnshire. In the distance, the gentle rise of the Lincolnshire Wolds blocked the view of what Nigel knew to be the North Sea.

"Are we almost there, yer grace?" asked Archie.

"Not yet," said Nigel with faint irony, "but if you ask again, it will surely make us arrive sooner."

Gyles had good-naturedly lent Nigel the Audeley carriage and coachman to take him and Archie to Lincolnshire. After all, Gyles had pointed out, as a newlywed couple, he and Louisa had no intention of leaving their bedroom for at least a month. Nigel had thanked Gyles for the loan of the carriage—and informed him that he could have done without that bit of explanation. Now, after two days of easy travel, they were getting close to the location of Nigel's country estate.

Grimsbald was a chimera of a castle, or—perhaps described more accurately—a history lesson of a manor house. The original tower, thick and squat, had been built shortly after the Conquest. Later, the Lymingtons of the Tudor Era had constructed a quadrangle, with the tubby tower on the northeast corner. And still later, Nigel's grandfather had remodelled the entire south wing of the quadrangle in the Palladian style.

Grimsbald sat on a vast swathe of land. Nigel had no exact idea of the area although he had heard his father say that it approached seven thousand acres. It was nearly a half hour after the carriage passed the stone fence demarcating Lymington land before they arrived at the circular drive in front of Grimsbald's Palladian entrance.

"Mayhap we're earlier than they was expecting?" said Archie, peering out the window at the empty stone steps that led up to the house.

"I didn't send word ahead of time," said Nigel. Better to surprise the skeleton staff that he had inherited from his brother and see the worst of things all at once.

Jumping down from the box, John opened the door, and Nigel climbed out with Archie close behind him. They ascended the grand steps, steps that Nigel had not walked up in nearly a dozen years. Nigel caught sight of movement in the window. In a location this isolated, the servants must have been peering out the upstairs windows since the carriage came into view five minutes prior.

Nigel lifted the knocker.

The door opened sombrely. An old man in a faded black coat stood there, alone but adorned with respectability. "Can I help you, sir?"

"Indeed, I hope you can," replied Nigel.

The old man, hands shaking, took hold of the doorpost. "Can it be? Master Nigel? Home at last!" Then collecting himself, he straightened and folded his hands behind his back. "Welcome to Grimsbald, your grace."

"Er, yes, Thank you."

The butler opened the door and Nigel entered, followed by a gaping Archie. Although the other older parts of the house contained exposed stone and rough-hewn beams, the northern wing was a luxurious confection of crystal chandeliers, decorative mouldings, and gilt-framed paintings. "We were not aware of your visit, your grace, or we would have prepared the master bedroom. Would you care to sit in the breakfast room while I locate some refreshment?"

"Of course," said Nigel, noting with satisfaction that the entrance hall and adjoining salon were clean and well-kept. "How many staff members are there at present, Randall?"

"Eight, your grace. Myself, Mrs. Grenville, two footmen, two housemaids, the stable master, and of course, Mr. Billings."

Nigel readily remembered the housekeeper Mrs. Grenville, but another name on the list gave him pause. "Remind me who Mr. Billings is."

"He is your steward, your grace."

"Ah," said Nigel, the name drawing some recognition from the recesses of his mind. Jonathan Billings—the steward who had written back to him. He took a seat in the breakfast room, ordering Archie to go ahead with Mr. Randall and unpack his trunk. Then he waited, looking about the light green room with a faint smile. It was just as he remembered it when he had sat in here as a child with a steaming cup of chocolate. His mother had always taken breakfast in her room. His father had rarely been at home to have breakfast. And his older brother, Louisa's father, had been too impatient to sip chocolate when he could be riding horses, shooting pheasants, or harassing pretty housemaids. This room had been Nigel's domain. He would read while he sipped his chocolate or set up tin soldiers on the breakfast table.

He heard a sound at the door and looked up to see a grey-haired woman in a dark dress enter. For a moment, he thought it was a vision of Belinda Morrison, forty years into the future, having grown old with him at Grimsbald—but within seconds, he saw that the lined face was that of the housekeeper, Mrs. Grenville. He stood up to greet her, with the same civility that he would have shown his mother.

"Welcome home, your grace." Her voice was laced with emotion. "It's been a good long time, it has."

"Yes, it has, Mrs. Grenville." Nigel's voice caught as he spoke.

"I'm afraid the ducal chambers are not cleaned and aired, but if your grace does not mind, your old bedroom is ready for tonight."

"My old bedroom?"

"Aye, we've had it at-the-ready each night for nearly thirty years, ever since you went away to Eton. Just so that your lordship—I mean, your grace—would have something to come home to."

Nigel's eyes grew misty. "Thank you." It was more than a thank you for the room. It was a thank you for making Grimsbald a home for him all those years ago. For giving him happy memories at Christmas. For remembering him every night for the last thirty years, even when he had forgotten who he was and who he ought to be.

CHAPTER TWENTY-FOUR

Fixing It

"Billings," said Nigel, sleeves rolled up as he examined the ledgers in the Grimsbald study. "When was the last time we increased the rent for the tenant housing and farmland?"

The black-haired man crossed his arms. "Never, in my tenure."

"Never?" asked Nigel in astonishment. His brother had no soft spot for the wellbeing of tenants, so it surprised Nigel that he had never raised the rent. But then, perhaps his brother had paid as little attention to the Lincolnshire estate as he had, preferring to toss his steward's letters in the fire too.

"No, your grace." Billings cleared his throat. "You'll recall I broached the matter in my introductory letter to you two years ago when you took the title—"

"No, I don't recall," said Nigel. He paused. "Although, it would probably be more truthful to say that I did not read your letter with the thoroughness it undoubtedly merited." He clucked his tongue against his teeth. "And my neighbours have raised rents for their tenants?"

"Oh, more times than I can count," said the steward with some chagrin.

"Would it be...unjust for me to raise the rents? I daresay no one is expecting it."

"Not unjust at all. And especially not if you put the tenant houses to rights with a few repairs."

Nigel leaned back in his chair. "Do we have the men for that?"

"We could if you paid them."

"Ah, therein lies the trouble. You're certainly aware that I'm short of ready cash at the moment."

Billings grunted. Nigel hoped that the steward's beetle-browed frown was more a sign of perpetual thought than a reflection of his opinion of his employer.

"I believe a swift infusion of cash could be contrived, if your grace is willing to cede some autonomy regarding the acres nearest the Wolds."

Nigel stared.

"I am referring to the mining rights," said Billings severely. "Which I mentioned in my initial report. But your grace may not have read that section either."

Nigel had the grace to blush. "No, I confess I also missed that."

"You have significant coal deposits on the acreage abutting the Wolds. There have been offers more than once from investors looking to acquire the rights to mine that land. You can doubtless see how present circumstances would make the benefits outweigh the detractions of such a plan."

"Ah," said Nigel, never having considered mining rights at all, save as a feeble excuse to Miss Morrison for his presence in Derbyshire. "Could you perhaps outline those benefits for me?"

"A lump sum from an investor for mining rights on the land could be used immediately for tenant repairs and bettering the current growing season on the rest of your acreage. In my mind, it more than makes up for the loss of revenue if you mined those coal deposits yourself."

Nigel could not dispute the wisdom of this. "How long would we cede the rights for?"

"Seven years."

It seemed a long time, but then again, a short time to learn the ins and outs of managing his estate. God willing, in seven years he would have the means to reclaim his own mines and increase the profits by starting his own mining operation.

"Very well, you can see about contacting investors who have approached the estate in the past. Let them know that we have multiple irons in the fire. Perhaps they'll bid higher because of it." He paused. "And besides the tenant housing and the spring planting, perhaps we can also use the money to increase our flock of sheep."

Mr. Billings grimaced. "If you'll let me speak plainly, your grace, sheep are a poor use of funds. We have a flock of a hundred or more, but the lambing season was dire. Too many stillborn creatures or feeble ones that lasted no more than a week."

"Hmm," said Nigel, tapping his fingers on the desk. "When do you breed them?"

"When do we—what do you mean, your grace?" Mr. Billings was clearly surprised by the question.

"When do you introduce the rams? Come, you must know what month."

"September, I think."

"Then postpone it a little later. The end of October this year. And it will be warmer in Lincolnshire with a better chance of survival for the lambs. Or, at least, that's the advice I received from a friend. A friend who is quite *expert* in these matters."

"We can try it, your grace," said Mr. Billings, his frown still expressing his doubt.

"Yes, we shall," confirmed Nigel. He had no intention of dismissing Mr. Billings' experience on any matters agricultural, but he also had no intention of ceding his own responsibility for the estate once again. He would listen and learn and make his own decisions about each matter. For now that he had taken the reins in hand, it was up to *him* to stay the course.

—— *ele* ——

"Clarissa told me you were determined," said Ned Haverstall as he helped Bel into the hackney.

"Indeed, I am," said Bel. She had dressed herself in one of her dark mourning dresses with a black veil pinned over her dark bonnet. "I must see Mr. Digby, and I thank you for accompanying me." In her reticule was a roll of banknotes larger than she had ever seen. It was good that she had such an imposingly muscular escort.

Mr. Haverstall gave the driver an address and then took a seat beside her in the hackney. "Digby's been trying to buy his way into the ton for the last five years, but most won't have anything to do with him."

"Why is that?"

"I would like to say it's because they sense something criminal about him, but I'm afraid it's more that they scent new money and deplore his disgusting manners."

"I've met aristocrats whose manners leave much to be desired," retorted Bel. In her mind was a picture of the tittering Lady Maltrousse.

"Yes, well, there's something decidedly plebeian about Digby," said Mr. Haverstall with a shrug. "I wonder that your friend did not take one look at him and run."

Bel lifted an eyebrow. "I believe my friend was at Point Non Plus."

Mr. Haverstall leaned forward in the hackney, his elbows resting on his thick thighs. "Am I right in thinking that this friend is a *gentleman*, not a lady, Miss Morrison?"

"You are right." Bel looked out the window, hoping to avoid any further questions on the subject.

They soon arrived at Mr. Digby's house in Leicester Square, and Bel was pleased to see that it was at least in a decent part of town. From Nigel's comments about Digby's thugs, she was afraid that they would have to travel into Seven Dials or some such slum. Apparently, Mr. Digby was eager to have a suitable address as he sought to buy his way into the ton.

Mr. Haverstall made an earnest appeal. "When we get inside, you had better let me pretend to be your brother, Miss Morrison. And let me do the talking to Digby."

That opened a wound that Bel had thought fully closed by now. If Charlie had been here, would *he* have gone with her to Leicester Square? Or would he have forbidden her from doing any such thing?

She smiled wanly. "I suppose we are almost brother and sister now that your uncle is marrying my aunt."

"Just so," said Mr. Haverstall, helping her down from the hackney and then turning about to pay the driver. The hackney wheels stayed firmly in place, so Mr. Haverstall must have also bid the driver wait in case they had to beat a hasty retreat.

The marble columns at the door of Solomon Digby's house were wholly out of place with the rest of the architecture; Bel could only surmise that they were expensive and that Mr. Digby had installed them to add to his consequence. A butler, pompous in the extreme, opened the door and waved them inside. The entryway brimmed with red velvet, gold edging, elaborate moulding, and classical artefacts. It was almost as if Mr. Digby fancied himself the Prince Regent.

Lounging against the wall were three burly fellows who looked at them curiously, one of them openly leering at Bel. No doubt these were Mr. Digby's associates, paid to bully a man into accepting an offer or punish him for reneging on a promise. Bel was gladder than ever that Ned Haverstall had accompanied her.

"Mr. Digby will see you in his study," said the butler, after checking to see if his master was at home. Bel kept her veil over her face as she entered the study on Mr. Haverstall's arm. Her eyes darted from side to side as she took in the tall bookshelves with perfectly glossy spines. It was clear Mr. Digby had bought his library all at once as a showpiece and that it was not a gradual accumulation of books he had read.

"Haverstall?" barked Mr. Digby as they came in. The butler had given him Ned's card. "I don't think we've ever exchanged more than three words before. What is it you want from me?"

Bel looked across the desk at a fat, balding man with a bright purple waistcoat. So, this was the mighty Mr. Digby. He did look coarse and common. He also looked like someone that even a non-Corinthian, non-prize fighter like Nigel Lymington could topple over with one blow to his flabby paunch—no wonder he hired so many brawny fellows to laze around his house.

"My sister and I have a friend indebted to you," began Ned Haverstall. He paused and looked at Bel. She had never actually told him the name of the debtor, the one for whom they were going to all this trouble.

"His name is Nigel Lymington, the Duke of Warrenton," said Bel firmly, "and he sent us to fulfil his obligation."

She felt Ned Haverstall's arm flinch as she gave the name. Apparently, he knew Nigel, at least by reputation.

"Warrenton!" said Digby. He stood up from his chair and swore vociferously. At least, Bel assumed that he was swearing, for they were words she had never heard before in all her life in Derbyshire. "He owes me two thousand pounds! And a thousand more for the humiliation of it all!" Digby's fist pounded the desk. "Did you know that she tied me up? That sharp-tongued niece of his. And then, when I determined to have my revenge, the other one, the Trafford girl, assaulted me with her boot."

Bel lifted an eyebrow. "I'm certain his grace feels very badly about the whole situation." She had no doubt that he regretted ever associating with Solomon Digby in the first place. She also had no doubt that Solomon Digby deserved to be tied up and battered with a lady's boot.

But Digby was not done. "And then there's Landsdowne—smooth as butter to the toffs and ugly as they come to anyone he thinks beneath him. He took the Trafford girl's part and blackened both my eyes so I couldn't show my face in London for a month. Urgh! Warrenton!"

This was more than Bel could follow, but she gathered that Mr. Digby considered Nigel the root cause of all his calamity. "We would like to repay what the Duke of Warrenton owes you," said Bel evenly. "If you would please name the amount."

"Four thousand pounds," said Mr. Digby promptly.

"Come now," said Bel, "that is double what he owes you. Surely, the interest cannot have increased so mightily in less than a year." She had let go of Mr. Haverstall's arm and was beginning to enjoy herself. This was not unlike haggling over sheep prices at a Derbyshire market. Thankfully, Mr. Haverstall had realised that she knew what she was about and was willing to stand back and watch her work.

"Interest as well as a penalty for defaulting on his word," growled Mr. Digby. "I won't take a penny less than thirty-five hundred."

"You must be aware that the duke has pockets to let," said Bel dryly. "Two thousand is the utmost he can repay."

"Three thousand," snapped Mr. Digby. "It's only just after what I've suffered."

It was good that Bel's flashing eyes and curling lips were still covered by a veil, for her opinion of Mr. Digby's suffering was written quite clearly on her face.

"We are authorised to give you no more than twenty-two hundred pounds," she said firmly.

"Twenty-five hundred pounds, and that's my last offer!" Mr. Digby beat a pudgy fist against his desk.

"Done," said Bel with alacrity. "And I shall require the original note and a signed receipt indicating that it is paid." She opened her reticule and removed the twenty-five hundred pounds that she had withdrawn from Hoare's the day before.

Muttering under his breath, Mr. Digby slid open a desk drawer and began rifling through a sheaf of papers. After a few moments, he found the required document, scrawled a note about receipt of funds, signed it, and shoved it in her general direction.

Bel lifted the receipt and placed it in her reticule. "I trust the Duke of Warrenton will not be troubled any further with your threats of reprisals."

Mr. Digby continued to mutter.

"I happen to be well acquainted with Viscount Landsdowne," interjected Mr. Haverstall, as if that were pertinent information.

"Cursed bully!" said Mr. Digby, standing up from his chair and uttering a few more unflattering opinions about this unknown viscount.

It was only after they had passed the lounging bravos in the entryway and the supercilious butler at the door that Bel stopped to ask a question. "Who is the Viscount Landsdowne, Mr. Haverstall? His name was as good as a talisman in there."

Mr. Haverstall snorted as he handed her into the waiting hackney. "A young friend of Kendall's, but more of a Corinthian than most. Dashed handy with the blade and his fists, and not too nice to apply a bit persuasion when needed. He rescued Penny from that Digby fellow when he kidnapped her this autumn and gave Digby a beating afterwards that he clearly has not yet forgotten."

"Ah," said Bel, finally understanding the matter that Mrs. Haverstall had alluded to in the Half Moon Street drawing room. She was glad that they were to take tea with the Haverstalls the following day, for she was eager to meet this Penelope Trafford.

"Didn't realise Warrenton was the fellow you were keen on saving from Digby's clutches," observed Mr. Haverstall, as the hackney rattled through the streets back to Bel's temporary residence. A deep frown sat between Ned Haverstall's brows.

"No, I thought it better not to mention it," said Bel frankly, "for fear that you would not have come."

"I wouldn't have. The fellow's a profligate fribble."

Bel arched an eyebrow and kept her opinions quiet. *Was* a profligate fribble, she thought to herself, but not anymore. And as the carriage rolled to a stop, she said a little prayer that this thought would prove to be true.

Chapter Twenty-Five

Loneliness

18 June 1811

Dear Uncle Nigel,

It is good to hear that Grimsbald is becoming profitable again. How marvellous that you were able to lease the eastern acres to mining investors under such good terms.

I own that I cannot think of Grimsbald with much affection. My childhood years there were not filled with happiness. I am certain that my haughty temperament did little to endear me to the servants there, for though I remember Mrs. Grenville and Mr. Randall by name, I remember little else than the demands I often made of them. I daresay I knew no better than to copy my mother and father in my arrogance of demeanour and thoughtlessness towards the servants. Fortunately, I still have time to remedy that in my new role as mistress of Audeley House, and I have Gyles to imitate in the care he shows for those of all stations in life.

Mrs. Garrick has agreed to become our housekeeper at Audeley House. She sends her love to Archie and hopes that he has scorched no more of your linens. She also begs that you tell him to stop sending home part of his earnings, for she intends to have grandchildren someday and would rather that he save his money for a wife.

You asked for news of our Upper Cross neighbours. Jack Ferris was wed to Lucy Morrison recently, but we've seen neither hide nor hair of the couple since the event. They have taken a wedding trip somewhere—something Gyles and I laughed about since we travelled so extensively *before* we were married that neither of us has any inclination to leave the house for the next year or ten.

The Brownlees prevailed upon Lucy's niece Belinda to stay with them as a houseguest so she would not be left at Morrison House, a single lady on her own. She is a strange creature. I do not think she cares a whit for bonnets, embroidery, theatre, or art. You know what a frivolous creature I am, so you can imagine how we get on. I have gone walking with her twice to attempt to be companionable, but I have seen the vicar walking with her a half dozen times or more. Perhaps they are well-matched, for he dislikes all things cosmopolitan—which is to say, all things that I was raised to adore.

Gyles works sun-up to sun-down in his rose garden, save the hours he spends with me, and I must own that the prospect of the Audeley House garden in the summer, when every variety is in bloom, is one of the finest sights that England has to offer. I have begun to try my hand at watercolour paintings of the different varieties to help him catalogue and record them. He is writing a book, you see, on the proper care and cultivation of roses. If he ever manages to finish it, it will be the most thorough manual for rosarians ever published. I am happy that my paintings can help contribute to it in some small way.

Your affectionate niece,

Louisa

NIGEL FROWNED AND RAKED a hand through his dark hair. He slapped the folded letter against the desk. Blast! He had hoped that Bel would send that officious clergyman about his business. But it sounded like Horace Townsend was still sniffing about like an overly eager sheepdog.

Was she lonely now that her aunt had married? And would that loneliness drive her to do something desperate? She had made no promises of waiting for him until he could reform his life and set his affairs in order. She owed him nothing. She could marry if she chose.

Nigel wondered if there was something he could do, either to dispel her loneliness or to open her eyes to Townsend's unsuitableness. Pulling out a sheet of paper, he scrawled a quick letter to his London solicitor.

Childers,

I have two errands for you to undertake. First, there was a ship that went down seven years ago on the western coast of Africa. The *Belladore* was its name. Were there any survivors? If so, who are they and where are they now? Perhaps the newspapers would have this information, or perhaps you can locate the owner of the ship.

Second, in a somewhat opposite conundrum, I have the name of a navy man, and I would like you to locate his ship. Townsend was the fellow's surname, but I do not know his first name. I believe he was an officer and that his ship saw adverse military action, causing his death, some thirty years ago. Can you find record of a Townsend deceased in naval action? Or alternatively, can you find record of a naval pension paid to a Mrs. Townsend for the past thirty years?

I have implicit faith in your abilities. Write as soon as you apprehend the information on either count.

Warrenton

Franking the letter himself, Nigel gave it to Mr. Randall to send with the next post.

Within a week, a reply came from Childers. The second piece of information he was still working to ascertain, but the first piece of information sent a shock of surprise through Nigel that had him gripping his desk and pouring a glass of brandy.

"Billings!" called Nigel, once the glass of liquid courage was empty. He leaned his head out of the study, hoping that the steward was somewhere nearby.

"Do you need something, your grace?" asked the steward, coming out of his own much smaller office next door.

"I need to go to London." Nigel took a deep breath. "Tell me, what do you think my townhouse is worth?"

Mr. Billings grunted and crossed his arms. "I have not seen it myself, and there is no recent valuation of it included with the deed that you have here in your files."

Nigel sighed. Sometimes, he wished his steward had more of an imagination. "Give me your best estimate, Billings."

"Impossible, your grace."

"Humour me."

"Ten thousand pounds," said Mr. Billings, throwing up his hands.

"Perfect," said Nigel, although he suspected that was far too large an estimate for a townhouse of medium size. "Tomorrow, I'll take the carriage to London. I'll be back for the early harvest but stay diligent on ensuring that the tenants pay their dues by working at the home farm." By custom and right, those who had cottages on the estate were obliged to work a set number of days at the home farm during each season. But, as this had never been enforced, it had been an uphill battle forcing a lazy pack of tenants to do their fair share of work. But Nigel was determined that his own crops would succeed this year as well as theirs.

He would make Grimsbald profitable if he had to spend his whole strength doing it.

—ele—

It was strange for Bel to no longer live in the home where she had been raised. The newly married Mr. and Mrs. Ferris had taken their wedding trip to Scotland, and at Aunt Lucy's insistence, Bel agreed to stay with the Brownlees for propriety's sake.

She had known the Brownlees almost since her birth. Harold had married Madge when Bel was just four years old, and Bel had dined at Mullhill Manor countless times since she had left the schoolroom. But still, to stay in someone's home as a guest was more of a revelation of their character than to eat an occasional dinner at their table. Bel discovered that Madge Brownlee would try on all her gowns at least three times a week and spent a large part of each day observing herself in a mirror. She would inform Cook she was on a reducing diet for meals but then request biscuits and other sweets at regular intervals throughout the day. She would make grand plans of travels she wanted to undertake and places she intended to see but then be too indolent to walk outdoors more than one day in seven.

Harold was an even more neglectful husband than Bel had previously suspected. He would dine elsewhere in the neighbourhood without notice to Cook or Mrs. Brownlee, and he spent far more mornings with his steward than he did with his wife. It was not the sort of marriage her parents had enjoyed—although from Nigel Lymington's stories, it seemed that his parents had been little different than the Brownlees. She wondered whether Harold and Madge had begun with affection that had withered over the years or whether they had rubbed along like this from the very beginning.

Although he had little time for his wife, Harold always greeted Bel with a jovial smile. And he always managed to be present on afternoons when the vicar came to take tea with them. "It's fine weather," he would urge. "You young people must take a walk together."

In this manner, Bel found herself thrown together with Mr. Townsend far more than was her liking. Now that she was out of blacks, the vicar felt free to renew his addresses. And indeed, Mr. Brownlee would have driven him to do so if he had not been so inclined. Bel almost wondered if the insistent landowner had made the persistent courtship a condition for the vicar to retain his living.

During their walks, the vicar's manner continued to vary between enthusiasm for parish duties and censure for the frivolity of those he could not understand. Bel, depending on her mood, could not always resist teasing the vicar and drawing his criticism, but it was never so much that he ceased conversing with her.

Periodically, Bel would stop by the Morrison farm to make sure that all was well with field and fold. Tam, despite being a man of few words, had taken charge of the farming operations, so much so that Bel was not even sure her direction was needed for a successful harvest. Had she always been this non-essential? Had her frenetic activity simply been a way of assuaging her loneliness and longing for Charlie's return?

Whenever she stopped in at the house, she asked Jenny for news of Archie, and in a roundabout way, for news of his employer. "Have you had another letter from him?" asked Bel circumspectly. "Is he still in Lincolnshire?"

"Aye, miss, and finding it quite easy to keep up with work boots and buckskins, for 'parently, his grace hasn't put on evening wear since he retired to his estate. Archie says he's almost forgotten how to tie a fancy cravat, but he's been tying them on himself in his free time, he says. Needs to stay in practice in case his grace goes to London."

"Does his grace anticipate returning to London soon?" asked Bel. If so, the attractions of the metropolis had just increased fivefold. She wondered if Lucy and Jack would return to London for a visit and if they would invite her to go with them.

"Well, he'd hardly tell Archie that, would he, Miss? I s'pose if he does it will be decided in an hour. The duke's a bit of a here-and-thereian, ain't he?"

"Do you think so?" replied Bel lightly. She hoped not. The solid three months he had already spent in Lincolnshire proved that he had the inclination to remedy his estate. If he had the staying power to last out the year, perhaps he could affect some real change. She took a deep breath. She could only hope that in all the work of becoming solvent and balancing his ledgers, he would not forget about the lady he had left behind in Derbyshire.

Chapter Twenty-Six

Digby

Mr. Childers evinced a good deal of surprise to see the duke in town. "The scandal rags intimated that your grace had been banished to the countryside."

"Banished by whom?"

"The heartless Lady M., or so my wife informs me."

"Hmm, well, yes. One could also say I was forced to *flee* to the countryside due to being hunted by the lady in question."

"Aha!" said Mr. Childers, eager to have a titbit of news to share later with his wife. "I might have known your grace would have other reasons. Now about that question on the deceased navy man—"

"Yes, yes, you can give me the details on that later. Right now, what I need to know is how much my townhouse is worth."

Despite his interest in gossip, Mr. Childers was a competent solicitor and more conversant than Mr. Billings with the price of housing in London. "It's a fine location you have," he said cautiously. "You'll not find another townhouse so pleasantly situated should you want to take up residency in London again."

"But what is it worth?"

"Three thousand pounds and a pile of regret if you sell. If you really need the money, perhaps Lady Louisa and her new husband would buy it from you—keep it in the family?"

"Thank you for your advice, Childers," said Nigel firmly, "but I have other plans for it. I brought the deed with me. Could I simply give it to...a certain individual as payment of a debt?"

"Yes, you *could* do that," said Childers with a sigh, audibly deploring the lengths his client must go to pay his vowels. "Is it too presumptuous to wish that your grace would stay away from the gaming tables?"

"Presumptuous indeed," said Nigel, "but I daresay my future wife wishes the same."

"Does your grace mean to be married then?" asked Childers in excitement, hoping to have another piece of exclusive news to bring home to Mrs. Childers that evening.

But Nigel ignored that question, adjusted his cravat, and picked up his cane to leave the solicitor's office on Jermyn Street. He had instructed Archie to turn him out in the smartest attire possible. After all, if a man were braving his own funeral, he ought to look his best.

From Childers' office to Solomon Digby's house in Leicester Square was only a walk of five or ten minutes. Nigel's lip curled in disgust as he looked at the tasteless marble columns in front of the house, their fluted Corinthian tops altogether too ornate for the rest of the architecture. By the side of the house, he saw one of Digby's muscle-bound minions leaning nonchalantly, hat pulled low over his face. Nigel was not a small man, but he knew he would have no chance if two or three such fellows cornered him on the street. He hoped that Digby would simply accept the deed to the townhouse and abandon any grudge.

The butler, an offensively supercilious fellow, kept him kicking his heels in the cluttered entryway for five minutes or more while he alerted the master of the house of his arrival. Nigel, trying to find a wall to lean against, wondered why Digby felt the need to display three urns on three separate plinths. Surely, a bench would be more useful in the entryway. Finally, Nigel was shown into Digby's study.

"Ah, Warrenton!" said Digby, rising from his desk and moving forward to shake Nigel's hand. Just as if nothing had ever happened between them. Just as if this were a regular morning call. Just as if he were actually pleased to see him.

"How's business, Digby?" Nigel asked cautiously. That was all the man usually talked about.

"Can't complain," said Digby. He began to speak of a mill he had acquired recently and two others that he had sold for an indecent profit. And then he began to discuss shipping, a pie into which he had inserted a very large finger.

"Shipping's exactly what I wanted to talk to you about," said Nigel. "But first, that little matter of me borrowing two thousand pounds—"

"Don't tell me you want to borrow again?" said Digby with a grunt. "I had my doubts if you would ever repay me without a good deal of *persuasion*. But I suppose you were—in the end—good for it. I *might* trust you again if we agree on the rates of interest ahead of time."

"I was good for it?" echoed Nigel stupidly.

"Yes, although I'm not sure why you sent a gel to pay, instead of coming to see me yourself."

Nigel pinched himself to make sure that he wasn't dreaming. "Just when did the girl arrive to pay it?"

"Oh, let me see, it must have been three months ago now. And she had that puritanical Haverstall with her. Said he was her brother. I didn't know you kept company with the likes of him—or rather, that he kept company with the likes of you!" Digby gave a coarse laugh.

Haverstall? Nigel racked his brain and finally put a face to the name. He had no notion why Ned Haverstall would be interested in paying off *his* debts. And who was the lady he came with? Nigel strongly doubted that she was truly Ned Haverstall's sister!

It was possible that Lady Maltrousse would want to buy up his promissory notes so that she could hold them over his head. But the arrival on Ned Haverstall's arm surely negated any possibility that the woman was Lady Maltrousse. The only woman he could think of who might be charitably disposed towards him was the former Mrs. Audeley. However, he could not imagine Lord Kendall letting his wife anywhere near Solomon Digby's residence. And besides, had she not gone to Brighton for her health?

"Did the woman give you her name, or did she keep you in suspense?"

"The latter," said Digby with a snort. "A typical woman's trick. And she never removed her veil so I could see if she was even worth looking at. Who was she then?"

Nigel gave a faint smile. "A friend."

His right hand patted the breast of his coat, feeling the deed to the townhouse still securely tucked away inside. Apparently, he would *not* have to disappoint Mr. Childers by giving up such a prime piece of property to pay his debt.

"You own several merchant vessels," observed Nigel.

"Aye, half a dozen."

"Have you ever had any mishaps with them?"

"Not for half a dozen years. I know how to pick my captains now. My first ship—now that was a disaster."

"Oh? What happened?"

"The *Belladore*. I'll never forget that name. I don't mind a bit of blue ruin myself, but not when I need all my wits about me. And every sane man knows that drink ought to be avoided if you're on the machinery, up in the carriage box, or at the ship's wheel. But the *Belladore* had more grog than they ought aboard ship, and the captain was drunk with the men...at least that's what the midshipman who survived said. The ship ran aground off the western coast of Africa."

"So, there were survivors?"

"Aye, a Dutch sloop picked up two crew members who eventually made their way home to England. And I found out later that an American slaver snatched up some of my cargo." Digby made a fist of fat fingers and growled.

"How do you know?"

"Because it was being sold in Charleston six months later! Marked wares specifically from one of my textile mills."

Charleston. Nigel filed that information away in his mind. It was a long chance, but if Charlie Morrison had not been picked up by the Dutch ship, perhaps he had been rescued by the American one?

"You're a busy man with your mills and your merchantmen," said Nigel, retreating towards the door of the study. "I'll let you get back to it."

Digby cocked his head. "But what did you come by for? Did you want to invest in shipping? Or perhaps you have another aristocratic bride in mind to help me enter the ton?" He patted the jonquil waistcoat that covered his large belly. "I've been practising my dancing for the next time I'm invited to a ball."

Nigel laughed. Why had he ever thought he could condemn his niece Louisa to marriage with this disgusting fellow? "No, no brides to recommend. Although I've heard that Lady Maltrousse can introduce you to elevated company...for a price."

"Hmm," said Digby, smacking his lips as he considered the notion of engaging that lady's services. "The price better be worth the product." He walked out into the corridor and entryway with Nigel. "What do you think of my Greek urns?" he said, proudly gesturing to the plinths.

"Er, very shapely," said Nigel. He might not have inherited money or morals from his family, but at least he had inherited a sense of taste. And he was almost positive, from the bright colours on the decorative vessels that they were modern reproductions, not artefacts from antiquity.

"I had an artist touch them up with a fresh coat," said Digby in a confiding tone. "Dashed things were so faded that I don't know why anyone would want them. But they sold for a pretty penny at auction, and I hear Greek pottery is all the crack with the toffs."

"Ah," said Nigel, trying to maintain an impassive face as Digby described the horror he had perpetrated. At least, thanks to the offices of an anonymous friend, he would never have to endure the humiliation of Digby taking possession of his townhouse and outfitting it in a style that was "all the crack."

When Nigel returned to Childers' office, he handed him the deed. "It turns out I won't be needing this after all."

"Thank heaven!" said Mr. Childers, taking the papers to lock them up somewhere safe. "My wife and I were driving by the townhouse just the other day, and I told her it was the best location in Mayfair. Perhaps after your grace's nuptials, you'll refurnish the place and resume residence in London?"

Nigel refused to answer that question, even to satisfy Mr. Childers' wife's curiosity. It was still too soon to know if the lady from Derbyshire would have him—or if she had already made up her mind to have someone else. But at least he could try to find out if that someone else was worthy of her. "You said you found information on the naval man I had you investigate?"

Childers motioned Nigel to an armchair and took a seat across from him. "I have searched high and low for a Townsend who perished in some naval action. There were several naval battles during the year you mentioned. Clinton's fleet in the American War was scuttled at the siege of Charleston. Several naval skirmishes occurred in the Caribbean with France and Spain. But none of the naval records and newspapers of the period mentioned a fellow with the surname Townsend. And they were quite thorough in listing the officers' names."

"If he did exist, what pension would his widow have received?"

"A lieutenant makes only one hundred pounds a year on regular pay, and a fraction of that when he is on shore. The pension would be barely enough for a widow to keep bread on the table and keep a table in the house."

Nigel had known the number would be small, but Mr. Childers' words were confirmation. "So, if this Townsend did exist, his widow would have no means to send a child to Eton and Oxford."

"Only as a charity case at the institution, or if she had other means from relatives to pay the fees."

"Hmm," said Nigel. Childers was clearly curious what all these inquiries were for, but this was not a story that Nigel was ready to share...yet.

Did it really matter if Horace Townsend's father was a deceased naval man or not? Why should he care whether the vicar was lying about his parentage?

But if the vicar was lying about his father, what else was he lying about? There was something havey-cavey about the whole business, and he'd be damned if he let a sharper of a parson make a May game of Bel Morrison. She was the most self-sufficient woman he knew, but even she could be bullied—or made to think that her duty lay in effacing all her own desires.

"I've one more task for you, Childers," said Nigel rising from the chair.

The solicitor followed suit. "Of course, your grace."

"What do you know about American newspapers?"

Childers blinked. "Not much. Why?"

"Would it be possible for me to place an advertisement in a South Carolina newspaper to run for, say, a month?"

Childers scratched his head. "I don't see why not. I have a distant cousin there, and I daresay he could make the inquiries for me. What do you want the advertisement to say?"

"This," said Nigel, and moving towards Childers' desk, he seized a pencil and a scrap of paper and began to write out exactly what he would like printed.

Chapter Twenty-Seven

Charleston

October 1811

T HE HARVEST SEASON HAD come and gone. The grain had been cut, the sheep had been sheared, the profit had been tallied—and somehow, throughout it all, Bel's heart had been completely absent. For the first time, she had even been tempted to let Harold Brownlee's steward negotiate the sale of her wheat and wool simply so that she could stay away from any crowds or questions.

Aunt Lucy was too happy in her new connubial bliss at Amsworth Park to notice the gloom that hung over her niece. Whatever listlessness lay in Bel's manner, she ascribed to the change in residence. "I realise that Jack's house is not quite to your taste," she said—and, indeed, Bel could not feel at ease in the Rococo flamboyance of a residence that had been decorated half a century ago— "and that you cannot come and go as you please in your trousers in all times and all weathers, but please remember how fond of you we both are. And it is ever so kind of you to play piquet with James after dinner so that he is not so cross to lose his brother's constant companionship."

The presence of Gyles and Louisa Audeley added other "young" people to the neighbourhood, but Bel found little in common with the lively Louisa. And besides, seeing Louisa only reminded her of the lady's absent uncle. She was cordial whenever Louisa came to call, but she could not find friendship there.

The periodic visits of Horace Townsend continued to punctuate the monotony of autumn in Derbyshire. The vicar—and his sensitive nose—was relieved that Bel had left Magpie at Morrison House in Jenny's care, rather than taking the cat to her aunt's new home. "I see you've had the kindness to dispense with your feline companion for my sake," he said with feeling.

Bel's left eyebrow answered that impertinence eloquently, but the vicar—unlike the duke—was not fluent in the language of the face. The sole reason for Magpie's absence was that old James Ferris considered all cats to be of a devilish disposition; the vicar's sneezes had nothing to do with the matter.

The long-legged vicar was fond of a brisk walk and loved to find the differences between this countryside and his home county of Shropshire. Bel often took the air with him when he came calling, finding it easier to endure his conversation when it was wafting through the fresh, loamy air rather than echoing loudly in the drawing room.

"I daresay you're relieved to have your new uncle's guidance with the Morrison estate," said the vicar, on his last visit. "A heavy weight off shoulders not created to bear such a burden."

Formerly, Bel would have bridled at such a comment, but now, she felt only a mild annoyance that she managed to overlook. She still cared deeply about the Morrison land, but without the hope of Charlie's return, her single-minded passion had lost its fuel. The vital spark inside her had burned low, and she did not know if would ever flame to life again.

"Have you completely accustomed yourself to the parish duties?" she asked, changing the subject.

"More or less. You will be delighted to hear that I have prevailed upon your tenant Mrs. Hogg to attend divine services."

"Yes, I saw her there last week." Bel did not mention that she had promised the old woman an extra basket of provisions each fortnight if she would be more civil to the vicar and heed his admonition to attend church. It was better than hearing Mr. Townsend complain about the old woman every time he came to call.

"It's further proof that I can do some real good here. The people are not so entrenched in their sin that they cannot experience a change of heart. They have not experienced the soul-poisoning miasmas of the metropolis."

"So, you have no hope for sinners in London?"

"Did not Our Saviour say *it is easier for a camel to enter the eye of a needle than for a rich man to enter the kingdom of God?*"

"And did He not conclude that, despite that difficulty, all things are possible for God? After all, Mr. Brownlee and Mr. Ferris are quite well-off, and surely you do not doubt their salvation?"

"I doubt no man's salvation unless he gives me cause to do so. But even so, there are few that live godly lives in our present time. Our recent visitors from London only illustrate the truth of that. *Wide is the gate and broad is the path that leadeth to destruction*, Miss Morrison. The less intercourse that we have with London, the better."

As the month of October ended, Bel began to feel increasingly despondent. She was usually too busy to ask her heart why it felt the way it did, but in this season of enforced inactivity, she had a surfeit of time for self-examination. Was this depression still grief over Charlie? Or was it grief for something else?

When she and the Duke of Warrenton had parted, she had hoped that he would have the fortitude to change the life he claimed to deplore. But ten months had gone by since then. She could not keep begging her maid-of-all-work for scraps of information via the duke's valet. It was common knowledge that a rake's interest was short-lived, and in the last ten months she had received no indication that Nigel Lymington still thought of her at all.

One afternoon, she was staring out the elegant window of the first-floor parlour when she put a hand to her face. Her calloused forefinger pressed against the place where Nigel's lips had met her own. It was not a practical gesture, but it was a practiced one—one she had repeated daily these last ten months. "What's in a kiss?" she whispered softly. What made the sensation of it linger so long after the loved one was gone?

He had worried that she would hate him afterwards. But somehow, she did not. She remembered him longingly and missed him. And she was afraid that she would go on missing him for the rest of her life. There was no moratorium on affection of this kind. No hope that after seven years her desire for Nigel Lymington would be declared deceased.

As she stared out the window, a post chaise turned off from the road and approached the house. The carriage belonged to no one from the neighbourhood, and Jack and Lucy had not mentioned any impending arrivals. Who could this be?

Slowly, Bel's hand moved away from her lips until it came to rest at her side. She would not say aloud what she wished. She was too sensible. She was too cautious. She was too afraid of being wrong.

From the window, she saw a man, whose brow was shaded by a very tall top hat, alight from the carriage. He handed down a tall, well-formed woman in a carriage gown of deep purple. The man gave the woman his arm and they ascended the steps to Amsworth Park. There was something familiar about the man, but Bel could tell at a glance that he was not the Duke of Warrenton.

Bel seated herself on the sofa in the parlour and waited for the butler to assuage her curiosity. The door to the parlour opened with a slow, almost trepidatious, swing. "Miss," said Uncle Jack's butler, clearing his throat more times than was natural. "There's a gentleman and lady downstairs claiming to be Mr. and Mrs. Charles Morrison."

At those words, Bel, who had barely been taken ill a day in her life, fainted dead away on the sofa.

—ele—

"There, there," cooed an unfamiliar voice. "Let me put this blanket on you." A woman adjusted a pillow under Bel's head and laid a counterpane over Bel's collapsed form. Bel felt the woman press her hand and offer repeated assurances that everything was going to be all right. The woman's accent was strange—Bel could not place where it was from, but she felt too tired to lift the leaden weights that sat upon her eyes and discover who the woman was.

"Butler, are there any smelling salts?" said a deeper voice, a voice that Bel had not expected to hear again on this side of eternity.

Bel's eyes flew open of their own accord. "Charlie!"

"I never thought you would become one of those elegant females who swooned to become the centre of attention." Her brother—older, more weathered, but still his same incorrigible self—was standing before her, teasing her as if he had never gone away.

"Charlie Morrison!" Bel pushed herself up into a sitting position. "How dare you surprise us like this!"

Charlie ignored her outburst. "Bel, meet my wife, Hester."

Bel stared at the pretty woman in the purple carriage gown. "But you don't look at all like you're from India."

"India?" said Hester with a laugh. "Certainly not."

"Then where did you meet her, Charlie? And where have you been all this time?"

"Where have I been? That's a story, by Jove!" He took a seat to tell it. "The ship I took passage in was damaged off the Ivory Coast and the hull completely stove in. The water rose faster than a spring flood, and it was only by committing myself to the mercies of the sea that I found a piece of cargo buoyant enough to hold me. I was on the ocean, under the beating sun for three whole days, without a drop of Adam's ale to drink, when—mercy of all mercies—I saw a white sail in the distance, shining like the pearly gates of heaven. My parched throat could barely call to them, but they saw me. The captain brought me—and my floating cargo—aboard. I was another human pulled from the coast of Africa to take to America, but above decks rather than below due to the colour of my skin."

"You were on a slave ship!" gasped Bel.

Two spots of colour appeared high on Hester's cheeks.

"Indeed, it was legal at the time. Although it's been two years and more now since that trade was abolished in America. The captain of the ship brought me back to South Carolina with him. I made myself useful on the voyage, and by the time I reached Charleston, I had warranted a word of commendation to the ship's owner, Mr. Jeffries. I'd enjoyed learning the craft of sailing, and the owner agreed to make me a first mate on the next voyage. In five years' time, I'd worked my way up to captain and he sent me out with a ship of my own."

"A ship's captain," marvelled Bel, looking at the dandy in front of her. In his immaculately cut coat and pantaloons, he looked nothing like the life he was describing although she could see a weather-beaten, sun-bronzed look about his face and hands.

"After my third voyage, however, Mr. Jeffries' daughter decided that she liked me better on land than on shore. And so I was forced to swear my services to a different admiral and take a different commission. I now oversee a plantation, sit in the shade sipping rum punch, and host other inhabitants of Charleston who enjoy sitting in the shade and sipping rum punch too."

"What he's trying to say in his circumbendibus way," interjected Hester, "is that we married last year, and since then, he's been in South Carolina. With me."

"Oh," said Bel, pushing herself up to a sitting position on the sofa. "So, you are Mr. Jeffries' daughter?"

Hester nodded shyly.

"And during all that time, you never thought to write? Never thought to let us know that you were alive?"

Charlie's eyes goggled and he gave a shrug. "I can't say that I did. Relations haven't exactly been friendly between America and England, so the mail is unpredictable. I always knew I would visit home eventually—and it's not like the farm or the house were going to pick up and leave."

"You nitwit!" said Bel, seizing the pillow from the sofa and beating him over the head with it as he held up a sturdy arm to stave off her blows. Finally, she exhausted her outrage and took a deep breath. "Mother and Father are dead, thinking you went to a watery grave."

"Yes, I heard that at the house," said Charlie, as if he had already accepted the fact. "From your maid there—Jenny, is it? She told us you were living here at Amsworth with Aunt Lucy, and that the old girl has married at last!"

"Yes. And no wonder the butler looked as if he'd seen a ghost when he came upstairs to announce you. You were declared dead ten months ago! In the eyes of the law, you don't even exist anymore, Charlie."

"Well, I like that!" said Charlie in an offended tone. "A man goes on a little adventure, and his pigeon-hearted compatriots immediately give him up for lost." He stamped his foot. "Why did you have me declared dead if you were still searching for me? I came as soon as I saw your newspaper advertisement."

"Newspaper advertisement?"

"Hester was the one who saw it—what did it say, love?"

"I have it right here." Charlie's American wife took a scrap of paper out of her reticule.

INFORMATION WANTED

The subscriber requests news of a certain Englishman named Charles Morrison, likely a resident of Charleston,

having arrived thither in the year 1803 or 1804.
If any gentleman has news of him,
he will be so kind as to inform his sister
by directing a line to her at Morrison House
near Upper Cross in Derbyshire, England.
—August 1811

"That was my first hint that Father and Mother had passed," said Charlie, "for if they hadn't, they would have written the advertisement rather than you."

"But Charlie," said Bel in shock. "I didn't write this."

Charlie stared. "You didn't?"

"I didn't even know you *were* in Charleston. I thought you were lost in the jungles of Africa or, in the best of all providences, rescued and taken on board a new ship to India."

"Stap me! How peculiar," said Charlie. The three of them looked at each other in befuddlement as the door to the parlour burst open.

"Charlie!" said Aunt Lucy, home with her husband from a nuncheon at the Jester's Arms. "Charlie, you rascal! Jack, darling, you remember Charlie!" Charlie rose to his feet in greeting, and she flung herself into her nephew's arms.

"Of course," said Jack, who had purchased his estate near Upper Cross several years before Charlie's departure to see the world. "Welcome back, my boy." He reached around the effervescent Lucy to shake Charlie's hand.

"Aunt Lucy," said Bel, rising to her feet. "Did you perchance place an advertisement in America searching for news of Charlie?"

"In America? Good heavens! Why would I do that?" She stopped hugging him long enough to look him up and down. "Is that where you've been all this time, Charles Morrison?"

"Yes," said Charlie proudly. "And I would like to introduce you to my wife Hester, Jewel of the Carolinas."

Lucy immediately altered the object of her embrace to her new niece-in-law while Jack bussed the tall woman on the cheek. "Welcome to England, my girl." His twinkling eye took in the slight curve of her belly beneath her purple walking dress, something Bel in all the turmoil had failed to notice. "Is it too much to hope that there are little Morrisons on the way?"

Once again, Hester's cheeks pinked. Bel reflected that she was much shyer than any American had the right to be.

"Yes, Hester's in the family way," said Charlie, answering for her. "I thought it might be better for her to stay on the plantation. But then again, if war is declared and the return home is delayed, I didn't want to be trapped here and separated from her."

"Return home," repeated Bel. "So, this is just a visit then. You're going back to Charleston now that you've done your duty and answered the newspaper advertisement."

Charlie looked at her in surprise. "But, of course. Haven't you been listening? My life is there now, with Hester. We have a whole plantation depending on us."

"But what about the farm?" Bel asked in desperation. "Your inheritance here in England?"

"Morrison House?" Charlie shrugged. "You keep it. You always did care more about the land than I did."

"Yes," said Bel faintly, another bout of light-headedness coming on. "I suppose I always did."

Nigel had never felt such elation. The harvest had exceeded his expectations, and even Mr. Billings—arms crossed and eyebrows beetled—had admitted that it was a job well done. The tenants, after having a good grumble about the enforcement of home farm service, ceased their complaints once they saw much-needed repairs made on their roofs and fences.

Nigel had celebrated his triumph by purchasing more agricultural books, these ones on the proper breeding of sheep, and he was considering purchase of new stock to strengthen the flock when a letter arrived for his valet.

"Yer grace! Yer grace!" Archie came bounding into the study, interrupting Nigel's conference with the steward. "Jenny says that Master Morrison's come home."

At the name *Morrison*, Nigel's head looked up sharply. "What's this?"

"Charlie Morrison's back in England. He's alive, yer grace!"

Nigel's face split into a slow smile. So, Bel had been right all this time, and her sisterly intuition had proved true. "Did she say where he's been keeping himself?"

"The Americas. An' he's brought an American wife with him who, Jenny says, has never even eaten a proper puddin' before."

"Well, I'm certain Jenny can rectify that," said Nigel. "I remember her being a worthy baker of biscuits." It was true, if one liked his ginger biscuits on the dry side.

"Yes, she is," said Archie with a broad grin.

Nigel's face was just as gleeful. So, his seedling efforts to find the truth had paid off in another glorious harvest. Charlie Morrison had made it to Charleston with the rest of the flotsam from Solomon Digby's *Belladore*. And now he was back in

Derbyshire, after all these years, with a wife in tow! Now, the magistrates would reverse their ruling, and Harold Brownlee's hopes would deflate like a balloon. Nigel could imagine the joy on Bel Morrison's face, and that kept a smile on his own. The dead had come to life again.

He turned back to Mr. Billings and instructed him to go ahead with the purchase of a half dozen new rams. They were a slightly hardier species from a farmer in Northumberland. By breeding them with his own stock, he had high hopes that the lambs would be sturdier in the spring.

And he also had high hopes that he was close to fixing all those things that needed fixing. And when that process was concluded, he could travel to Derbyshire, throw himself at Bel Morrison's feet, and beg for her hand. For if the dead could be raised, then the prodigal could be transformed, the rake could be remade, and a fool of an English duke could find happiness in the end.

Chapter Twenty-Eight

Shropshire

December 1811

N IGEL HAD INTENDED TO wait until the spring to call on Bel—for once the spring planting was done, he would have a year of roots set down in Lincolnshire, a year of careful living behind him, and a year of expectations met. But another letter from Jenny at the beginning of December precipitated his plans.

"Yer grace, yer grace!" Archie's anxious face bounded into view as soon as Nigel dismounted from his horse in the dark cold of the early evening. The duke was tired after a long day of digging. The winter rain had sent a stream of runoff through the corner of the main barn, and it had taken a dozen men with shovels—one of them Nigel—to cut the stream a new, less destructive path.

"What is it, Archie?" Nigel said with a groan. "Can it wait till I have my supper?" He knew that Mrs. Grenville would have ordered something warm and filling to take the chill out of his bones.

Archie gulped. "I'm afraid it can't. Jenny says if I'm going to marry her, I'd better come and do it quick, for she won't cook and clean for Mr. Townsend if she must hear a lecture at every dinner and a sermon on every wash day. If you have a place for her in Lincolnshire, she'd take it in a trice. An' perhaps, if we're man and wife, we might have our lodgings in the gatehouse?" He looked at Nigel hopefully.

"Hold now," said Nigel, removing his riding gloves, his face growing hard. Suddenly, the soreness in his shoulders and fore-arms was the least of his concerns. "Explain yourself. Why should Jenny have to cook and clean for Townsend?"

"She overheard Mr. Charlie telling Miss Bel she ought to marry him."

"What the deuce!" Nigel slapped his riding gloves against his leg. "Are you sure of that?" Had he really gone to all the trouble to bring Bel's brother here from America for the fellow to give her the worst advice since Job's wife?

Archie nodded. "'Parently Master Charlie's leaving again for his wife's country, and he wants to see Miss Bel settled before he goes. An' since the vicar's been callin' on her—"

"Pack my trunk, Archie. We're leaving tomorrow."

"Yes, sir. R-right away, sir," stammered Archie. "To Der-byshire?"

"Aye," said Nigel. "To Derbyshire." He paused to consider. "But not directly. We'll go by way of Shropshire."

"Yes, yer grace. Right away, yer grace," said Archie. "An' if it's not too much trouble, might I tell Mrs. Grenville to tidy up the gatehouse while we're gone?"

—ℯℓℯ—

Nigel instructed the coachman to set him down at Mullhill Manor. Then he sent Archie on ahead in the carriage to beg lodging for them from his niece at Audeley House. There had been no time to send word, but he hoped that Louisa would be kind enough to accommodate him. Otherwise, he would have to make do with the Colemans' hospitality at the Jester's Arms—and awaken all sorts of village rumours about why the Duke of Warrenton had returned to Upper Cross.

A quick knock on the door gained him access to the house where he had first eaten dinner with Bel. The entryway brought back memories of the first time he had noticed her attractiveness in the blue silk evening gown.

Mrs. Brownlee intercepted Nigel in the corridor before the butler could bring him to Mr. Brownlee's retreat in the library. "Your grace, how splendid to see you again. To what do we owe the pleasure?"

"A little misunderstanding that I need to clear up with Mr. Brownlee," said Nigel. "But I'm delighted to see you again as well, Mrs. Brownlee." He gave the plump woman a kind smile. It was not her fault that her husband was a thoroughgoing cad.

"Ah, your grace!" said Harold Brownlee, clapping his hands together as he met Nigel at the library door. "Down from town again, I see. Have you brought a party of Londoners with you? I still remember your friend Lady Maltrousse—a delightful woman. Welcome here any time."

"I've brought no one but myself." Nigel advanced toward the sofa and sat without invitation. As soon as Harold Brownlee's stooped shoulders settled against the chair opposite, Nigel came straight to the point—or, at least, straight to the point where he intended to begin the conversation. "I will eventually need to find a candidate to fill the living on my estate in Lincolnshire, and I wonder, Mr. Brownlee, could you remind me how you came across your own vicar, Horace Townsend?"

Harold Brownlee pursed his lips. "Er, yes. I was a friend of his father's."

"His father who died in the course of his naval duties?"

"Yes, that's right, your grace."

"Causing his widow to receive an annual naval pension to support herself and her son?"

"Yes, I believe so." Mr. Brownlee's brow wrinkled. "But why don't you ask the vicar about that—he would know better than I." He grinned. "You're not trying to steal our vicar away to Lincolnshire, are you?"

"Certainly not," said Nigel. He looked up at the ceiling as if in thought. "Is it difficult to attract a vicar to a living if the stipend is small? I recall you suggesting to Mr. Townsend that it would be possible for him to supplement his income by marrying well."

"There are so many curates looking for posts that the number of candidates is endless. But yes, Mr. Townsend has additional prospects. I believe there might be a happy announcement any day now, and Mr. Townsend will be reading his own banns from the pulpit this Sunday."

"You refer to Miss Morrison, I presume?"

"Just so."

"It was a lucky chance that her brother was declared dead, so she could inherit all the property." Nigel managed to avoid sneering as he said this. "But I heard a rumour that the brother has lately returned?"

Harold Brownlee leaned forward in his chair. Nigel could tell that the old fellow loved a good gossip. "Yes, returned and has submitted proof of his identity to the magistrates. The property would have reverted to him—and Mr. Townsend would have stood to be very much the loser. But as it turns out, Mr. Morrison is already quite wealthy by right of his wife's fortune. He was no sooner declared alive again than he formally ceded all the land and money from his parents to his sister. So, she gets the whole of it—as will her husband—just as if her brother had been dead all along."

"How fortunate," said Nigel dryly. "I wonder, Mr. Brownlee, why is it that you take such an active interest in Mr. Townsend's situation?"

"Why, what do you mean? I take an interest in him, just as I would any of my neighbours. A little more so, I suppose, since he receives his income from my hand."

"And if Mr. Townsend were able to increase his income, he could afford to bring his mother from Shropshire to Derbyshire."

Harold Brownlee looked at Nigel in surprise. "Yes, what of it?"

Nigel leaned back in his chair and yawned. "I happened to pass through Shropshire on my way here—beautiful countryside. And I happened to meet Mrs. Mary Townsend."

"Did you indeed?" Mr. Brownlee's eyes lost their friendly gleam and narrowed with suspicion.

"Yes, she was quite hospitable. She invited me in for tea and we found we had a host of mutual acquaintances." Nigel's voice deepened. "The story she told me about her son's father was quite different from the one you've just told me."

Harold Brownlee stared at him. Nigel stared back.

"Does Horace Townsend know that he is your son?" demanded Nigel.

Harold began to protest, but Nigel's voice grew louder and more masterful. "Don't lie to me. It's plain as a Puritan's prayer book to anyone who really looks at the two of you. Your bearing and mannerisms are the same. Mrs. Townsend's word only confirms it. There never was a death at sea. There never was a naval pension. There never was a Mr. Townsend."

"Now see here," objected Mr. Brownlee. "Did you come to Derbyshire just to dig up a scandal and meddle in my affairs? What possible interest can you have in the matter?"

"A very personal interest. You may have as many bastards as you like, Brownlee, but once you begin imposing on Bel Morrison, that is when I take issue with it. I am highly opposed to Horace Townsend making a match of it with Bel Morrison, and I am highly opposed to you manipulating affairs to get her money into his hands. Were I to reveal Townsend's connection with you, Miss Morrison would certainly cut all ties with him."

Mr. Brownlee rose from his chair in alarm. "No. I beg you to reveal nothing of the sort. The vicar is unaware of the connection. He would be horrified to hear that he is of illegitimate birth, that his mother was not—" He sank back into the chair. "But then, your grace certainly understands the ways of the world. She was not a loose woman by nature. I was in love with her, but she hadn't a penny, and my father objected to the match. He needed an infusion of cash, you see, for the Brownlee estate; and that meant I was not free to settle for anyone less than an heiress."

"An unlucky situation, to be sure," said Nigel, standing up as well. He was more than familiar with attempts to rescue financial imprudence through forced marriages.

"By the time my father threatened to disown me, Mary was already in the family way. And so my father made me a bargain—if I would promise to marry a bride of his choosing, he would put Mary and her child up in a cottage far away from here and send her a monthly stipend. I agreed to it. And when my father died, I continued to send the stipend to Shropshire. I have never seen Mary since our separation, although we have written letters to each other over the years. I knew my son had taken orders, and when the living came available, I approached him as a friend of his father's and offered him the position. I wanted to know him, you see, to further his way in the world and thus redeem my youthful mistake."

"A touching tale," said Nigel dryly. He might have trusted it wholesale twenty years ago; he might have believed it in the main ten years ago. But he had seen enough of Lady Maltrousse's set in the last two years to know the kind of man Harold Brownlee truly was. It was far more likely that he had lured Mary Townsend into lifting her skirts with promises of love and marriage and then deserted her at the first opportunity. He wondered if it was the father who had forced Brownlee to do the right thing with the cottage and the stipend. "It would bear more semblance to the truth if you did not continue to take advantage of other women's charms, like the widow Mrs. White."

Mr. Brownlee's shifty look confirmed Nigel's suspicion on that account.

"Are you hoping for a renewal of your intimate acquaintance with Mrs. Townsend under your son's very nose? It would be most convenient if you could convince your son to bring your former paramour here to Upper Cross."

Mr. Brownlee's wrinkled cheeks flamed red, and his hands fell into fists. "You devil!"

"It takes one to know one," said Nigel coolly, convinced that he had Harold Brownlee's measure.

"What do you want from me?"

Nigel leaned forward and spoke with clear intensity. "Stop promoting a marriage between Horace Townsend and Belinda Morrison. I overheard you at that dinner party last December—it was you who put the idea in his head, you who furthered the acquaintance. You know how to steer that man like a ship—so steer him in a different direction."

"I fear you are too late, your grace," said Harold Brownlee. "He told me yesterday that he was planning to declare himself. And if I know anything about Bel Morrison, I know that she'll hold fast to her word once it's given. She would never jilt a man just because he discovered he was illegitimate. Your interference will change nothing in that quarter. She will marry Townsend regardless. Yes, you will damage my reputation and sully his. But do you really want to expose *her* to the scorn of the world simply to satisfy your own jealousy?" Brownlee smirked, convinced that he held the trump card to win this match.

Nigel gritted his teeth. Had he really come too late to stop a betrothal? The halt in Shropshire had delayed him by a day, but his conversation with the buxom and overly friendly Mrs. Townsend had been necessary to solidify his suspicions regarding Harold Brownlee. And yet, Harold was right about Bel's character. If she *had* already plighted troth with Horace Townsend, she would see it as her duty to continue.

Without answering Mr. Brownlee's question, Nigel turned to leave the library.

"Where are you going?" demanded Harold Brownlee. "What do you mean to do?"

"I mean to give Miss Morrison all the facts," said Nigel, "and let her decide fairly." He walked to the door. "Oh, and Brownlee," he added. "Pay a little more attention to your wife. She's a good woman. She doesn't deserve your infidelity or even your indifference."

"Giving sermons now, are you?" said Mr. Brownlee with a sneer. "It seems that you missed your true calling, your grace."

"As a parson?" Nigel laughed. "No, no, I have every intention of becoming a sheep farmer. Good day to you."

Chapter Twenty-Nine

Perfectly Clear

C HARLIE AND HESTER'S TRUNKS had no sooner been carried out the front door than Bel began to pack her own. She carefully folded her navy-blue evening gown and all the dresses she had bought in London. Her trousers, coat, and cap she left hanging in her wardrobe—she would not be needing those.

She tied the ribbons of her simple straw bonnet around her chin, tugged the heavy trunk down the stairs one at a time, and then walked to the kitchen for some last instructions. "Jenny, you'll take good care of Magpie and all the rest, I trust?"

"Oh, yes, miss," said the maid. "You needn't worry yourself on that score. But won't you change your mind? Mrs. Lucy will be beside herself with worry."

"Just give her my note," said Bel. "There's nothing for her to worry herself about. I am thirty years old, and a short journey by stagecoach will not hurt me one whit. Besides, I've written to Mrs. Haverstall, and she's expecting me."

Thankfully, Charlie and Hester's coach was headed to Plymouth, *not* London, for she was more afraid of what Charlie would say than her aunt, especially when he learned that her future was not as secure as she had led him to believe.

She went up from the kitchen and was waiting in the entrance hall when she heard a crunch of wheels on gravel outside. That would be Jer with the wagon.

She slid the trunk close to the door, opened it without hesitation, and nearly ran straight into a pair of broad shoulders in a caped greatcoat. "Steady there," said a man's voice as a pair of hands caught her by the elbows.

Bel knew that voice. She looked up at a chiselled jaw, a curious half-smile, and a pair of dark eyes. "Nigel!"

"I'm glad to see that we're still on a first name basis."

Bel's breath caught as she heard the flirtatious drawl in his voice. How was it possible for the timbre of the human voice to be so heart-hammeringly attractive? "What are you doing here?"

"Calling on you."

Bel realised that his hands had never let go of her elbows. They were still locked into a formal frame on the doorstep of Morrison House, looking for all the world as if they were about to dance. The winter wind whipped wildly about them, catching the capes of his coat and the skirt of her dress.

"But you look like you're going out," he continued, sliding one set of fingers down her forearm and over the edge of her gloved hand. He peered into the entryway behind her. "Where are you going? And why have you packed a trunk?"

"Jer is taking me to the Jester's Arms."

"Oh? Is the house infested with fleas? Or do you have builders coming? Is there some reason you need to put up at a public inn?"

"No, you gudgeon," she said, finally feeling steady enough to pull away from his grip. "I was planning to go to the Jester's Arms to catch the stagecoach."

His nostrils flared. "Dare I inquire about your destination?"

"London."

"But whatever for? It's all crowds, and smells, and cheap folderols. You would hate it." He looked at her suspiciously. "Are you going to buy your trousseau?"

"My trousseau?" Bel raised an eyebrow. "Explain yourself, your grace."

"No, *you* explain yourself." Nigel looked around the open yard. "But perhaps the doorstep is not the best place for this discussion."

Bel folded her gloved hands in front of her waist and looked up at him beneath the brim of her straw bonnet. "Where would you like things explained?"

"I have fond memories of the barn."

There was that flirtatious drawl again. Bel stopped her fingertips from reaching unconsciously for her lips. "You're not dressed for the barn. And the parlour would be more convenient."

"Hmm...my memories are less fond of that room, but very well."

Bel retreated inside and Nigel followed her without removing his hat and coat until they were both standing, clad in their outerwear, in the centre of the parlour.

"Why did you ask if I was going to buy a trousseau?" demanded Bel.

"I heard you might be planning to marry."

She hesitated. "I did receive an offer of marriage yesterday." She looked up at him. "From Mr. Townsend."

"I thought so." He lifted a hand in explanation. "Archie had word from Jenny that such an offer was imminent. Something she overheard your brother discussing."

"Ah, so your valet and my maid have both been spying on us."

"Why? What has Archie told Jenny about me?" His voice was eager, anxious.

"Far too little," said Bel, letting the disappointment in her voice be heard. "I know next to nothing about what you've been doing for the last year. Good things, I hope?"

Nigel looked down at her, and the gaze was so intense that it nearly took her breath away. "I can tell you. But shall we sit down?" He nodded toward the sofa.

They sat down, Bel first, and then Nigel nearby, his body angled towards hers. "I've been in Lincolnshire. Fixing things. I won't bore you with the details but suffice it to say that Grimsbald had its best harvest in three decades, and I have great plans for enhancing the pedigree of the sheepfold by purchasing new rams."

"Why would that bore me?" said Bel with a grin. "You know how dull I am."

"Let's just say that it would bore *me* at present, for there are a great many other things that I would rather talk about right now...like that offer of marriage from Townsend."

"Ah," said Bel lightly. "You want to know what I said."

"Are you determined to be the most provoking woman of my acquaintance?" Nigel leaned closer. "Well, out with it. Are you betrothed to the vicar?"

"No," said Bel slowly, "although I may have led my brother to believe as much. It was the only way he felt easy leaving the country, and they needed to sail soon before my sister-in-law was too far advanced in her pregnancy."

"What?" exclaimed Nigel, his tone so sharp that Bel almost thought he was angry with her. "He comes all the way home from Charleston after no word for seven and a half years and then thinks he can dictate whom his sister must marry?"

No, he was not angry with her. But there *was* strong feeling behind his words.

"Charleston?" Bel repeated, catching the name of the city. "Did Archie learn that from Jenny as well?"

She looked at him narrowly, but he made no answer.

"It was *you*, wasn't it? You looked for news of the *Belladore,* and you posted the newspaper advertisement in America!"

"You entrusted me with the name of the ship—that day you were weeping in the barn. It was the least that I could do with that trust."

"I don't know how you managed it," she said, laying her gloved hand on top of his larger one, "but thank you! You are an angel of mercy."

He laid his other hand atop hers, pressing it lightly. "I think I have my own angel to thank. I discovered this summer that there was a veiled woman who visited Solomon Digby and paid my debt to him. It took me a while to work out who that was, but in the end, I could not think of any woman of my acquaintance who would have done that, save one."

She looked away. "I couldn't stand the thought of you being beholden to such a monster. Thanks to Mr. Brownlee's hastiness, the money was mine, and what better use could I have for—why, what are you doing?" She looked down. "No, please, don't take off my gloves."

"Why?" he demanded, having already extracted three fingers from their leather sheaths.

"Because my hands...they're not beautiful," she said, casting him an apologetic look. It was true. They had callouses and scars and signs of time spent in all sorts of weather. And Nigel Lymington was a connoisseur of beauty—

"My dear girl," said Nigel, pulling the glove off her right hand in one fell swoop. He took her bare hand and held it against his cheek. "I will be the judge of what is beautiful to me. Have I ever mentioned how much I love your thumbnails? Those perfect half-moons on each hand."

"Flatterer," she said, but she did not pull her hand away.

They sat there in silence for a moment, each enjoying the closeness of the other, and each aware that they were on the brink of something even better.

"Why were you going to London?" he asked, his voice low and intimate.

This was no time for anything but the truth. "To look for you." She stroked a thumb against the edge of his jaw. "I couldn't exactly show up on your doorstep in Lincolnshire. But I thought there was a chance you might come to London for the season. And a chance that I might meet you by happenstance—at a ball, or at the park, or...at church."

Nigel's face came even nearer to her own. "I will attend church quite happily as long as a different vicar than Mr. Townsend is telling me my sins—you'll be glad to know that the vicar in Lincolnshire does his job quite admirably. And London parks are well and fine, although I must say I prefer walking my estate." He shook his head teasingly. "But as for balls, I've no interest in those at all unless a certain Derbyshire lass is dancing with me."

He smiled down at her. "I'm glad you were coming to look for me, but it's too little too late, Miss Morrison, for I had already made up my mind to come looking for you."

"Well," said Bel, regaining her hand and using it to remove her other glove. "You've found me. What now?" She kept her tone carefully neutral.

"Now we pledge our troth, and marry, and say never a word about it by letter. And when your brother sails back from Charleston in seven more years, he'll find you married to a duke instead of a vicar. What do you say to that?"

"Yes." The word was out of her mouth almost before he had finished his question.

"Yes?" he repeated.

"Yes," said Bel without hesitation. "I like this plan very much."

They moved toward each other in unison, in an embrace as impassioned as the winter wind. It was mere seconds, however, before Nigel released her and began to fumble with the ribbons beneath her chin. "This dashed bonnet," he gasped. "You have to get rid of it."

"Mmm, do I?" replied Bel, but she had no time to answer anything further before he tossed it on the floor. Then his hands were on her shoulders, her neck, her cheeks, and his lips devoured hers with the pent-up longing of twelve months gone.

The kisses had only just begun, however, when a ball of fur sprang onto the sofa and nuzzled its way into Nigel's lap. "Ah, not now, Magpie," said Nigel, reluctantly releasing Bel to deal with the interloper. He looked down. "What's this? That's not Magpie!"

"No, indeed. She had kittens this summer, and the whole litter survived. Now there are half a dozen magpie cats running about the place. I kept them all, so that if you ever came back, I could give you your pick of them."

"What did you name them?" asked Nigel with a glitter of challenge in his eye. "Not Patches, I hope?"

"No," she said primly. "I named them Romulus, Scipio, Hannibal, Magellan, Newton, and George. All tomcats, I'm afraid, so I couldn't use any of your suggestions."

Nigel clicked his tongue against his teeth. "Poor George seems rather outclassed with so many heroic names for his brothers."

Bel shrugged. "He was a very fat kitten, so I named him after the Prince Regent."

Nigel almost snorted with laughter. "And so you would, darling. And so you would. Which one is this?"

Bel cocked her head and looked at the cat for a moment. "Romulus."

"Well then, Romulus," said Nigel, seizing the cat about the middle and depositing it on the floor, "I'm pleased to see that I'm already your favourite. But I'm very busy right now, so if you return in, say, an hour or so, I shall see that you get your plate of ham."

"Surely, you won't let this poor cat starve for a whole hour?" asked Bel, her left eyebrow curved like Cupid's bow.

Nigel put his hands about her waist and pulled her closer, depositing a kiss on that cynical arch as he worked his way back down to her mouth. "I've been starving for you for a full year, you minx. And this cat can learn to wait his turn like the rest of us."

A knock sounded on the parlour door. Nigel groaned.

"The wagon's ready, miss, to take you into the village," said Jer's muffled voice. "I loaded up your trunk."

"Well, you can jolly well *unload* it," roared Nigel, releasing Bel momentarily, "for she won't be going anywhere."

A pause followed that declaration, and Bel began to wonder if it was safe for them to resume their activities. But within seconds the parlour door had burst open, and spotty-faced Archie Garrick was running in with Jenny in tow. "Yer grace, yer grace. She said yes. I'm the happiest man alive. Can we send Mrs. Grenville word that the gatehouse *will* be needed?"

"Archie," said Nigel firmly, standing up from the sofa, removing his greatcoat, and tossing it towards his valet. "You may send any message you like to Mrs. Grenville. You may even spend the next hour kissing the future Mrs. Garrick in the kitchen, if you like. But the occupants of this room are to be left undisturbed for the next hour *at least*. Have I made myself clear?"

Archie gaped and looked from Nigel to Bel and back again. "Perfectly, yer grace." He bundled the greatcoat under one arm and took hold of Jenny's hand with the other, and they scuttled away through the open door.

"And now, Miss Morrison," said Nigel, shutting the door and sinking back onto the sofa. "Where were we?"

"Here," said Bel, and she took his face in her hands and kissed him with all the sweetness of the sunshine after a storm.

Epilogue

MARCH 1812

"Hannibal, Scipio, come away from there," said Bel. With a brisk wave of the hand, she shooed the two cats off the bench of the pianoforte where Nigel was sitting. He glanced up from the music to flash her a smile and continued to play without missing a single note of the complicated arpeggios. The cats, rather than disappearing from the music room, continued their adoration of him by slinking past his boots and purring against his toes.

"Your husband is an excellent musician," said Mrs. Haverstall. She and her husband Ned had travelled with the Ferrises to Lincolnshire to attend the Lymington newlyweds' first house party. It was a small and intimate gathering, the perfect way for Bel to practice being a hostess in the grand old house of Grimsbald.

"Yes, indeed," said Bel. "I'm afraid I have no such accomplishments, but his grace more than makes up for my deficiencies."

Nigel's fingers stopped mid-phrase. "I believe it is common knowledge that my real deficiencies far exceed any imagined ones on your part." The notes began again.

"Ha!" said Uncle Jack, slapping a hand against the knee of his old-fashioned breeches. "Are you always this complimentary to each other? Or is it solely for our benefit?"

"Jack, dear," said Lucy reproachfully. "They are in love. It is to be expected." She nodded happily to Bel as her niece took a chair beside her to listen to the rest of the music. "I'm so glad to find you happy. And a duchess! Who would ever have thought?"

"Not I," said Bel promptly. "I forget that I *am* one, most days. For we haven't gone into society—Nigel's had no interest in visiting town. I shall need someone to teach me the finer points of town manners if we ever do."

Lucy nodded at Jack's niece, Mrs. Haverstall. "Perhaps Clarissa could help. She has done an excellent job guiding Miss Trafford through the pitfalls of town living."

"Are you chaperoning Miss Trafford again this season?" asked Bel.

The Haverstalls exchanged a glance. "No," said Clarissa lightly. "Lord and Lady Kendall are back in town, but dear Penny has been sent away to Bath."

"Sent away?" said Aunt Lucy. "That sounds ominous. I hope the poor girl is not in any...trouble." She and Bel had briefly encountered Penelope Trafford at the Haverstalls' house during their visit to London a year ago, and although she seemed high-spirited, she did not seem the kind of girl to fall in with bad company.

"No, nothing at all of that kind," replied Mrs. Haverstall. "But lest you think the worst of her, I see I must tell you all. Last summer, her younger sister Ginny, who was not even out yet in society, had the good fortune to contract an excellent match. And poor Penny…well, she has taken it hard to be 'beaten to the altar,' as it were. She has had dozens of suitors, but somehow, none of them has managed to—what is it the young people say? — 'come up to scratch.' Lady Kendall had much ado to console her, and Lord Kendall finally had enough of her histrionics and banished her to Bath in the care of an aged relative of his."

The pianoforte came to a cadence, and the small crowd applauded the duke's performance. Even the cats gave a short meow of approbation.

"Good heavens!" said Aunt Lucy, continuing the conversation as the clapping came to an end. "In all my time chaperoning Bel, I never had to deal with tantrums. She was far too sensible for that."

"She was saving them all for me," said Nigel cheekily. He gave his wife a wink and stood up from the instrument to rejoin his guests.

"What's that?" cackled Jack. "Tantrums from Bel? So, all these compliments are pre-emptive measures, eh? What do you say to that, Bel?"

"I wouldn't call them tantrums," said Bel. "Differences of opinion, perhaps."

"On what?" asked Ned Haverstall. "Politics?"

"No, not that," said Nigel with a laugh. "I don't think I've even asked her if she's a Tory or a Whig."

"Household management?" guessed Clarissa Haverstall.

"Er, no. Mrs. Grenville and Mr. Randall have everything running so smoothly that neither of us have changed a thing indoors."

"The keyword there must be *indoors,*" said Aunt Lucy. "If I know Bel, it's some sort of dispute about agriculture. She was forever wrangling with Harold Brownlee about the proper way to farm in Derbyshire."

"You are as astute as ever, my dear Lucy," said Nigel. He looked at their houseguests with a grin and entertained them all with a longsuffering sigh.

"We subscribe to different systems of crop rotation," Bel explained. "It makes for some lively dinner conversation." She turned to Nigel with a superior smile. "I should remind you, my dear, that your steward Billings agrees with *me*."

"And I should remind *you*, my dear, that I have read the most up-to-date science on the matter, and Billings has not."

"Reading and practice are not always of equal value—"

"Do you see what I mean?" said Nigel with mock severity. "I can't even stop her from arguing in front of guests." He took his wife's hand and brought it close to his lips, letting it hover there in expectation. He swept a thumb over the back of her fingers in a wordless sign of affection. Her eyes fastened on his for a little longer than was comfortable for their guests.

Ned Haverstall snorted and whispered to his wife. "I don't think they like arguing as much as they like making up afterwards."

"Well, they *are* newlyweds," Clarissa whispered back, "so let's leave them to it." She raised her voice to speak to the others in the room. "Uncle Jack, Aunt Lucy, what do you say to a game of whist? You can partner each other against Ned and me, unless the gentlemen would prefer to take us ladies on?" The two couples rose from their chairs and drifted toward the card table on the other side of the room.

And meanwhile, pleased that their guests had found something to occupy themselves, Nigel and Bel slipped away to their own rooms upstairs for further discussion on the proper care, management, and husbandry of one's beloved.

FINIS

Author's Note

T HANK YOU FOR READING the third instalment of the *Kendall House* series. From the moment the Duke of Warrenton stepped onto the page in *The London Rose*, I knew that, someday, he must have a book of his own. Despite my usual dislike for the "reformed rake" trope, Nigel Lymington has been one of my favourite characters to write.

Rakes in Regency England are not simply the figment of a romance novelist's imagination. There were always scandalous goings-on with members of the upper class, from the royal family to the peers of the realm. In the story, the fictional Lady Maltrousse mentions staying with the real Duke of Devonshire at Chatsworth. This duke was infamous for keeping a mistress in the same house as his wife, a mistress whom he married after his wife passed away. The Duke of Devonshire is a perfect example of the "rackety set" that Nigel gets himself into when he becomes a duke.

Horace Townsend, the vicar who disapproves so heartily of Nigel, is an example of a curate who is lucky to have connections---albeit connections unknown to himself. Many curates waited years to receive a "living," subsisting on a meagre wage that was not enough to start a family. Wealthy landowners like Harold Brownlee who had the right of advowson (the right to appoint a clergyman to a living) could exercise nepotism if desired. In Jane Austen's *Mansfield Park*, Sir Thomas Bertram does so when he offers the living connected to Mansfield to his brother-in-law, Mr. Norris.

Harold Brownlee's plan for Mr. Townsend to obtain not only the living but the Morrison land and money was certainly possible at this point in history. A daughter might inherit an unentailed piece of property if her brother was dead, and once a marriage took place, a wife's possessions legally became her husband's. How easy was it for a missing man to be declared dead by the magistrates? Seven years was the minimum amount of time for a man to be absent before the courts would consider such a thing. The courts sometimes delayed this declaration (for fear the man should unexpectedly return), but the fact that Charlie Morrison's ship had gone down at sea would have facilitated a declaration of presumption of death.

The advertisement that Nigel placed in the Charleston newspaper to seek out Charlie was inspired by similar "missing persons" advertisements from the period. These advertisements always started with the heading INFORMATION WANTED. Then they gave details about the missing individual, encouraging either the missing person or someone with knowledge of the missing person to write to a given address to "hear something to their advantage."

Charlie and Hester travel from America to England while tensions are high between the two countries, shortly before the "War of 1812" breaks out. At this time, the journey between the two continents took approximately four to six weeks, so it is conceivable that a woman could travel there and back during a pregnancy.

Although my village of Upper Cross in Derbyshire is fictional, the Jester's Arms is inspired by another Derbyshire inn that is purported to be haunted. Allegedly, the ghost of a jester who was murdered there plays pranks on guests by hiding their belongings, much in the same way that Archie Garrick hides the personal effects of Lady Maltrousse.

While I cannot say that any of the individual characters in the book are inspired by real people, many of the individual episodes in the story are. The "meet-cute" for Nigel and Bel was inspired by the "theft" of our outdoor cat when our neighbour decided to consistently feed the cat superior meals to the food we were providing. Bel's lack of imagination in naming pets was inspired by the many names my children have proposed for pets over the years ("Let's call the fish...Fishy!"). And Nigel's attempts to fix his financial situation before offering for Bel were inspired by my now-husband rectifying his own financial situation by working for a military contractor in Qatar for eight months before we were engaged.

The next instalment of the Kendall House series will continue with Ginny Trafford's story in *The Brighton Imbroglio*. Sent to the seaside with her family for the sake of her aunt's health, good-natured Ginny encounters the charmingly carefree officer, Felix Comfort. But when Felix's older brother, Cassius, comes to put a stop to the unacceptable relationship, trouble ensues....

Cheers,

ROSANNE E. LORTZ

Books

by Rosanne E. Lortz

Pevensey Mysteries

To Wed an Heiress

The Duke's Last Hunt

A Duel for Christmas

An Inconvenient Journey

Allen Abbey Romances

The Gentleman in the Ash Tree

The Lady in the Moneylender's Parlour

The Vicar and the Village Scandal

Kendall House Regency Romances

The London Rose

The Paris Footman

The Derbyshire Dance

The Brighton Imbroglio

Comfort Quartet

A Brother's Wager

Sketches by the Serpentine

The Brighton Imbroglio

Cousins of Cavendish Square (multi-author series)

The Discarded Companion

Printed in Dunstable, United Kingdom